# "The target is down. Repeat. The target is down. I'm moving out."

Tony wasn't completely surprised by the ambush. The CIA's south of the border security was generally sloppy, and already there'd been numerous security breaches in Central and South America in recent days. What did surprise him were the words of his boss, now coming through the headset.

"Is Guiterrez carrying a backpack or a briefcase?" Jack Bauer demanded.

Almeida spied Guiterrez sloppily dodging moving cars and vans. Jack was right. The man was clutching something. Tony was also aware of the assassin on the sidewalk, still trying to get a clear shot at the injured agent.

Almeida spoke into the pinpoint microphone. "Jack, why do you need to know—?"

"Is Guiterrez carrying something? A bag, a parcel? *Anything?*"

"He's got an attaché case—"

"Retrieve that case at any cost. Even if it means abandoning Guiterrez. Do you understand me, Tony?"

*No, Jack. I don't understand,* Almeida thought, but said—

"Roger, Jack . . . I got it."

## 24 DECLASSIFIED Books
*From HarperEntertainment*

VANISHING POINT
CAT'S CLAW
TROJAN HORSE
VETO POWER
OPERATION HELL GATE

*Coming Soon*

CHAOS THEORY

# DECLASSIFIED

## VANISHING POINT

# MARC CERASINI

**Based on the hit FOX series by Joel Surnow & Robert Cochran**

**HarperEntertainment**
*An Imprint of HarperCollinsPublishers*

HARPERENTERTAINMENT
*An Imprint of* HarperCollins*Publishers*
10 East 53rd Street
New York, New York 10022-5299

ISBN: 978-0-06-084228-4
ISBN-10: 0-06-084228-8

HarperCollins®, ®, and HarperEntertainment™ are trademarks of HarperCollins Publishers.

First HarperEntertainment paperback printing: March 2007

Printed in the United States of America

Visit HarperEntertainment on the World Wide Web at
www.harpercollins.com.

10  9  8  7  6  5  4  3  2  1

To Chuck Hoffman and Bob Langer,
who were instrumental in the creation of this novel.
And to my brother, Vance, who helped me out of a
couple of technical dilemmas I'd written myself into.
But most of all to my wife, Alice Alfonsi,
who helped immeasurably with the preparation
of this complex and difficult manuscript.

# ACKNOWLEDGMENTS

The author sends out another hearty "w00t" of thanks to Sharon K. Wheeler, software engineer, for her helpful guidance in things digital. And to Vance Cerasini, who offered me a quick lesson in the ARPANET. If there are any errors, or if literary license was taken in the depiction of computer technology in this book (and yes, it was), the responsibility falls entirely with the author.

Special thanks to Will Hinton of HarperCollins for his vision, guidance, and especially for his abundance of patience. Thanks also to Virginia King of 20th Century Fox for her continued support.

Without the groundbreaking, Emmy Award-winning "24" creators Joel Surnow and Robert Cochran, and their talented writing team, this novel would not exist. Special thanks to them and also to Kiefer Sutherland for breathing life into the memorable character of Jack Bauer. An extra-special, extra-hearty thanks to Carlos Bernard, too. Tony Almeida, you *will* be missed.

A personal thank-you to my literary agent, John Talbot, for his ongoing support. And a very special thanks to my wife, Alice Alfonsi. A guy couldn't ask for a better partner—in writing or in life.

After the 1993 World Trade Center attack, a division of the Central Intelligence Agency established a domestic unit tasked with protecting America from the threat of terrorism. Headquartered in Washington, DC, the Counter Terrorist Unit established field offices in several American cities. From its inception, CTU faced hostility and skepticism from other Federal law enforcement agencies. Despite bureaucratic resistance, within a few years CTU had become a major force in the war against terror. After the events of 9/11, a number of early CTU missions were declassified. The following is one of them. . .

# PROLOGUE

*CTU Headquarters, Los Angeles*
*Four months ago*

The door opened without a knock. Jack Bauer looked up from the daily threat assessment file to find his former boss standing over his desk.

"Busy, Jack?"

Christopher Henderson hadn't been on this coast in over a year, not since he'd become CTU's Director of Covert Operations. The promotion required a temporary move east, to CIA headquarters in Virginia.

Jack rose and shook the man's hand. "Christopher. How are things at Langley?"

His old mentor had arrived sans jacket. The sleeves of his starched white shirt were rolled up to expose sinewy biceps. A platinum Rolex glittered on his knobby wrist.

Outwardly the man hadn't changed much since being cast into Washington's bureaucratic vortex. Still tall and lanky with dead gray eyes, he'd obviously staved off an administrator's bulge by making use of the Company's gym. Then again, his early years in the Agency had earned him the nickname "Preying Mantis"—although that had as much to do with his rangy physique as his ability to convert vulnerable hard targets into Agency assets.

"I read about the biological threat you neutralized in New York," Henderson said. "Exposing a renegade FBI agent didn't endear you with the boys in the Bureau."

Jack tensed, still chafing over the lack of follow up on his recommendations. "Frank Hensley was more than a renegade. He was a mole with ties to—"

"I'm not here to talk about Operation Hell Gate or Hensley's Middle Eastern puppet master—although the official assessment is that your conclusions are shaky at best, your theories unsubstantiated."

"*Unsubstantiated*? But the evidence we gathered—"

Henderson raised a hand. "I came here on another matter. I have a critical situation down in Colombia, and I need a favor . . ."

Jack's momentary defensiveness dissolved into curiosity. He studied Henderson's expression, even though there wasn't much to read beyond a relaxed confidence, which was typical Henderson.

"Go on," Jack said, settling back behind his desk.

Henderson pulled up a chair. "Three days ago, one of my agents, Gordon Harrow y Guiterrez, went missing. For the past six months, he's been posing as a gadget guy for the Rojas brothers."

The Rojas family—a father and three sons—ran cocaine out of South America. They were a successful and ruthless gang, but not yet the top of the food chain among Colombia's many drug cartels.

"I don't understand," Jack said. "Guiterrez didn't call in a code red? Request emergency extraction?"

Henderson shook his head. "He just vanished. Went black without warning, ditching the false identity Central Cover created for him. We only learned he'd gone missing through intercepts. From what we gleaned eavesdropping on cartel chatter, Guiterrez had stolen something the Rojas family feared he would sell on the black market."

Jack's eyes narrowed. "And is that what really happened?"

"I wasn't sure at first. Within twenty-four hours, all chatter ceased inside the cartel. Even the loquacious Señora Rojas stopped calling her mother in Bogotá, so we knew something was up. After forty-eight hours, Guiterrez still hadn't made an appearance at the CTU safe house in Cartegena. So we assumed the worst."

"Was Guiterrez executed?"

"He's alive and for a very good reason. He knew something we didn't. The Cartegena safe house had been compromised. Yesterday it was attacked."

Jack frowned. "I saw the alert on that. Six dead, one wounded. . . . but Intel said the attack was a reprisal for a raid on a cartel factory last month."

"A cover story. The raid was staged by the Rojas family. They knew about our safe house, how many agents and staffers worked out of the facility, the daily schedule . . . the *works*."

"I see." Jack exhaled, knowing the implications for a hit like that. "I assume the attack compromised more of the Agency's operations in Colombia?"

Henderson nodded. "You'll see the reports soon enough."

"Reports of . . . ?"

"The hits, Jack." Henderson's easygoing mask momentarily slipped. "CIA and DEA operations in Cartegena, in Medellin, in Cali and in Barranquilla . . . They've all been quietly taken out in the past several hours," he said.

Jack took a few seconds to process this. He leaned forward, resting his forearms over the threat assessment file. "Christopher, that can't be the work of the Rojas gang. They're too small time to hold sway in Cali, Bogotá, or Barranquilla. They couldn't act on rival turf without cooperation. A deal of some kind must have been made . . ."

Henderson nodded but hesitated before saying more.

"What do you know?" Jack pressed. "I need all the facts before I can help. Are the Rojas consolidating power? Going national? International? Is this a political situation?"

Henderson moved to the edge of his chair. "The target of these raids was my agent. The Rojas family and its rivals are desperate to find him. They're trying to recover what Gordon stole from them."

"But you don't know what he has," Jack assumed.

"That's not ... precisely ... true." Henderson stared at Jack, unblinking. The mask was back. "Guiterrez contacted me again last night, through a ... back channel connection."

Jack didn't care for Henderson's sudden vagueness of wording. It smacked of legalese. "What kind of 'back channel' connection?"

Henderson lowered his voice. "He called me on a sat phone I maintain privately."

Jack didn't know why Henderson was sidestepping Agency monitoring, but he didn't ask. If anyone understood the occasional need to violate protocol, Jack did.

"Gordon told me what he'd grabbed, and I understood why he had to get out, and take it with him. He snatched a prototype of a portable electronics device that can render an airplane virtually invisible to conventional radar."

Jack blinked. "Is that possible? I thought an aircraft's stealthy characteristics came from its shape ... along with the composite materials used in its construction?"

Jack knew all about the Hopeless Diamond configuration of the F–117 Stealth fighter, and the flat-surfaces, angular design and non-reflective fuselage of the Raptor. The shape and materials of both aircraft were engineered to deflect radar, rendering them practically invisible.

Henderson nodded. "Our advanced fighters do rely on materials and shape, but they also have electronic sub-systems that can generate a field around the aircraft. This field effectively absorbs, deflects, or dissipates radar waves. Guiterrez claims the prototype he snatched can make *any* aircraft appear to vanish—even one without the stealthy materials or shape."

"My god . . ." Jack rubbed his neck as he considered the possible uses of a handy little package like that one. "If smugglers can use this technology to fly across America's borders undetected, then so can terrorists. Only they'll be delivering weapons of mass destruction, not nose candy."

"That's affirmative."

"No cartel could have invented something like that." Jack stared at Henderson, waiting for him to say more, but he simply shrugged. "*Where* did it come from, Christopher? The Pentagon? A foreign defense lab?"

"We'll know more once we get hold of the device. We can take it apart, analyze its components, reverse engineer the little sucker if necessary—"

Jack considered pressing harder, but instead took another tack. "Do you know where Gordon Guiterrez is now?"

Henderson shook his head. "On the run, somewhere in Colombia . . . I had to come up with an extraction plan on the fly. Guiterrez is paranoid—not that I blame him—but he gave me less than five minutes before he broke off communication and went dark, this time for good."

"A rural extraction would be best," Jack noted. "Far away from the urban areas a strike team could move without detection. We wouldn't need much.

A Delta squad, a Pave Low helicopter, a Little Bird, maybe a reconnaissance team on the ground to secure the perimeter—"

Henderson waved aside Jack's suggestions. "No can do. Security all over Colombia has been compromised. Half our agents are dead or on the run, the rest we can't trust for fear they're under surveillance—or on the cartel's payroll."

Jack released a breath. He wanted to help his old mentor, but . . . "This is a job for *Delta*, Christopher."

"If we send a big team into Colombia—or anywhere down there for that matter—word will get out in a minute. Anyway, Guiterrez isn't prepared to hump the boonies like you and me. He spent his childhood in Colombia, but he was educated at Princeton before coming to us. Nineteen years ago he won a collegiate fencing title, and he's had our standard weapons training, but that's the extent of his martial arts skills. In other words, Gordon Harrow y Guiterrez wouldn't last two days in the jungle."

"What did you tell him?"

"He claimed he had a safe way to get out of Colombia, so I told him to go to Nicaragua, to the capital. There's a construction site on the corner of Bolivar Avenue and Calle De Verde in Managua. The site is managed by Fuqua Construction, which is really a CIA shell company."

"Why Nicaragua?"

"It's a quiet assignment since the Sandinistas were tossed out of office in 1990. I doubt the Colombian cartels have a reach long enough to touch someone in Managua." Henderson paused, leveled his gaze. "I want you to go down there and bring Guiterrez back. I've already cleared it with Walsh."

Nodding, Jack reached toward the keyboard of his computer. "I'll assemble a team immediately—"

"No team. I told you, a large group will attract unwanted attention. Take *one* agent besides yourself—someone you trust. But don't mention the stealth device. Let your partner think your mission is a simple extraction from hostile territory."

"What do I tell the case officers in Managua?"

"Concoct some cover story as the reason for your visit. You'll think of something. But, again, I can't stress this enough. Don't mention the device—not even to other Agency personnel. It's small enough to hide in a suitcase or backpack. Chances are nobody will even notice Guiterrez has it with him when you bring him in."

*Managua, Nicaragua*
*Three days later*

Even before he opened the dented cab's squeaking door, Gordon Harrow y Guiterrez sensed he was being watched. He clutched the attaché case just a little bit tighter. Under the sweat-stained band of a worn baseball cap, perspiration painted his forehead.

More than anything, Guiterrez wanted to shift his gaze and check his six. That would, of course, be a fa-

tal error. If he really was being tailed, turning around
would alert his pursuers that he was on to them—
which would no doubt force their hand. They'd take
him out right then and there, before he had a chance
to get near the CIA safe house.

Feigning indifference, the undercover agent paid
the driver with a fistful of *córdobas*, exited the vehicle
and melted into a loud and festive lunchtime crowd.
Among the throng of Nicaraguan office workers,
Guiterrez began to wonder.

*Am I really being tailed?*

His senses were jangling from the amphetamines
he'd been swallowing like candy for far too many
days, and Guiterrez realized he could no longer trust
his judgment. Lifting his bloodshot eyes, he squinted
at the hazy blue sky. Strong sunlight shimmered above
the ten- and twelve-story structures that flanked this
commercial street. Almost all of Managua had been
rebuilt since the mid '70s, after an earthquake killed
tens of thousands and leveled ninety percent of the
Nicaraguan capital. Unfortunately, the graceful pre-
colonial buildings were replaced by boxy, utilitarian
structures that made much of the city resemble a particularly decrepit American strip mall.

Even worse, this time of year Managua's air was hot
and sticky under a scorching sun. Moving through the
crush of office workers, food vendors and street mer-
chants was painfully slow—made worse by blue-gray
puffs of car exhaust fumes, and clouds of charcoal
smoke, redolent with the scent of charred meat.

On busy Bolivar Avenue, a long thoroughfare between Lake Managua and the muddy Ticapa Lagoon, the humidity was especially thick and uncomfortable. Buffeted by the crowd that hemmed him in, Guiterrez had trouble catching his breath. His grimy, unshaven neck itched, and the cotton shirt clung to sweat that trickled down the small of his back. Perspiration dampened his scalp as well, but Guiterrez dared not take off his cap.

His Anglo features had helped him with the Rojas family. They'd more willingly bought his cover story—that he was a pissed off software engineer who'd gotten sick of his American company passing him over for promotion. But he was on the run now, and his shock of light blond hair would stick out in this homogenous crowd like a *sabana* in a Mexican prison. At least his deep tan disguised his fair skin and helped him blend with the environment.

Sun glare blazed off a shop window. Guiterrez's eyebrow twitched uncontrollably. The simmering heat, his lack of sleep, the drugs, days of constant movement and ceaseless vigilance were finally taking their toll on the overweight agent. Even worse, the amphetamines no longer kept Guiterrez alert or focused—only twitchy and paranoid

But at least he'd gotten out of Colombia, with the device intact. Now that he'd reached Managua, the odyssey was nearly over. Guiterrez was almost home. Five days ago he'd stolen a pleasure boat in the Colombian seaport town of Barranquilla and sailed up the Atlantic to the shores of Panama. He scuttled the engine and sunk the boat in a lagoon, then hiked to

Panama City where he hot wired a car. Guiterrez drove north, across the Costa Rican border, all the way to Nicaragua.

The car died outside the town of Upala, so he ditched it and paid off some farm workers to stow away in a vegetable truck. Guiterrez bailed at Galpa, a tiny Nicaraguan fishing community transformed into a housing development for middle-class government workers. There the agent mingled with the workers' morning rush hour to board a rusty commuter ferry, which crossed Lake Managua.

Once in the capital, Guiterrez lingered near the harbor until lunchtime, waiting for the streets to be filled with traffic so his movements would be less noticeable. When lunch hour rolled around and the sidewalks were jammed, he hailed a cab and asked the driver to take him to Bolivar Street.

The car deposited him a block from the CIA safe house. Over the heads of the crowd, Guiterrez could see the steel-girded skeleton of a building, a large white sign halfway up that read *Constructores De Fuqua* in black block letters. Guiterrez's grip tightened on the briefcase—a movement that sent pain signals up his arm and caused his shoulder muscles to ache. The agent shrugged off the discomfort, increased his pace. Just a few more minutes and his sleepless nights and days of running would be over.

Guiterrez limped down Bolivar until he was just across the street from the construction site. Near the corner, the door to a small bistro opened, blocking his path. Two women emerged, laughing and talking. Guiterrez paused as the giggling young women stepped around him. One flashed Guiterrez a smile, but the agent didn't notice. His eyes were locked on the glass door, at its reflection of the crowded street and the sidewalk directly behind him.

In the instant before the door closed, Guiterrez spied a familiar face—Francesco Rojas, the youngest member of the crime family he'd betrayed. Rojas was the cartel's enforcer and murderer, and he never missed his target. The assassin was standing behind him, not twenty feet away, his eyes black pools focused on Guiterrez's back.

Instinctively, the agent's free hand reached for the weapon he no longer possessed—he'd been forced to ditch the handgun he carried at the border crossing at Costa Rica or risk arrest. Now his futile gesture, made out of fear, surprise and exhaustion, had been spotted by Rojas. The cartel enforcer reached into his jacket and drew an Uzi. In one smooth motion, Rojas dropped to one knee and opened fire.

As a stream of bullets shattered the restaurant's door and windows, showering the sidewalk with sparkling shards, Guiterrez leaped between two parked cars. The two women were caught directly in the Uzi's deadly spray. Grotesquely, they seemed to dance under the impact of the high velocity shells, their colorful skirts billowing as they tumbled to the pavement. A waiter dropped limply through the restaurant's window, the top of his head a shattered, blood-filled cavity.

Feeling no bullet impact, no jolt of pain—and not quite comprehending his good fortune—Guiterrez stumbled into the middle of the busy street, crossing against the light. But as he attempted to weave between passing cars, Guiterrez's legs suddenly felt weighted, a pounding throbbed in his ears, and he realized he *had* been hit. He was losing blood fast. . . .

"The target is down. Repeat. The target is down. I'm moving out."

CTU Field Agent Tony Almeida reached behind his back, grabbed the handle of the Glock tucked into the belt holster of his black denims. A moment ago, he'd spied Gordon Guiterrez strolling along the sidewalk, but Tony barely had time to report the sighting before the firefight erupted. Two women had been torn apart by the automatic weapon's fire. Guiterrez had lunged out of the way, but he'd been struck too. Now he was stumbling into the middle of the street, trailing blood.

Tony tried to move quickly through the panicked crowd, pointing his weapon to the ground in case of accidental discharge. The vigil for Guiterrez had been a long one. According to Jack Bauer's uncharacteristically sketchy briefing, this was to be a simple extraction, complicated by the fact that Guiterrez was being hunted by Colombian assassins.

Bauer maintained that the cartel's reach probably didn't extend far enough to cover operations in Nicaragua. The moment the gunman stepped out of the crowd and fired, Tony knew Jack's assessment had been wrong.

Tony wasn't completely surprised by the ambush. The CIA's south of the border security was generally sloppy, and already there'd been numerous security breaches in Central and South American in recent days. What did surprise him were the words of his boss, now coming through the headset.

"Is Guiterrez carrying a backpack or a briefcase?" Jack Bauer demanded.

Almeida spied Guiterrez sloppily dodging moving cars and vans. Jack was right. The man was clutching something. Tony was also aware of the assassin on the sidewalk, still trying to get a clear shot at the injured agent.

Almeida spoke into the pinpoint microphone. "Jack, why do you need to know—?"

"Is Guiterrez carrying something? A bag, a parcel? *Anything*?"

"He's got an attaché case—"

"Retrieve that case at any cost. Even if it means abandoning Guiterrez. Do you understand me, Tony?"

*No, Jack. I don't understand*, Almeida thought, but said—

"Roger, Jack . . . I got it."

Jack Bauer cursed as he drew his Glock. "*Salga de la manera. ¡Muévase! ¡Muévase!*" he shouted at the crowd around him. He raised his weapon high enough for everyone to see, barrel pointed to the sky. "*¡Muévase! ¡Muévase!*"

He pushed through the mass of people. Pedestrians who heard him—or saw the weapon—instantly obeyed his shouted command and got out of the way. Those who didn't were dodged or elbowed aside.

Jack heard screams, outraged shouts and startled cries.

"¡Él tiene un arma!"

"¡Ese hombre va a tirar a su arma!"

People dashed into shops, cowered in doorways. Jack kept going. He regretted causing a panic, but at least the civilians were scattering. *That's one break in this whole rotten mess.*

Like Tony, Jack had been waiting for hours, lingering near a food cart on Bolivar Street—on the wrong side of the construction site, as it turned out. Feet pounding the pavement, he wondered where he'd screwed up.

When he and Tony had first arrived in Nicaragua, they'd hooked up with Case Officers Ben Burwell and James Cantrel at Fuqua Construction—their CIA shell company cover. But in Jack's quick estimation, Burwell and Cantrel had been recycling the same reports for some time. The eyes and ears of United States intelligence in Nicaragua were nothing more than career floaters, coasting toward retirement, and their entire Nicaraguan operation had been lax probably since the Sandinistas were voted out of power in 1990.

After observing the two men conduct business, Jack concluded that the "organization" in Managua was riddled with cartel informants, and he and Tony were better off working on their own.

The fact that Rojas assassins were lying in wait for Gordon Guiterrez proved Jack correct on the first count—not that this validation brought him any satisfaction. But at least Jack now understood the reason why he'd been ordered not to tell Tony about the device unless it became necessary.

Christopher Henderson didn't trust Tony Almeida any more than Jack trusted agents Burwell and Cantrel.

For a few seconds, all Tony could see were people running, all he could hear were fearful shouts and high-pitched screams. As he moved toward Guiterrez, he tried in vain to keep his eyes on the Uzi-wielding assassin, but his path was constantly blocked by panicked civilians.

*Screw this. . .*

Without slowing, Tony swerved off the sidewalk and into the street. A horn blared. He spun to see a red Toyota. The driver wasn't stopping—but Tony wasn't moving. Instead of dashing out of the car's path, he threw himself onto the hood. The thin aluminum crumpled under his weight. The vehicle's momentum slammed Tony's spine against the windshield, cracking the safety glass.

Glock extended—finger off the trigger—Tony rode the hood as the vehicle continued to veer down Bolivar. When the stunned driver finally slammed on his brakes, momentum threw Tony forward. He landed on his feet, stumbled, then quickly regained his balance.

The assassin was now standing directly in front of Tony. The man still held the Uzi in one hand, but his attention was focused on the retreating Guiterrez.

Unnoticed, Tony took two steps forward, halting behind the assassin's back. As he raised his Glock, the man whirled. His dark eyes went wide, his mouth opened in surprise. Tony could smell the gunman's breath as he placed the Glock's muzzle against his temple.

The assassin lifted his Uzi.

Tony pulled the trigger.

Blood and brains splattered the restaurant wall, the spent shell shattering harmlessly against the bricks. Francesco Rojas jerked once, then dropped to the pavement.

Amid the chaos, Gordon Guiterrez managed to reach the opposite side of the street. Still leaking blood, he'd stumbled through traffic, then dropped to his knees at the curb.

He heard gunfire again, a single discharge from . . . *a Glock?*

He dragged across the sidewalk, using his arms, because his lower body had become oddly numb. Chest heaving, daggers of pain traveling up his torso, he braced his spine against the construction site's rough wooden wall and sat up.

With a rush of triumph, he realized his right hand was still gripping the handle of the attaché case. His misty vision became even hazier, casting a red veil over the world. Still, Guiterrez could see that the sidewalk was nearly empty now . . . except for one man. A pale Anglo resembling one of Henderson's CTU men appeared to be running toward him, gun in hand.

Not sure whether Jack Bauer was an illusion, Guiterrez attempted to focus his fading vision when a hard jerk jolted his right arm. Someone was pulling at the attaché case in his grip. He turned his head to find a boy about sixteen in a New York Mets T-shirt, his thick brown forearms mottled by the telltale scars from the coca labs. Behind the boy's back, an older Colombian *cholo*, this one wearing a red bandana and holding an Uzi, was obviously watching the boy's back.

Amid the screams and traffic noise, Guiterrez heard Bauer's voice. "*!Caiga su arma y paso lejos!*"

The *cholo* with the Uzi turned—Jack's two quick shots tore the top of the *cholo's* head off, bandana and all. At the same moment, the handle broke away so suddenly from the attaché case that the teenage boy toppled to the sidewalk.

Guiterrez stared numbly at the handle still clutched in his fist. *This shouldn't have happened,* he thought in a cloud of shock and pain. *I would have used handcuffs, if I'd had a pair. One cuff around the handle, another around my wrist. No one would have snatched the case away from me then.*

Problem was, inside the Rojas compound where he'd been living, handcuffs were hard to come by. Explosives were easier to find. Much easier. So Guiterrez had rigged something up.

The bomb was inside the case, right next to the device he'd stolen. A brick of C4, more than enough to do the job. The handle was the detonator, the timed delay only five seconds—long enough to catch Jack Bauer's eye, gesture a warning.

The boy tucked the case under his arm, scrambled to his feet.

"No, wait!" Jack cried, backing away.

The C4 detonated in a bright orange flash.

*CTU Headquarters, Los Angeles*
*Three days later*

Jack Bauer was surprised by the sheer number of personnel packed into CTU's soundproofed conference room. Christopher Henderson had cobbled together an impressive operation in under thirty-six hours, one of the largest undercover stings Jack had ever joined.

Along with Agents Tony Almeida and Nina Myers, Curtis Manning, a former member of Chet Blackburn's strike team, was also at the table. Manning's quick thinking and initiative during Operation Pinstripe had attracted the attention of Administrative Director Richard Walsh, who immediately moved Curtis over to Field Ops. This would be his first real assignment.

On the communications side, Programmer Jamey Farrell was present, along with the young computer protégé, Doris Soo Min. Jack also noticed the shiny bald head of portly Morris O'Brian, CTU's cyberspecialist. He'd recently come over from Langley, just ahead of a sexual harassment suit, according to the sealed portion of his personnel file.

What was amazing to Jack was that what had once been a shoestring operation involving only the late Agent Guiterrez and his CIA case officer, Christopher Henderson, had suddenly ballooned into a full-fledged black operation requiring the bulk of CTU's West Coast resources.

While Jack watched Director Henderson bring those who were just now joining the operation up to speed with past events, Jack realized he was once again working for his old boss—and his feelings about that were mixed.

"Though explosives in the briefcase destroyed the device that Guiterrez had stolen, our team in Nicaragua managed to recover enough of its components to determine the origins of the cloaking device," Henderson explained. "So if you look at it from a certain perspective, then the Nicaragua mission was a success . . ."

*Tell that to Gordon Guiterrez*, Jack thought with self-disgust. From the expression on Tony Almeida's face, Jack knew he felt the same.

Sleeves rolled, tie tossed over his shoulder, Henderson paced the front of the glass-enclosed conference room. On the opposite side of the window, Jack spotted Ryan Chappelle and George Mason huddled in conversation. Both surreptitiously glanced at the conference in progress. Both wore sour expressions.

*Chappelle's out of the loop*, Jack realized, a little surprised Henderson had the clout to stonewall CTU's Regional Director.

"Through the use of advanced cybernetic forensics techniques, Morris O'Brian gave us our first break." Henderson focused his expressionless gray eyes on the British-born cyber-technician.

O'Brian's round face gave a little nod. He adjusted the cuffs of his Joseph Abboud sport coat, then glanced at the open file on the table.

"It's clear we're dealing with advanced technology. *Classified* technology," he said, the Cockney lilt still evident in his voice. "I was able to trace a partial serial number from the remains of a silicon chip, and the lot number from a tiny data compressor. Both were manufactured by a Japanese firm and imported for use by the United States Air Force. But our big break came when a piece of the motherboard was found at Santa Theresa Hospital in Managua—"

Nina Myers, Jack's second in command at CTU, cocked her head. "Found *where*?"

"During an autopsy of one bomb victim, a nine centimeter bundle of silicon and copper wire was found embedded in the corpse . . ." Morris paused, flipped a page and squinted as he read. "Through a close examination of this component, I surmised that the board was manufactured by Systemantics, a division of the defense contractor Omnicron International."

Morris closed the file and looked up. "By hacking into Omnicron's database, I discovered that the motherboard was purchased by and delivered to the Technology Acquisition Department of the Experimental Testing Range at Groom Lake Air Force Base in Nevada, exactly twenty-three months ago."

Morris raised an eyebrow, his fleshy cheeks lifted in an elfin grin. "To UFO buffs and conspiracy theorists, Groom Lake is known by another name. It's called Area 51—"

Henderson interrupted him. "Okay, O'Brian, let's skip the little green men and focus on reality, shall we? Groom Lake is a top secret advanced research facility managed by the United States Air Force. The entire compound, including the runways, testing range and bombing range, is larger than the state of Delaware. The facility, located in the middle of the desert, just fifty miles outside the Las Vegas city limits, is both remote and well guarded . . ."

Tony Almeida shook his head. "Sounds like this is a problem for Air Force security."

"If only that were true," Henderson replied. "Unfortunately, Air Force Intelligence denies it has a problem. Claims this particular motherboard was incinerated six months ago. They have the paperwork to back up that claim, too."

Agent Almeida shifted in his chair. "But we have the motherboard, which means somebody's lying—or covering their asses."

"Once again, Agent Almeida has cut to the chase," Henderson said with a humorless grin. "And as it turns out, this isn't the only time the folks at Groom Lake have misplaced classified technology."

The Director of Covert Operations dropped a sealed Mylar evidence bag in the middle of the conference table. Inside was a black box the size of a cigarette pack, connected to what appeared to be a gold wedding band by a single, thread-thin insulated wire thirty inches long.

"This handy gadget was seized by the Las Vegas police six weeks ago, on the gambling floor at the Babylon Casino Hotel," Henderson declared. "The wedding band—made of copper, incidentally, with insulation inside to protect the wearer—is worn on the finger. The wire runs to the black box, which contains a classified Air Force digital scrambling chip."

"And this does what?" Jamey Farrell asked.

"The wearer tries his hand at the slots," Henderson said, mimicking the movements he was describing. "Our con man puts a coin into the slot, while placing his left hand on the side of the machine, like this. Electronic impulses are sent through the ring, into the slot machine. These impulses override the digital randomizer inside the slot's software. Suddenly you're winning one out of every five pulls instead of one in ten thousand—"

"Enough to cheat your way to a luxurious lifestyle. if you're playing fifty or hundred dollar slots and didn't get too greedy," O'Brian interjected.

Tony's dark eyes narrowed. "You're saying the chip inside this device came out of Groom Lake?"

Henderson nodded.

"Obviously the guy who was arrested using this device knows where he got it?" Tony demanded. "Why not pump him for the information?"

"Funny thing about that," Henderson replied. "The cheat's name was Dwayne Nardino, a small time racketeer out of Reno. Within hours of his arrest, Nardino was bailed out of jail—which cost someone close to fifty thousand dollars in cash. It was an amount they were willing to lose, because Nardino was discovered behind the wheel of his car the next morning, with two thirty-eight caliber slugs in the back of his head."

"Obviously someone didn't want Dwayne talking out of turn," Nina Myers said softly.

Henderson's movements became more animated, his gray eyes seemed alive for the first time. "Here's the interesting part. Two years ago the Drug Enforcement Agency identified Dwayne Nardino as a major distributor of Rojas cocaine. The DEA even has surveillance photos of Nardino meeting with the brothers at their hacienda in Colombia . . ."

"It's clear that someone at Groom Lake is peddling classified technology," said Jack. "Any theories about who or why?"

Henderson placed the palms of his hands on the table, his gaze sweeping everyone seated there. "The why is simple. They did it for money. The theory we've come up with is that someone on one of the research teams at Groom Lake, or maybe someone in supply or the classified material disposal unit, has a big-time gambling problem. In order to pay off a large debt, we're guessing this person passed along classified technology adapted for criminal use. Of course, once a syndicate has their claws into someone who can provide such technology, their debt would never be wiped clean. The mob would naturally squeeze them to supply more and more gadgets, until there's no juice left." Henderson's narrow face flashed a humorless smile. "And that's how we'll nail the bastards."

Pushing away from the table, Henderson strode to the front of the room. "We're going to use a two pronged investigation to plug this technology leak." He held up two fingers. "That's two teams, working at separate locations toward a single goal. One team will operate in conjunction with an undercover agent planted inside of Groom Lake. This agent will be working on one of the research teams conducting experiments at the testing range."

"Need a volunteer?" Nina asked.

"Agent Almeida will coordinate all surveillance activities with Ms. Farrell and Ms. Soo Min, who will monitor activities from here," Henderson replied.

"And the second team?" Jack asked.

"We're placing a three-member team undercover, right in the middle of a crooked casino in Las Vegas," he declared. "One agent will impersonate a mob lieutenant—that's *you,* Jack. Your cover story is that you're on the payroll of Kansas City mobster Gus Pardo. It's Pardo who owns the Cha-Cha Lounge."

Jack folded his arms. "I can tell you now, there's no way this will fly. What if someone contacts Pardo and asks questions?"

"Gus Pardo will vouch for you and your team, to anyone who asks. Even his own lieutenants."

Morris O'Brian scratched his forehead. "Why would this criminal help us?"

"Simple. We own him." Again, Henderson smiled. "Pardo's college-aged son was arrested for cocaine possession in South America. He's facing hard time in one of the worst prison systems in the world. If

Pardo cooperates, he'll see his son again, compliments of the U.S. State Department. If Pardo screws us, his kid rots in a Peruvian jail for the rest of his short, miserable life. Naturally, we're convinced Pardo will cooperate . . ."

Jack blinked. "What am I supposed to do at this casino?"

"Loan shark. Launder money. Load the dice and water the booze," Henderson replied. "The one thing you will not do is catch professional cheats. We want the word to get around Vegas that the Cha-Cha Lounge is an easy mark. Sooner or later someone using classified technology to run a scam will walk through the doors, and we'll have them."

"And the rest of my team?"

"While you're watching the dealers, croupiers and pit bosses, Curtis Manning will provide overall security. Meanwhile Morris O'Brian will be up in the catwalk monitoring the customers using CTU's best surveillance equipment. The next time a cheater shows up with classified technology, we'll be ready."

Jack frowned, surprised at the sheer audacity of Henderson's plan.

"The Director's approved a three month operation. I'll petition to renew for another three if we come up empty . . . but I don't expect us to come up empty. Get creative, if you have to, but get results. In the next twelve weeks, I want at least one solid lead to take back to the Director. During that time, Jack, you and your team will be surrounded by a criminal element that is completely unaware of your true identities and motives. As far they're concerned, you're mobsters working for Gus Pardo's Kansas City crime syndicate, dispatched to Sin City to operate his casino . . ."

Henderson paused. "You all know what that means. This is deep cover. If anyone feels they are not up to this assignment, see me after the meeting."

Jack Bauer sat in silence, processing. He felt Christopher's hands on his shoulders. "Relax, Jack. How many agents get an all-expenses-paid assignment in Las Vegas?"

1 2 3 4 5 6 7 8 9
10 11 12 13 14 15 16 17
18 19 20 21 22 23 24

. . . . . . . . . . . . . . . . . . . . . . . . . . . . . . . . . . .

THE FOLLOWING TAKES PLACE
BETWEEN THE HOURS OF
12 P.M. AND 1 P.M.
PACIFIC DAYLIGHT TIME

. . . . . . . . . . . . . . . . . . . . . . . . . . . . . . . . . . .

*12:00:04 P.M. PDT*
*The Cha-Cha Lounge, Las Vegas*

The holding room was located three levels below the
gaming floor, in the casino's deepest subbasement.
Yet even here the clatter of coin and the jangle of five
hundred clicking, ringing slot machines penetrated
the insulated brick walls and seeped through the
cheap soundproof ceiling panels—an incessant car-
nival buzz that rose and fell like a demented organ
grinder's squeeze box.

Jack Bauer closed his ears to the noise and barely
registered his dismal surroundings; gray, unpainted
walls, avocado-green phone without a press pad or

dial, a steel fire gate that led to a concrete corridor, and a windowless steel door that led to the tiny holding cell behind the one-way mirror.

Jack approached the glass. He studied the man on the other side, absorbing every detail of the stranger's clothing, physical characteristics, and mannerisms.

Though the man wore a bland, relaxed expression, he'd been alone in that locked room for fifteen minutes and he was still perched on the edge of a Cha-Cha Lounge-orange fiberglass chair, as if he were going to bolt the moment the door opened. Occasionally he'd gingerly touch his face, and Jack noticed a fresh bruise under his left eye.

Jack pegged the man's age as well into his fourth decade, though he tried to appear younger. His sandy brown hair—disheveled from the rough treatment he'd received at the hands of "casino security"—was white-gray under a clumsy dye job. His addict-thin body was clad head-to-toe in denim, the faded blue jacket torn at the sleeve, buttons missing from his shirt. A crumpled cowboy hat lay on the concrete floor next to the man's scuffed leather boots.

"What's his name, Driscoll?" Jack asked the casino's pit boss. "Where'd he come from?"

Don Driscoll had the strength of a bull and the face of a bull dog, but the manner of a fastidious cat. With meaty hands, he adjusted the lapels of his bright orange sports jacket.

"Midnight Cowboy calls himself Chester Thompkins. Says he's a truck driver. He's got a North Carolina commercial license to prove it. Of course, that don't mean squat—'specially not with that South Jersey lilt tucked in the back of his throat."

Driscoll was born and raised in Atlantic City, so he would know.

"Did he have anything else on him?" Jack asked. "Drugs? A weapon?"

Driscoll shook his dark head, his perfectly pomaded hair didn't move. "Just the gimmick, Jaycee."

The pit boss used Jack's alias because that was the only name he knew. Driscoll also believed J. C. "Jaycee" Jager was using this low-rent, off-the-beaten track casino as a front to launder mob money and pull a little loan sharking scam on the side.

"Where's the device?" Jack asked.

"Morris is examining it now."

"What about his wallet?"

"Curtis took it. He's running a make on the guy." Driscoll chuckled. "My bet, it'll come back light, if you know what I mean. The Lone Ranger had over forty Gs in his wallet. Ill-gotten gains, says me."

"Who spotted the scam?"

"Chick Hoffman, the croupier at table five." Driscoll displayed pride. "The roulette table was reset yesterday and the balance was good. Then along comes Jon Voight here, who's betting careful and winning big. Been here since nine-thirty in the AM. Hoffman got suspicious—naturally, 'cause I trained Chick myself."

"Did Hoffman find the device?"

Driscoll frowned. "Nah. It was Morris, up in the catwalk. Chick couldn't scope the scam, but he tripped the silent alarm anyway. O'Brian used X-rays or heat vision or some magic crap to sniff it out. The gizmo was in the guy's jacket. There were wires in his sleeve, a laser lens hidden behind the cuff button."

Driscoll rubbed his clean shaven jaw. "When we established for certain that he was cheating, I had security snatch him up and bring him down here. I saved him for you."

Jack dragged his eyes away from the man behind the mirror, faced Driscoll. "Tell Hoffman there'll be an extra grand in his envelope at the end of the day. There'll be a couple of Gs in your envelope, too." Bauer forced a half-smile. "Good work, Driscoll."

The pit boss brightened considerably. "Thanks Jaycee."

"Do you want me to stick around and help break this bunco rat?"

Jack shook his head. "I'm going to handle it myself. Do me a favor and find Curtis. I need to know what he dug up on this guy."

"Sure thing, boss. Right away."

Driscoll paused when he reached the fire door, one hand poised on the push bar, he seemed to be gathering his thoughts. "It's good what you're doing, Jaycee. It's the right thing."

"What are you talking about?" Jack's tone was prickly.

Sensing his annoyance, Driscoll talked faster. "It's good to finally make an example, Jaycee. That's all I meant. Things were getting sloppy around here, across the board. The croupiers, the dealers, the Eyes in the Sky, even the goddamn cocktail waitresses. And the word's out, you know? Sorry, but for nearly three months now, ever since you came on board, this casino's been drawing grifters like a cesspit draws flies."

Driscoll's watery gray eyes drifted to the man behind the mirror. "Nailing that bastard, dealing with him without the law . . . It'll send the right message to the right people. After this, nobody's gonna think Jaycee Jager is an easy mark. Nobody."

Jack fixed a cold stare on Don Driscoll. "I came here from Kansas City to make my mark. And that includes making this dive profitable. That's what I'm going to do, no matter what it takes, no matter who I have to take down in the process." Jack shifted his gaze back to their cheater. "Now go find Curtis and send him down here. I'm going to need some muscle to take care of this son of a bitch."

The pit boss practically stood at attention. "Right, Jaycee. I gotta get back to the floor anyway."

The steel door clanged behind the pit boss and Jack was alone. Staring at the man behind the glass, he steeled himself for what might happen next, what he might be compelled to do.

The phone rang. Jack snatched the receiver off its cradle.

"Jager," he answered, pronouncing the name *Yah-ger*.

"It's Morris, Jack," the man said, but O'Brian's Cockney accent would have been recognizable without the I.D. "I've had a look-see at that little gizmo your drugstore cowboy had in his tuck. It's the real deal. Just what we were lookin' for. That guy in the cell's our first lead . . ."

Jack's focus suddenly sharpened. The investigation into technology leaks at Groom Lake had been stalled for weeks, despite the resources expended—not to mention the difficulty of placing an inside man at the base without the United States Air Force knowing about him.

"What does he have, Morris?"

"A little black box, with a predictive roulette computer inside."

Jack frowned. "That's no big deal. They've been around since the early 1980s. Computers have been used to rip off casinos from the Riviera to Atlantic City."

"Ah, but this particular beast is smarter than the average bear. It's the Einstein of predictive computers."

Jack could envision the smug grin on Morris O'Brian's face.

"Get to the point, Morris."

"As you know, predictive computers use lasers to scan where the ball is in relation to the wheel, and then asks the computer to predict the section of the wheel where the ball will most likely land. Most predictive computers increase the probability of winning to say . . . one in three, or thirty-three percent. Good but not great. You can still lose your shirt with those odds. But the little bugger I'm holding in my hand is much better than that. Maybe as good as ninety percent, or better."

"That's impossible."

"I watched the security tapes, Jack, and I've tested it myself," Morris replied. "It's that good. And that's not all. The software . . . it's cribbed from the new, improved Patriot Missile system."

"How did that help him cheat?"

"The point of the Patriot system is to hit an incoming missile with a missile you fired. That's like hitting a flying bullet with another flying bullet. Measuring the speed of a steel ball on a roulette table is child's play to this software."

Jack stared at the man inside the cell. "Do you think this guy built it?"

Morris chuckled. "Our boy Thompkins? Hardly. Frankly, I'm surprised he learned how to use it."

"So where did he get it?"

"Actually, predictive computers are readily available from certain unscrupulous types, for a rather punishing outlay—say fifty or sixty grand. I haven't seen one this good, however, so I'd bet it's worth a couple of hundred thousand on the open market. When I'm through testing it, I'm going to take it apart and we'll know more."

"Do it quick," demanded Jack.

"Yes, yes, but it's a shame though." Suddenly Morris' tone brightened. "The good news is that once I dissect this, I can reverse engineer it. Build us both a pair and we could clean up, make us a fortune."

"I don't gamble."

Morris chuckled again. "Au contraire, Jack. You gamble every minute of the day."

Jack ignored O'Brian's talk show psychology. "Right now, as a matter of national security, we need to know where Thompkins bought this device and who made it."

"That's the long and short of it. I leave that job to you, my friend . . ."

Jack hung up just as the fire door opened. Curtis Manning entered, drew a sheaf of papers from the pocket of his bright orange Cha-Cha Lounge sports jacket.

"I gave him a drink of water, took the fingerprints off the plastic glass and sent it back to CTU," Curtis said, handing Jack the top page. "He's not who he says he is."

While Jack scanned the pages, Curtis spoke. "His real name's Max Farrow. Currently he's wanted for the assault of his ex-wife and his stepdaughter in New Jersey, where he's a convicted rapist. He also has one felony and a variety of misdemeanor convictions that are gambling-related. Got himself banned from the Atlantic City casinos for passing bad dice, counting cards, fishing in the dealer box—you name it."

"And the rape conviction?"

"Sentenced to five years, paroled in two," Curtis said. "Farrow bailed out of a halfway house in Passaic last year, probably to avoid that state's sex offender registry, which is public record. At least one member of the victim's family has vowed revenge . . ."

Jack stuffed the rap sheet into his black leather jacket. "Unlock the holding cell and wait here."

The man didn't look up when Jack Bauer entered.

Instead he shifted in his seat and appraised the newcomer with a sidelong glance. As Jack circled the chair, Farrow thrust out his long legs to block his path. Bauer's eyes narrowed, but he said nothing. Instead he stepped around the man, turning his back on his prisoner for just a moment.

Max Farrow leaped out of the chair and lunged at Jack, hands outstretched and reaching for Bauer's throat.

Jack was ready. He effortlessly sidestepped the clumsy charge, then grabbed the man's wrist with his left hand. He stepped around Farrow, twisting the man's arm behind him. Farrow was thin, but he was sinewy, and his resistance was substantial. Using leverage, Jack applied even more pressure, until the pain was enough to drop Farrow to one knee.

Bauer attempted to rattle the man further by raising his voice. "You want to hurt me?" he shouted. "Is that what you want? You want to hurt *me*?"

With his right hand, Jack reached into his leather jacket. When it came out again, the hand was circled by a carbon steel knuckle duster. With soft rubber surfaces to grip the hand and protect the wearer, the high-tech version of the old brass knuckles hugged Bauer's right fist like a glove.

Farrow saw metal and his eyes went wide. "What are you gonna do to me? I have rights! You can't hold me prisoner! You have to turn me over to the cops, you bastard!"

He'd made demands, but Farrow's panicked voice was anything but commanding.

"You're going to tell me a story, Max." Jack voice was a hoarse whisper. "You're going to tell me where you got that computer in your pocket."

"No way, asshole. I'm not a rat—"

Jack brought his brass fist down on the man's chin, cutting the sentence short.

"You're going to tell me where you got that computer, Farrow. Do you hear me?"

Farrow spit blood and stared at the floor. Jack yanked the man to his feet, and shoved him into the chair so hard the cheap orange fiberglass cracked.

Grunting, Farrow kicked out. His boot heel barely missed Bauer's knee.

"Where did you get it?" Jack demanded again.

Farrow tried to rise. Jack backhanded him, then shoved his own boot into the other's chest. With a sharp snap, the chair broke in half, spilling Max Farrow along with dozens of fiberglass shards onto the concrete floor. Jack avoided another kick, hauled the man to his feet again and shook him by his lapels.

"The computer, Farrow . . ."

"Go to hell."

*12:14:58 P.M. PDT*
*Hangar Six, Experimental Weapons Testing Range*
*Groom Lake Air Force Base*

The mast had been constructed overnight, a fifty-foot steel skeleton rising from the middle of a concrete square exactly five hundred feet away from the hangar itself. The tower's spidery struts were painted in a dun and rust-colored pattern, which blended perfectly with the desert terrain. This was part of strategy to render it nearly invisible to satellite surveillance, even in the brilliant glare of the scorching afternoon sun.

The massive microwave emission array that would soon be mounted atop that tower was impossible to camouflage, however. Roughly the size and shape of Subzero refrigerator, with what appeared to be a thousand little radar dishes mounted on a side panel, the system weighed over a ton. It had to be towed to the site by tractor and lifted into place with a crane. The device's visibility had forced the two hour delay in its final placement—a wait that infuriated the Team Leader of the Malignant Wave project.

Regal in high heels and pearls, a spotless white lab coat draped on her ballerina physique, Dr. Megan Reed pushed a cascade of strawberry blond hair away from her freckled face. Frowning, she whirled to confront a young Air Force corporal from the Satellite Surveillance Unit at Groom Lake.

"How much longer before it's clear and we can proceed, Corporal Stratowski?" she barked in a voice that belied her feminine appearance. In fact, a few airmen remarked in private that her harsh, demanding tone sounded more like a drill sergeant's.

"Three minutes, sixteen seconds, Ma'am," the corporal replied. "I'm tracking the satellite now. It's nearly out of range."

Clad in crisp blue overalls, Corporal Stratowski hunkered down in front of an open laptop, eyes locked on the animated display. The computer rested on a stack of packing crates, on its screen a red blip marked the space vehicle's path and trajectory on a digital grid map.

With an impatient glare, the woman turned away from the corporal and strode to the hangar door. With each step, her cornflower blue summer skirt billowed around her long legs. At six-foot-one, Megan Reed was taller than almost everyone else on the Malignant Wave team. But she didn't need her Amazonian presence to intimidate others. Her harsh managerial style, acerbic personality and drive for perfection in herself and others had been quite enough to alienate her from most of her staff.

Ignoring the thick framed glasses now tucked in her pocket, the team leader stooped low, to squint through a small porthole set in the wall-sized hangar door. Outside the sky was blue and cloudless. Beyond the boundaries of the Air Force facility, the desert horizon was a series of stacked layers of browns, mauves and rust reds fading into the firmament. The wind kicked up, and the camouflaged tower was momentarily obscured by a tornado of swirling sand.

*I can't see the damn thing with my naked eyes from five hundred feet away! How can any satellite—even the most advanced—spot it from Earth's orbit?* Dr. Reed mused, convinced this was another futile exercise. *Another way for Air Force Security personnel to justify their pointless existence!*

With an impatient gesture she turned her back on the desert, scanned the interior of Hangar Six. Her

team of technicians, researchers, and support personnel—numbering seventeen in all—lolled casually on
packing crates or in folding chairs. The air conditioning inside the hangar was inadequate and many had
succumbed to the sleepy warmth.

For an instant, Dr. Reed locked eyes with Beverly
Chang, who was fully alert and fidgeting with a plastic cup of tea. The thirty-something cyber specialist
appeared as tense and nervous as Megan Reed felt.

*At least one other person is taking this demonstra-
tion seriously.*

"Ninety seconds and we're in the clear. The satellite will be out of range," the corporal announced—a
statement that elicited a groan from Dr. Reed.

"Why did this have to happen today, of all days.
Just hours before a critical test in front of a VIP from
the Senate Defense Appropriations Committee?" she
complained.

"Actually, you should be flattered, Dr. Reed. You
got their attention," Stratowski replied.

"Who? The Chinese? Are you telling me they're
interested in my demonstration? How do they even
know about it? This project is top secret. Or did you
security boys drop the ball again?"

Scratching his nose, Corporal Stratowski peered at
the tracking screen. The young man's pale pink complexion had been cooked lobster red in places by the
desert sun. His hair had been cropped so short it was
hard to tell whether the color was blond or brown.

"This is no coincidence, Ma'am," the Corporal
explained patiently. "*Something* piqued their interest.

The Chicoms went to a lot of trouble to stage this fly over. They have a whole bunch of photo reconnaissance satellites that pass over this facility on regularly scheduled visits. We know their trajectory and adjust our schedules accordingly."

"Yeah," said Dr. Phillip Bascomb. "But those are old fashioned film-return satellites using technology that's twenty years out of date. By the time the payload is dropped back to earth, the film recovered by the Communist Chinese military and evaluated by their intelligence service, the information is twelve hours old and likely obsolete."

A microwave specialist and a critical member of Dr. Reed's team, Bascomb often displayed a wide range of knowledge that reached beyond his academic field of study. Under his lab coat, he was a stylish dresser, but his affection for the latest designer casual was belied by his refusal to part with a ponytail and walrus moustache—both streaked with gray, both holdovers from his late '60s Berkeley days.

"If these satellites are so outmoded, then why all the paranoia?" Dr. Reed demanded.

"Ask Big Brother," Dr. Bascomb quipped, jerking his head in the Corporal's direction.

"This fly over was unscheduled, Dr. Reed," the man explained. "US Space Command only warned us it was being repositioned two hours ago. And *this* satellite is a Jian Bing ZY–5, the Chicoms' most advanced space based photo reconnaissance vehicle launched to date."

Stratowski tapped the blip on his screen with his

finger. "The ZY–5 has real time capabilities. That means some technician at the Taiyuan Satellite Launch Center in Shanxi Province is watching this hangar right now."

"Smile. You're on *Candid Camera*!" Dr. Alvin Toth grinned. A retired physician and pathologist, the sixty-four year old was the oldest member of Dr. Reed's team. Portly and bald with bushy eyebrows that matched his worn lab smock, Toth leaned against the tow tractor, arms folded across his paunchy torso.

"Careful, Alvin. You're showing your age. Nobody under sixty ever heard of *Candid Camera*," Phil Bascomb called.

"I'm not showing my *age*," Toth countered with a wink. "What I'm demonstrating is my vast range of knowledge, experience, and expertise."

Dr. Dani Welles snorted. "*Candid Camera* was a TV show, not a breakthrough discovery in particle physics. But you know I love you, Doc!" She threw a dazzling smile at Toth. "'Cause, I think older men are hot."

Not yet thirty, Welles was down-to-earth friendly. No one who met her ever guessed that the breezy young woman graduated with honors from MIT. In fact, most of her *MySpace* friends thought "Ms. Cocoa Quark" was just another girl from South Central.

Steve Sable laughed. "So *that's* why you won't go out with me? You're waiting for me to get an AARP card?"

He'd been observing the conversation from a folding chair, munching a donut and sipping coffee from a Styrofoam cup. A cyber engineer and software designer, Dr. Sable was a relative newcomer to the project—only their newest technician, Antonio Alvarez, had less tenure since he'd joined them nearly three months earlier. But Sable had proven himself invaluable in the fourteen months since he joined them. Malignant Wave was Sable's second project at Groom Lake. The previous program had been cancelled.

"I never went out with you because you never asked," Dani replied with a sly smile.

The banter was interrupted when the airman's laptop beeped three times in quick succession. Dr. Reed watched over the Corporal's shoulder as the blip drifted off the grid map and vanished from the screen. A moment later Stratowski tapped a key and shut down the computer.

"All clear, Dr. Reed. Your team can proceed."

Dr. Reed sighed. "Finally."

Heels clicking on the concrete, she strutted across the hangar and punched a red button on the doorjamb. A warning siren wailed, reverberating deafeningly throughout the massive hangar—the signal that nap time was over. With a metallic clatter, the massive steel door began to rise, filling the dim interior of the hangar with bright sunlight and waves of oppressive heat.

After ten seconds, the warning siren went mute. Several young airmen, yawning and stretching, emerged from a tangle of packing crates. A young Hispanic woman in overalls climbed aboard the tow tractor, and the engine roared to life in a cloud of blue smoke. Rumbling, the tractor lurched forward, dragging an aluminum tow platform containing the microwave emissions array.

A split-second later, the tow tractor abruptly braked, tires squealing. Carried by momentum, the tow platform continued forward, colliding with the rear of the tow vehicle. The jolt rattled the sensitive microwave emitter strapped to the platform. Cries of alarm erupted from the research team and Dr. Bascomb cursed. Sable threw his Styrofoam cup to the ground and Beverly Chang took a step backwards, blinking in surprise.

Dr. Megan Reed went ballistic.

"What the hell is that . . . that *thing* blocking the door?" she cried. Reed pointed to a ten foot steel pole set in a concrete filled tire. A volleyball dangled from a long rope hooked to the top.

"It's a tetherball post," Corporal Stratowski declared.

"I know what it *is*," Dr. Reed said. "I want to know who owns it."

"It belongs to Antonio—I mean, Dr. Alvarez." Dani Welles regretted speaking before the words were out of her mouth.

"I should have known," muttered Dr. Reed. She looked around for the guilty party, but saw no sign of the project's energy system programmer. She shouted out in a voice that rivaled the decibel level of the warning siren.

"Alvarez, where the hell are you?"

"Yo!" came the call from the back of the hangar. Dr. Antonio Alvarez stuck his head out of the interior of a malfunctioning electrical generator.

"Front and center, now!" Dr. Reed commanded.

Alvarez hurried forward, a power coupler in one hand, the end of a long electrical cable in the other. The wire in his hand unwound until it reached its limit, nearly jerking him off his feet. With an embarrassed frown, Alvarez dropped the cable and tossed the power coupler onto a crate. Standing before Dr. Reed, he wiped his greasy hands on his white lab coat.

"You called?"

Dr. Reed stared at the newest member of her team. She'd known many "eccentric" scientists and researchers in her day, but few were as clueless as Dr. Alvarez. She studied the man, from the dark tangle of his unkempt hair; black, thick-framed glasses; and perpetual five o'clock stubble; all the way down to the baggy, oversized sweatpants.

If Dr. Reed applied some of the considerable powers of observation she used for her research, she might have noticed that Alvarez was as tall as she was—a fact disguised by his submissive demeanor and perpetually slumped shoulders. Also masked was the man's muscular, former-Marine physique, his strong shoulders and arms strategically camouflaged by a lab coat two sizes too big.

"Does that . . . that *pole* belong to you?" Dr. Reed asked through gritted teeth.

Alvarez followed Reed's gaze to the tetherball stand outside.

"Yes, Dr. Reed."

"Could you move it."

"Of course, sorry. I was trying to fix the backup generator. It blew yesterday, when we tested the coupler set up. I had to reconfigure a few of the—"

"Move the pole. NOW!"

Alvarez flushed red. Pushing up his thick glasses, he tucked his head into his chest and ran to the tetherball pole. He yanked on the rope until the pole toppled. Corporal Stratowski joined him and together they used the concrete-filled tire to roll the post out of the way. A moment later the tractor rumbled through the door of Hangar Six.

"Got it, partner?" Stratowski asked.

"Sure, Corporal," Alvarez replied. "Thanks for the help."

A crane rolled out of another hangar and approached the steel tower. Stratowski joined the others, following the tow vehicle to the base of the structure. Dr. Reed and Dani Welles passed Alvarez on their way out. The Team Leader glanced at the nerdy technician, who was struggling to position the pole as close to the hanger wall as possible.

"A grown man and he still plays tetherball. Can you believe it?" Megan Reed said incredulously.

Dani shrugged. "He plays solo squash, too. Last week I saw him over at the dorms before sunup. I'm sure he didn't know anyone was around. The dude's hot. He was wearing nothing but shorts, and

he whacked that ball like a pro. I was surprised to
see how trim he is. Hides it under those ridiculous
clothes." Dani glanced over her shoulder at Alvarez.
"A girl could do worse . . ."

Dr. Reed snorted. "Antonio? Please. It's lonely out
here in the desert, but not *that* lonely."

When everyone was out of earshot, Dr. Alvarez
reached around the pole, until his fingers located a
small hole drilled into the metal. He probed inside,
until he located two buttons hidden there. He tapped
them in a precise sequence, heard a faint beep over
the sound of the desert wind and rustling sand.

"Jamey, it's Almeida. Can you hear me?"

The voice that answered was faint, broadcast from
CTU Headquarters, Los Angeles, hundreds of miles
away.

"I hear you loud and clear, Tony," Jamey Farrell
replied after a split-second lag.

"How's the reception. Do you have a clear image?"

"Crystal clear. I don't know how you placed the
surveillance camera so close to a top secret test in a
photo restricted area. You have to tell me how you
did it when you get back."

Tony smiled. "Let's just say that sometimes the best
place to hide something is in plain sight."

"Okay, I've activated the digital recorder," Jamey
said. "You have unlimited memory available to you,
so you should have a complete visual recording of the
weapon's set up, the test, and the equipment break
down afterwards."

"Excellent. If anyone approaches that array we'll

have a photographic record," Tony replied, glancing over his shoulders. "I better join the others now . . . Over and out."

Jack Bauer's right arm felt like lead. It hung limply at his side. With his left hand he wiped a splash of blood off his cheek and stared down at the man slumped in the corner of the room, amid orange shards of the shattered fiberglass chair.

"Who sold you the device and when did you buy it?" Bauer asked in a soft voice.

Max Farrow winced at the sound. His chin was buried in his chest, rivulets of blood ran out of his nose. His left eye was swollen shut when he lifted his face to stare at Jack.

"It was Bix," Farrow croaked. "Hugo Bix. I bought it down at his garage . . . Paid seventy grand for it . . ."

"When?"

"Two days ago . . . Tested it out at the Chuck Wagon Casino yesterday . . . Big win . . . Then Bix sent me here 'cause he said the Cha-Cha was an easy touch . . ."

Farrow's voice caught in a muffled sob. "The son of a bitch lied, and now that bastard Bix is gonna kill me for what I'm telling you . . ."

Jack looked up, nodded to Curtis Manning on

the other side of the one-way mirror. The door lock clicked a moment later, and Jack left the cell. Manning glanced at the man huddled on the floor, then closed and locked the door.

"You heard?" Jack asked, wrestling the knuckle duster off of his swollen right hand.

"I'm not surprised," Manning replied. "Thanks to the DEA, we already have a direct link between the Bix gang and the Rojas Brothers. Now we've linked Bix to the technology thefts. I think Hugo Bix is our man, Jack. You were right to go up against him."

It was a tough admission for Curtis Manning. Initially he'd resisted the plan to begin undermining the most powerful gangster in Las Vegas. But Jack knew he wouldn't get bites unless he started baiting. He hadn't wanted to do it, either, but—

"We had no choice, Curtis," Jack reminded him. "The local DA and the Nevada Prosecutor's office have nothing on Bix, and when the FBI tried to trap him, their undercover agent ended up in a shallow grave in the desert."

"You better proceed with caution. Bix has got a real hate on for you."

To Manning's surprise, Jack laughed, short and sharp.

"Good. That's the way I want it," Bauer said. "The more Jaycee Jager threatens Bix, the more desperate he becomes. We've been cutting into his drug trade and stealing away his customers for three months. By sending that cowboy to shake us down, Bix showed his hand. That was his first mistake."

*12:52:09 P.M. PDT*
*Babylon Hotel and Casino, Las Vegas*

Jong Lee recognized his visitor the moment the man was ushered into the luxury suite. The face he had seen many times, on American television, and on the covers of American magazines and newspapers. Although Jong knew everything there was to know about this man—from his humble birth in the deep South to his impressive athletic and political careers—nothing could prepare him for Congressmen Larry Bell's size and physical presence.

*Hùnzhàng! Where does this brute purchase his clothing?* Lee wondered.

Smiling affably, Jong Lee rose and moved to greet the newcomer. At nearly six feet, Jong was tall for a Chinese man. But the former pro basketball player towered over him. When they shook, Lee's pale hand disappeared in the American's ebony fist. Protocol demanded Jong bow, so he did. Not deeply, but enough to show respect. Tradition also dictated that Jong's head should never be lower than his visitor's—symbolic of his own dominant position in the coming negotiations. But in this case, he would have to forego tradition.

"Please sit down, Representative Bell," Jong said. "I realize how busy you must be. You are quite generous to spare me even a moment of your time."

"You're the one who's generous, Mr. Lee," Representative Bell replied. "I know how busy you must be. Your firm operates five factories in Hong Kong alone . . ."

Jong crossed his legs. "I'm impressed, Congressman. You have done your homework."

Silently, Jong Lee's associate, a petite woman named Yizi, set a mahogany tray on the table between the two men. Aromatic steam rose from a porcelain tea pot. Gracefully she served. Her blue-black hair was swept to one side. Bell's eyes followed the cascade along one delicate cheek, past her pale throat. The only sound in the room was the rustling of her black dress, the tap of her heels on the marble floor. Mesmerized, Bell continued to follow her movements. When the woman placed the warm cup before him, her alabaster hand briefly brushed his.

"You were saying, Congressman . . ."

The man blinked, faced the speaker. "I was saying that I'm delighted you made this trip, Mr. Lee. But I also admit I'm surprised."

Jong Lee raised an eyebrow, but said nothing.

"What I mean to say is that you're a chip manufacturer from China, and the Pan-Latin Anti-Drug Conference chiefly involves business leaders and law enforcement officials from the major Latin American drug producing nations . . ."

"Ah, I see your point, Congressman," Jong said with a wry laugh. "I suppose I could plead altruism, mumble a collection of familiar platitudes about how we're all part of the global community, and in an ever-shrinking world no issue is truly local, but the truth is, my firm also operates a factory in Mexico, so I am no stranger to the drug epidemic in the West. My company also happens to manufacture an array of sensors and microchips that are quite useful in drug interdiction, so I also have a selfish motive."

Congressman Bell held the porcelain cup between his thumb and forefinger, then swallowed the contents. He placed the cup on the table with a click, then slapped his knees.

"That's a relief, Mr. Lee. As a United States Congressman from the great state of Louisiana, I get uncomfortable around too much altruism."

Both men laughed. Yizi stood beside the Congressman to replenish his cup. She was so close her scent made him dizzy. Larry Bell found himself wondering if she was wearing anything under her form fitting dress. He doubted it.

"Altruism has its own rewards, Congressman. But a smart man will always find profit in charity."

"Well said, Mr. Lee . . . I wonder if we might have some privacy?"

Congressman Bell glanced at the silhouette of Yizi as she peered through the picture window, at the Vegas Strip thirty stories below.

"Pay the woman no mind, Congressman. Yizi knows nothing of my business and she speaks no language but Mandarin. She is here for only one purpose—to serve my personal needs."

Bell's reply was a lecherous wink. "The benefits of the private sector, eh?" the Congressman said. "I haven't had a piece that fine since my days with the pros. You are one lucky man, Lee."

Jong brushed the lapel of his London tailored suit. "I believe we were about to talk business?"

Congressman Bell drained his second cup. "You've been very generous to my re-election campaign. Very generous. Now I think I can help you."

"Please."

"At the end of this year more than a billion dollars' worth of manufacturing contracts will be handed out by the Pentagon. What your firm does is pretty standard, and you do it well. But those contracts can go anywhere."

"Your point?"

"Later on, at the Conference, I can introduce you to one of the most influential members of the Senate Defense Appropriations Committee. Not only is he a powerful senator. There's also a strong consensus in both parties that this man—my old friend—is going to be our next president." Larry Bell paused. "Just imagine the kind of influence a generous donation to his primary campaign can buy."

Jong Lee nodded. "This friend of yours. Do you believe he will be open to my offer?"

"He's an ambitious man, Mr. Lee. He wants to be president, and that takes money."

"And you, Congressman Bell? You do this out of your own generosity?"

Bell snorted. "As you yourself said. A smart man finds a way to make altruism profitable. My introduction will only cost you a million dollars . . ."

Jong Lee smiled and reached across the table. Once again his hand vanished when it was enfolded by the American's massive fist.

Congressman Bell rose. "I think I'd better go. I

have plenty of work to do before tonight's dinner. You have your invitation?"

"Indeed I do, Congressman."

Bell stole a final glance at Yizi, who was re-arranging flowers in a vase. "You have fun . . . If you know what I mean."

The woman saw Congressman Bell head for the door. She hurried to open it. As he passed she bowed politely.

"You're a lucky man, Lee. A lucky man," Bell said before the door closed behind him.

Yizi drifted back to the vase, continued her task.

"I hope that animal did not offend you with his words, Yizi," Jong said.

"His words and opinions are of no consequence to me. All that matters is that Congressman Bell fulfills his part in the plan," the woman replied in perfect, accent-less English.

Holding a slightly imperfect flower between her exquisitely manicured fingers, Yizi studied the blossom. Rejecting it, she snapped the stem in half and tossed the remains into the waste can.

"He is going to introduce you to Senator Palmer?" she asked.

Jong nodded. "Today. As planned—though I doubt the Congressman is aware of the *true* reason for Palmer's visit. I'm sure Bell believes Palmer is here for his useless conference."

*12:56:47 P.M. PDT*
*The Cha-Cha Lounge, Las Vegas*

Flashing a tantalizing display of bronzed thigh, Stella Hawk stepped out of the cab. The doorman at the casino's entrance was dazzled even before her luminous topaz eyes cast him a warm greeting.

Voluptuous yet lithe, with slender waist, full hips and eye-catching cleavage, amply displayed by the extreme v-neck of her filmy saffron sundress, Stella Hawk radiated a vitality as fierce and sultry as the desert winds. Her raven hair, streaked with russet highlights, fell in glossy waves down her supple, sculpted back; and, with each confident stride, a thin chain of tiny platinum bell charms tinkled faintly around her ankle.

Heads turned as the woman strutted through the betting floor—there were even a few whistles and cat calls. But if Stella noticed their stares or heard their cries, she paid no mind. A star performer in *Risqué*, an erotic stage extravaganza performed nightly at the Babylon Hotel and Casino on the Vegas Strip, Stella wasn't just accustomed to the adoration of the opposite sex. She reveled in the attention and expected nothing less.

After passing through the casino, Stella entered the Tiki Lounge, walking between two fifteen-foot wooden totems imported from some unnamed South Sea island back when Frank Sinatra and the Rat Pack were a Vegas fixture. She sidled up to the pit boss, who was sipping a scotch at the end of the long, polished mahogany bar.

"Hey, doll," he said with a wink. "Long time, no see. Where you been keeping yourself?" the pit boss asked.

Stella sat on a stool, crossed her shapely legs. "Oh, you know. Here and there."

"Can I buy you a drink?"

"It's a little early, and I'm working tonight." She opened her leather handbag, pulled out a cell and checked the messages. Stella rolled her eyes in obvious annoyance when she found a voice message left by her roommate. Stella closed the phone without retrieving it.

The bartender placed a glass of iced water before Stella. She ignored it. "Where's Jaycee?" she asked.

Driscoll stared down at the brown liquid in his shot glass. "He's in the basement, working on a problem. He's busy. Real busy. You want I should interrupt him?"

"Of course I want you to interrupt him, Don," she said, her full lips curling into a lewd smile. "You tell Jaycee that his Stella's back in town, and she needs some attention real bad . . ."

1 2 3 4 5 6 7 8 9
10 11 12 13 14 15 16 17
18 19 20 21 22 23 24

. . . . . . . . . . . . . . . . . . . . . . . . . . . . . .

**THE FOLLOWING TAKES PLACE
BETWEEN THE HOURS OF
1 P.M. AND 2 P.M.
PACIFIC DAYLIGHT TIME**

. . . . . . . . . . . . . . . . . . . . . . . . . . . . . .

*1:00:57 P.M. PDT
Babylon Hotel and Casino, Las Vegas*

"Lev," Senator David Palmer whispered through gritted teeth, "what *is* all this?"

The hotel lobby was crowded with reporters, all of whom obviously had anticipated the senator's arrival. But David Palmer had been given no notice of this instant public appearance. He was tired, his throat was parched, and the long flight West had left him unkempt and irritable. To top it off, the limo's air conditioner had been on the fritz, so there were perspiration stains under the arms of his wrinkled white button-down.

Still, Palmer knew the power of the photo op; and, inside of fifteen seconds, his initial expression of surprise, then extreme annoyance, vanished. In its place came the well-rehearsed campaign smile. His grin was so firmly set that his lips barely moved when he quietly asked his chief of staff what the hell was going on.

Lev Cohen's fleshy face flushed under his red beard.

"Sorry, David. I didn't know about any event," he replied. "It must be something Congressman Bell's people set up—"

"You *should* have known about it." Senator Palmer's voice was an irritated rumble.

Sherry Palmer suddenly appeared at her husband's side, tucked her hand under his arm. "You've made this trip to raise your national profile before our run for the Presidency, David," she reminded him softly.

Palmer arched an eyebrow. "*Our* run?"

Sherry didn't miss a beat. "Yes, David," she purred, her eyes scanning the crowd for familiar media faces. "And I'll be right there beside you the whole way."

The crowd had assembled inside the immense sandstone and glass atrium of the ultra-modern Babylon Hotel and Casino, an architectural showplace that was the latest addition to the Las Vegas skyline. A huge banner hung from a balcony, proclaiming this hotel as the venue for the Pan-Latin Anti-Drug Conference. Flags of a dozen North, Central and South American nations dangled from the high ceiling.

David Palmer hardly noticed the décor. The brace of reporters was what concerned him, along with the cheering group of spectators, who'd suddenly recognized their choice for the next presidential election.

Palmer studied the throng uncertainly. His race for the U.S. Senate had involved local Maryland press, of course, but the glare of national media interest, now that he was about to announce his presidential run, was nothing like he'd ever before experienced.

Sherry touched his arm. "Wave, David," she urged through a tight smile.

Palmer waved.

"Now slip on your jacket," she whispered. "It'll cover those *nasty* sweat-stains." Sherry released the grip on her husband long enough for him to cover his wrinkled dress shirt with the blue suit coat draped over his arm.

"Look," she continued quietly, "I know you don't like to talk off the cuff, but it's time you practiced. Just say a few words. Keep things light and cheerful and don't let the press steer the conversation."

"They're the ones who ask the questions."

"Politics 101, David. Do I have to remind you? They ask. That doesn't mean you have to answer," Sherry Palmer said through a stiff smile.

The Senator glanced down at his wife and his grin became more genuine. "What would I do without you?"

"I shudder to think," Sherry shot back. Then she gestured with her expressive brown eyes. "Look, there's Larry. Go greet your old teammate and make nice with the people who came out to see you."

Palmer looked up, saw Larry Bell approaching. He

moved forward to greet him. Photographers flashed and spectators applauded as the famous Congressman and even more famous Senator clasped hands.

Both ex-basketball players were taller than everyone around them. But Larry Bell was lanky with gangly arms and legs. Broad-shouldered Palmer was built more like a linebacker than the former Big East Conference Defensive Player of the Year and NCAA All-American; and though both men had a full head of hair, Bell's closely trimmed Afro was peppered with gray.

Almost at once, the pair was surrounded by cameras and proffered microphones.

"Really great to see you, David." Bell's smile was warm, but his eyes remained fixed on the press.

"An impressive welcome, Larry," Palmer replied without a hint of rancor.

Bell faced his colleague eye to eye. "Nothing but the best for the guy who consistently passed me the ball in the greatest game of my career." Bell slapped Palmer's arm. "Even when he didn't have to."

Palmer shook his head. "I wasn't there to make you look good, Larry. I was there to win—and since you scored every time you got near the basket, I just thought I'd hand the ball off to you."

"We made a great team—" Congressman Bell faced the cameras, his voice rising. "And we'll make a great team again. Only this time we'll be doing more than winning the NCAA championship."

There was a smattering of applause, then a *Washington Post* reporter fired the opening salvo. "My question is for Senator Palmer. What brings you to Las Vegas, sir?"

David Palmer grinned. "Well, as Larry said, this time it's not the NCAA championship. In fact—"

"How about the presidency?" a woman from the *Los Angeles Times* shouted. "Are you here to raise your national profile, Senator Palmer? Is it true that you're planning a run for the White House next November?"

Palmer waited patiently for the battery of questions to end. "I'm in Nevada for only one reason," he told them. "I'm here to participate in a vital and important program that may someday end the scourge of illegal narcotics, not just in the United States, but through-out all of North, Central and South America . . ." Palmer paused, gestured to his colleague.

"Of course, Congressman Bell and I both know that solving this massive problem will require inter-national cooperation—which is exactly what the Pan-Latin Anti-Drug Conference exists to promote . . ."

Though shunted to the sidelines by her own staff and the press of reporters, Sherry Palmer's gaze never left her husband—even when Lev Cohen touched her shoulder and spoke softly into her ear.

"I just spoke to Bell's chief of staff, Doug Healy—"

"And?"

"Congressman Bell's going to make the introduc-tion himself. Later this afternoon. I have all the infor-mation . . ."

Sherry frowned. "Oh, you have all the informa-tion? Then you must know why we weren't notified about this press conference in advance. This was no spontaneous event, Lev."

Cohen bit his lower lip. "Healy claimed it was an oversight. Someone in his office didn't make a call—"

Sherry cut him off. "That's bull and we both know it. Larry Bell is jealous. Back in the day he thought he was a better basketball player than David, and now he thinks he's a better politician, too."

Sherry finally shifted her gaze away from her husband, to focus on his chief of staff. "Bell probably believes he should be running for president instead of David, too. But that will never happen because David has the one thing that Larry Bell will never have."

Lev blinked. "Actually David has three things, or did you forget our campaign slogan? *Competence, charisma, and experience . . .*"

Sherry smirked. *David Palmer possesses all those qualities, it's true,* she thought. *But he's only going to be President for one reason. Because he has* me.

*1:19:11 P.M. PDT*
*Hangar Six, Experimental Weapons Testing Range*
*Groom Lake Air Force Base*

CTU Agent Tony Almeida entered the hangar through a little used side door, pausing for a moment so his eyes could adjust to the building's dim interior. Outside, in the desert's afternoon glare, most members of Dr. Reed's research team were running diagnostic tests on the massive sensor array. By now, the apparatus was sitting on top of the tower, and the huge crane that had hoisted it here had crawled back to its holding area on clanking steel tracks.

After Tony finished running his own diagnostics—on the shielded generator unit that would power the microwave emitting device—he noticed the entire team wasn't present. Slipping away, he headed back to Hangar Six to track down the missing person.

Tony circled the building, moving off the pavement into the soft sand. With each step of his steel-toed work boot he kicked up red brown desert dust. No one had used this path for some time. Tony knew because some sign of foot tracks would have been visible, and there was nothing in the sand beyond the swirling tracks of a long-gone rattlesnake.

Near the rear of the structure, Tony climbed three steel steps that led to the side door. He knew the door was unlocked—Tony had made sure of that before the researcher team even rolled out of the hangar. Now he entered a darkened storage area just off the main floor of the hangar, well out of sight of anyone inside.

With the overhead lights powered down, what little illumination came through grimy windows set high in the walls. Most of the high-roofed interior was shrouded in shadows. When his eyes finally got used to the gloom, Tony cautiously stepped around a pile of empty wooden packing crates which formed a makeshift wall.

Suddenly he froze. A hushed voice was speaking in an urgent tone. . .

"I told you I can't come now . . . The project is on a lock down, that's why . . . That means nobody can leave, no matter what . . . I'm stuck here until the demonstration is over."

Though the echoing interior of the hangar distorted some of the words, Tony recognized the speaker at once. He was the missing scientist, Dr. Steve Sable. Tony trailed the sound, moving quietly from one dark patch to another, carefully approaching the caller.

"Look, I'll try to get there soon, but I can't promise anything," Sable said. "I—"

The man's excuses were cut short by the person on the other end of the line. Sable tried to stammer a few words in his own defense, but they were apparently ignored. Patiently following the sound, Tony finally located the cyber-engineer behind an idle tow tractor. Sable was there, leaning against a dented workbench covered with wires, chips and motherboards. His back to Tony, Sable was whispering into a slim silver cell phone.

The doctor had good reason to hide his activity in what he thought was a deserted hangar. Using a personal phone anywhere inside the confines of the Groom Lake Experimental facility was a flagrant violation of Air Force security protocols. At the very least, Sable could lose his clearance and face dismissal if he were caught in possession of a cell phone, even if he weren't using it.

"Threats won't help either of us," Sable said with a hint of irritation. "I know how important this is."

Tony couldn't read the man's expression because he

faced Sable's back. Risking discovery, Tony used the cover of packing crates and electronic gear to circle the man. All the while he strained to hear the voice on the other end of the line. Unfortunately, Tony was just too far away.

"Yeah, I know it's a problem," Sable said, his tone exasperated. "Money is always a problem, but the delay can't be helped. I'm not dodging my responsibility. It's just bad timing, that's all."

Suddenly another voice echoed inside the hangar. "Dr. Sable . . . Are you in here?"

Surprised by the call, Sable quickly slipped the phone into his lab coat and spun around—to come face-to-face with Tony.

"Jesus, Alvarez, you scared the hell out of me!" he cried.

Hearing their voices, the young airman standing near the hangar entrance called out again. Only then did Sable realize Tony's wasn't the voice he'd heard call out his name. A split second later it dawned on Sable that Tony had most likely seen the phone, and was maybe even eavesdropping on the conversation.

"Listen, Tony," Sable said in a whispered hiss. "You won't tell anybody about the cell, will you?"

Tony moved out of the shadows to face the man. Sable stepped closer, leaned into his ear.

"See, I got this girl in Vegas," he said. "She's a showgirl. A real hottie. But she kind of takes advantage, you know? This morning she totaled the tranny in her new Mercedes convertible and expects me to pay for a new one."

Sable flashed Tony a conspiratorial wink. "'Course, I'll ante up and she knows it. I mean, I'm not married, divorced, or responsible for any brats—that I know of, anyway. So what else am I gonna spend my money on, right?"

Abruptly, a young airman appeared between two mounds of electronic equipment. He halted in surprise when he saw them.

"Dr. Sable, Dr. Alvarez . . . Dr. Reed's been asking for you," he said.

"Yeah, well, Tony and I were just grabbing some cable," Dr. Sable replied, tucking a coil of thick, insulated wire under his arm.

"That's right," grunted Tony, grabbing another bundle and looping it over his shoulder. "Some of those old generator wires are frayed. Better to replace them all."

"Maybe I can help," the airman offered. The earnest young man grabbed two coils, each representing several hundred feet of wire—more than they would ever need. Spinning on his polished heels, the airman headed back to the hangar door.

Sable grinned, shot Tony a conspiratorial wink. Then he dropped his own coil and, whistling tunelessly, followed the soldier to the exit.

Meanwhile, Tony shouldered his own burden, while he pondered how he was going to get hold of Sable's cell phone in the next several hours, without the man knowing about it.

*1:32:05 P.M. PDT*
*Babylon Hotel and Casino, Las Vegas*

"This suite is certainly impressive." Sherry Palmer ran her hand across the sleek steel frame of an ultra-modern armchair.

Senator Palmer appraised the stark sandstone walls, glass partitions, black leather furnishings, and splashes of primary-colored pop art.

"It's nice," he said with a raised eyebrow. "But I still prefer the Venetian."

Sherry crossed the floor and threw open the balcony's glass doors. A blast of hot desert air filled the room—but only for a moment, until the suite's computer brain increased the air conditioning by forty percent.

"Just think, David. The last time we were in Las Vegas this place hadn't even been built yet."

"Casinos grow like weeds out here."

"You can't deny the view is impressive. The hotel's Hanging Gardens start right below us. I can smell the honeysuckle all the way up here . . ."

The senator had already removed his jacket. Now he rolled up the sleeves of his dress shirt, loosened his tie, and placed his hands on his hips. "The view is magnificent, no doubt about it. From forty stories up, even Las Vegas is a handsome city . . ."

"But you disapprove," Sherry observed from the edge of the balcony. "Because you really are a Puritan."

David smiled. "I prefer to think of myself as a Boy Scout."

Sherry laughed, walked back to her husband. "You're tense," she said, reaching up to massage his broad shoulders. "Are you still fretting about your performance downstairs? Well, don't. You were wonderful, David! Your words, your answers . . . they set just the right tone."

Senator Palmer shook his head.

"You didn't let Larry Bell get under your skin?" Sherry pressed. "I know he's a conniving dog, but you should be used to that—"

"It's nothing, Sherry, really," David replied, wrapping her in his arms.

"I know you too well," Sherry said, returning his embrace. "You're holding something back."

But Palmer refused to respond to her question. Instead, he changed the subject. "This is nice," he whispered, nuzzling his wife's hair. Sherry closed her eyes and leaned closer.

A gentle knock interrupted them.

"Ignore it," Sherry whispered, pulling him closer. But David Palmer frowned and stepped back.

"I . . . can't," he told her. His tone and his expression were brimming with regret.

Sherry nodded. "Now I know what's been bothering you. You're not only here for the drug conference . . . You've got some kind of committee business going on." Her expression shifted suddenly, from suspicion to alarm. "You're not doing something that would jeopardize your bid for the White House?"

"I can't discuss this right now," he replied.

"You don't have to. I know I'm right."

The knock came again. They stared at one another for a moment.

"You know that you can't shut me out . . . not even from policy decisions. When everything's said and done, I'm your only ally, David," Sherry said, then turned to call loudly towards the door. "Let yourself in, Lev! You have a keycard!"

The door opened. "Hey." Lev's gaze nervously darted between Sherry and David.

"Sherry was just leaving," the senator said.

"That's right, I'm leaving," Sherry repeated coolly. She snatched her bag from the glass and steel table. "I have a full schedule, too."

As she passed Lev Cohen, their eyes met. "I'll see you later," Sherry promised softly before closing the door behind her.

"Come in, sit down, Lev." Palmer sank into the leather couch and stretched his long legs. Cohen sat in the steel framed chair across from him.

"Before we begin, Senator, I want to apologize for what happened in the lobby. I . . . I should have been on top of that."

David raised his hand. "No apologies, Lev, or I'll have to apologize, too, for my initial reaction. My impatience was out of line, so let's just drop the subject."

Lev Cohen nodded, visibly relieved.

"Now, about this other matter," Palmer prodded.

"All the arrangements have been made, Senator. A representative from the Air Force Systems Command will arrive in—" Cohen checked his watch. "—a little less than two hours."

Palmer nodded, his expression a thousand miles away.

"Senator?"

He blinked. "Sorry, Lev. I guess I zoned out for a minute there."

"Yes, well, as I was saying . . . Your escort will be a Colonel Vincent DeBlasio, accompanied by a security staff. He's bringing a car that will take you to the airport."

Palmer sighed. "Thank you, Lev."

"Since I won't be going with you, I thought I'd assist Sherry with her afternoon schedule. She's meeting the Mayor's wife at four, then there's . . ."

Lev's voice petered out when he realized David Palmer was, once again, distracted by something. He cleared his throat and the Senator looked up.

"You're a wise man, Lev," Palmer said. "I trust your counsel as much as I trust anyone's."

"Thank you sir . . ."

"You know I'd take you with me today . . . if I could."

This time it was Lev who raised his hand. "What you're doing today is classified, sir. Part of your duty as the chairman of the Senate Special Defense Appropriations Committee. It's obviously beyond my security clearance level, and I completely understand."

Palmer offered his chief of staff a half smile. "Nicely put. Still, I could use some of your sage advice. I'm forced to make a very difficult decision today. It's a decision I'll make alone, and it's weighing heavily."

Lev nodded sympathetically. "The burden of command, David. It will only get heavier after you get to the White House."

Palmer's grin was genuine. "*If* I get there, you mean."

Lev shook his head. "Oh, you'll get there, Senator. You have what it takes and this country needs you."

"I appreciate your endorsement, but I'm afraid we'll have to leave it up to the voters."

Both men chuckled. Then the chief of staff rose. "You'd better get some rest, Senator. It's going to be a long day."

*1:56:43 P.M. PDT*
*Big Dean's Truck Farm*
*Two miles southeast of Route 582*
*Outside of Henderson, Nevada*

A billowing cloud of powdery dust followed the lumbering semi as it crawled up the slight incline. With each pit and bump of the rough, unpaved road, the trailer the truck hauled shuddered and boomed hollowly, rocking back and forth so violently it seemed poised to tip over at any moment. At the top of the hillock, the narrow path ended at a pair of eight-foot wooden doors adorned with curls of rusty barbed wire. Above the weathered gate the faded BIG DEAN'S sign was topped by a crudely rendered image of smiling cowboy tipping his broad brimmed hat.

The driver hardly slackened his pace as he approached the barrier. Instead, the truck's roar shook a pair of sun-browned workers in greasy overalls out of a dilapidated, sun-bleached shed. They loped to the gates, one lifting the latch, the other swinging the rickety doors open. Within a moment, the truck roared through the opening, followed by its cloud of grit and grime.

With a high-pitched squeal the semi braked, sand and gravel crunching under sixteen wheels. The vehicle ground to a halt in the middle of a dusty expanse occupied by the shack, and a battered mobile home with cracked windows resting on gray concrete bricks. The mobile home's dented sides were flecked with peeling yellow paint.

The driver popped his door just as the persistent plume of dust finally overtook his vehicle. Coughing once, the coyote hopped to the ground and disdainfully kicked the Nevada sand with a booted foot. Tall and rail thin, wearing faded jeans and a red bandana around his throat, the young man had dark hair that stuck out from under the brim of a sweat-stained cowboy hat. Brown face impassive, the human smuggler sauntered to the rear of the vehicle.

As he began to unlock the trailer's door, three Hispanic men emerged from the dilapidated mobile home on the opposite end of the enclosed lot. The trio were clad in dusty denim and heavy work boots. The two men on either end were well over six feet tall, muscular, with thick necks and shaven heads, dotted with stubble. The man in the middle was shorter than the others, and had a full head of brown, curly hair. Mirrored sunglasses covered his eyes. Each man cradled an AK–47 in the crook of his arm.

If the presence of automatic weapons troubled the coyote, he didn't show it. With an air of tedious routine, the man unlatched the steel door on the back of the trailer and swung it open. Eyes to the ground, he stepped back to allow the newcomers unobstructed access to the cargo inside.

Five men emerged from inside the cavernous trailer, blinking against the harsh desert sun. They wore worn work clothes and were armed like the others, their assault rifles slung over their shoulders, next to heavy backpacks. Joints stuff, muscles sore, the men slowly and silently climbed down from the trailer. Only one man out of the group approached the armed trio. Without preamble he hugged the man in the middle, muttering quietly in Spanish. The two stood in the sun, arms looped around each other's necks, heads bowed, foreheads together like boxers who'd just finished a grueling match.

While the reunion took place, the coyote crossed the enclosure to a rusty faucet sticking out of the ground next to the ramshackle hut. He slipped a canteen from his belt, turned on the tap, and filled the aluminum container. Moving quietly past the others, he jumped into the dark trailer.

"Where is he going?" the man with the sunglasses asked, finally breaking the embrace.

"We were not alone," the other man replied. "There are more people inside the truck. A banker, his wife, and their child. He's a businessman . . . *for-*

*mer* businessman . . . fleeing a financial scandal in Mexico City."

The man with the sunglasses moved between the others, to peer into the darkened trailer. He saw a man in a tailored suit, now dirty and travel worn. The man's eyes were large and nervous, his tie loose around a flabby neck. He squatted on the metal floor, a prominent gut hanging over his belt. A woman rested on her knees beside him. With the hem of her dress, the woman was brushing dirt off the pudgy face of a five-year-old girl, still sluggish from sleep. The man and wife viewed the armed men warily, while pretending indifference.

While the man with the sunglasses watched, the coyote offered the family his canteen. The businessman waved it away, still staring at the strangers through the open door. The woman took a few sips, then helped the little girl quench her thirst.

Sunglasses sneered. "This flesh smuggler had specific instructions. He was very well compensated to ferry you and your men across the border. *Only* you and your men."

The other nodded once. "He told me this . . . this banker paid more money than we did. He said if he was leaving anyone behind, it was us. In any case, it was too late to haggle. I thought it best to deal with the problem on this end . . ."

"And so we shall," Sunglasses said. Stepping back, he raised his right hand and gestured the two bodyguards forward.

"Use your weapons. Deal with them," he commanded.

Before anyone could register shock, the two men raised their AK–47s and threw the safeties. The woman inside the trailer jumped at the sound. The coyote whirled to face them.

The quiet desert suddenly erupted with the chattering bark of twin assault rifles. The long, sustained sound seemed magnified by the trailer's hollow interior, echoing back at the shooters in waves of booming sound. Only when the banana-shaped clips were empty did the men stop firing. The abrupt silence was nearly as jarring as the explosion of noise that preceded it.

The man with the sunglasses turned his back on the carnage, focused his mirrored stare on one of the men who'd opened the gate.

"Bury them in the desert," he said.

Then the man with the sunglasses turned and led the newcomers to the dusty mobile home.

• • • • • • • • • • • • • • • • • • • • • • • • • • • • • • • • •

THE FOLLOWING TAKES PLACE
BETWEEN THE HOURS OF
2 P.M. AND 3 P.M.
PACIFIC DAYLIGHT TIME

• • • • • • • • • • • • • • • • • • • • • • • • • • • • • • • • •

*2:01:21 P.M. PDT*
*The Cha-Cha Lounge, Las Vegas*

The woman beside him stirred. Jack Bauer opened his
eyes, instantly alert. A dark cloud was spread across
the pillow beside him; and then he remembered. . .

He'd drifted off, gazing at the ebony hair of Stella
Hawk, but thinking—and dreaming—of his wife.
It was a vision from a long time ago. He was surfing a shimmering aqua ocean, the sun-washed beach
gleaming white. Teri sat on the sand, laughing with
her art crowd friends around a small bonfire, her
body taut in a wetsuit, waiting for Jack to give her
that promised surf lesson. He did . . . and, later that

night, they'd made love for the first time. . .

Jack lay motionless for a moment, clinging to the vanishing threads of his deeply satisfying dream—only to feel the memory slip away, along with the feeling of contentment it brought him.

He raised his left arm to check the time. In the dim light filtering through the shuttered blinds he almost believed he could still see the faded circle around the third finger of his left hand. Jack immediately shifted his gaze to the illuminated face of the MTM Spec Ops watch. It was just after two o'clock in the afternoon. Forty-two days and seven hours since he'd last been with his wife.

In the beginning, Jack believed this undercover assignment would allow him time to visit his family—a weekend here and there, at the very least. Los Angeles was just a few hours away from Vegas by car, even quicker by plane. And Christopher Henderson agreed that an occasional visit would not jeopardize the success of the mission.

During the first two months, Jack had made several trips to see his family. But each homecoming proved more difficult than the last. There was a world of difference between Jack Bauer, loving husband and father, and the dangerous, violent double-life of Jaycee Jager. To his dismay, Jack discovered that he could not easily bridge that gap. After playing the role of Jager twenty-four hours a day, for weeks on end, shifting personas proved difficult. The last time he'd been home, Jack actually felt alienated from his own family. Instead of the respite it was supposed to be, life in his own home seemed to sap more of Jack's energy than his undercover existence at the Cha-Cha Lounge.

So Jack stopped going home, warning Teri that he would be "overseas" for an extended and as yet undetermined period of time. Of course, his wife accepted his explanation. She always did. Teri had learned to accept the nature of his work and no longer asked questions.

Jack secretly worried that if she knew the truth, she'd be as relieved to see him go as he was to be gone.

By his side, Jack felt Stella move again. She wrapped her warm, naked body around his. The woman's knee curled and he felt the platinum bells circling her ankle tickle his calf. Holding him close, she sighed and muttered something in her sleep. He noticed her bright pink lipstick was smeared from their quick, passionate coupling.

He'd brought Stella up to the tiny suite of rooms that doubled as Jaycee Jager's home and his office. As soon as the door had closed behind them, she'd thrown herself at him, her physical demands insistent and unconstrained. He'd surrendered, knowing she would be more pliable to his questioning after their tryst.

Jack hadn't heard from Jaycee Jager's volatile girlfriend in over a week, but he was impressed with the woman's timing. Stella was connected to the underbelly of this city; and, thus far, her knowledge had proven accurate and useful. Now he was hoping she'd gotten wind of Hugo Bix's scheme to peddle classified technology to lowlife gambling cheats. Why should she know? Because before Jaycee Jager had rolled in from KC, Stella Hawk had belonged to Bix.

Jack had already planned to grill the woman when their paths crossed again. If she hadn't shown up today, he would have sent Curtis over to the Babylon to fetch her. But she had shown up . . . and now that Stella had her "afternoon delight," as she put it, it was time to collect some answers.

Jack sat up and ran his hands through his hair. He pulled the sheets aside and slapped Stella's naked bottom. "Wake up, doll. I gotta get back to work."

The woman's eyes flew open and she squealed in protest.

"Get up or I'll give it to you again." Jack forced a grin, and she moved out of his way.

"Cut it out, Jaycee!" Stella cried, rubbing her tender flesh. "I've got a show tonight and I hate wearing that damn body makeup."

Despite her protests, Stella's luminous eyes laughed and her generous mouth was smiling. She sat up in bed, not bothering to cover her nakedness. Her wanton behavior came as no surprise. Stella had once told Jaycee that strutting completely nude on stage five nights a week had pretty much annihilated any shred of modesty she may have possessed, but Jack doubted she'd ever had a shred of modesty. The woman he'd gotten to know was the most uninhibited female he'd ever met.

"I need some coffee, Jaycee," Stella moaned, one hand pulling back her hair.

"I'll have someone bring it up."

While Jack made the call from a phone on the nightstand, Stella rubbed the sleep out of her eyes with the backs of her hands, then used the sheet to wipe away her ruined lipstick.

"Hungry?" Jack asked, receiver to his ear.

Stella shook her head.

"Just coffee," Jack said into the phone. He hung up and lay back, avoiding her eyes. Stella reached out and stroked his arm with long, fuchsia fingernails.

"Where have you been, Stella?" Jack asked with an air of masculine disinterest.

Stella rolled onto her back.

"I had to make myself scarce," she said with a sigh. "Lilly had custody of her daughter for the week. Her ex is coming to town today or tomorrow to snatch the kid back. In the meantime, she's stuck with the little rug rat."

Lilly Sheridan was Stella's roommate, a hostess at one of the Babylon's four star restaurants—the mammoth casino hotel had three of them. The women shared an expensive house on the outskirts of Vegas. Jaycee had met Lilly once or twice, but Jack never knew until now that Lilly had a daughter, or a failed marriage in her past.

"So where'd you go, baby?" Jack asked.

Stella stretched her arms over her head and yawned. "Drove to Reno and subbed for a friend. Three sets a night, two grand per show. Nice bling for taking my clothes off."

"How's the Babylon feel about you working for the competition?"

Stella threw back her head, shook out the long locks of raven hair. "They don't have an opinion. Why should they. I didn't sign an exclusive contract. I'm not that kind of girl."

Jack swung his legs over the side of the bed. "Seen Hugo Bix lately?"

Stella smirked. "Jaycee . . . Are you having me followed?"

"Should I?"

"Okay, sure," she replied. "I went over to Bix Automotive today. The radio stopped working in my Beamer while I was in Reno. I figured, since Bix bought the car for me, the boys at his garage could fix it."

Jack shot the woman a sidelong glance. Feigning annoyance he asked, "Did you see Hugo?"

Stella's smirk turned triumphant. "Are you jealous, Jaycee?"

When he remained silent, she rolled her eyes. "Honestly," she said, hand over her heart as she mimicked a southern drawl. "You two big strong men should stop fighting over lil' ol' me. Why, I'm hardly worth the trouble . . ."

Suddenly Stella's eyes narrowed into angry slits. "Anyway, this caveman bit between two bull apes is getting tired. I'm not property, Jaycee. Get it through your head. I'm with who I'm with 'cause that's where I want to be. You don't own me and neither does Hugo Bix."

She wrapped the sheets around her lush body, slid to the edge of the bed. She was hardly on her feet before Jack grabbed her arm and pulled her onto the bed again. Stella didn't struggle.

"Hugo's a son of a bitch, we both know that," Jack said. "And he's probably not very happy with you after you dumped him and took up with me. I don't want you messed with, that's all."

Stella's anger faded like a passing storm cloud. "I can take care of myself. That's what I was doing long before you blew into town."

She rolled over in Jack's lap and bit his arm. Jack felt the sting of sharp white teeth, then the silky caress of her tongue. Soon her lips were pressed against his.

A knock interrupted them and Jack pulled himself free. "That's the coffee," he whispered hoarsely.

With a theatrical sigh, Stella flopped onto her back, pulling the sheet with her. Her long legs stretched naked across the bed. Jack rose and slipped on his pants. Shirtless, he unlocked the door. Curtis entered the suite, tray in hand. The big man moved carefully to avoid stepping on the clothing strewn around the room.

"Hey, Curtis," Stella called with a casual wave.

"Hi, Stella," Curtis replied, eyes diverted.

Jack took the tray from the other man's hands. Curtis leaned close. "Driscoll had to get back to work, so his assistant Perry is watching the prisoner," he said softly.

"Call LA and tell them to expect a prisoner."

"Farrow?"

Jack nodded. "Get him ready for the move, then I want you to take him to the airport yourself."

Curtis glanced over Jack's shoulder, to the woman in the bed. "And you?"

"Call me on this phone in fifteen minutes," Jack replied. "I'm almost done here."

Curtis got the message and hastily departed. Jack set the tray on the nightstand, opened the warm carafe. Then he sat on the bed and waited for Stella to pour. She quickly got the message. With an exasperated groan the woman rose to her knees and slowly crawled across the bed to the night table, her naked curves brushing against Jack's body like a kitten petitioning for a bowl of milk.

Jack pretended not to notice.

"When you were at Bix Automotive, did you hear about any scams you old boyfriend is running," he asked, accepting a steaming cup, sans milk or sugar.

Stella stared at him. "No. Should I?"

Jack sighed. "Caught a cheat at the roulette wheel earlier today. This guy had a predictive computer. A good one. Claims he bought it from Hugo Bix."

Stella glanced away. "First I've heard of it."

"But he has sold that kind of stuff before, right? Cheating devices, I mean . . ." Jack knew he had to probe gently. He could see Stella was holding back.

The woman shrugged. "Doesn't sound like his style, but if you say so."

Jack stared at his coffee. "This is only the beginning. I think Hugo's about to make a move."

"Well if he is, he's making a big mistake." Stella took a long sip from her own coffee cup. "Hugo ain't that bright. Not nearly as smart as you, Jaycee. I doubt he's got the *cojones* to buck you, and why should he? He's got his share and you got yours."

"We're the two biggest punks on the block. We're

gonna mix it up sooner or later. I know it, and Bix knows it."

Stella rolled her eyes. "Well, I'm going back to the garage later, to pick up my car. I can ask around, quiet like."

"If you do, be careful."

"I told you I can take care of myself." Stella waved a dismissive hand, then put down her cup and threw her arms around Jack's neck. "Enough about him, Jaycee. I'm getting hungry again, and not for dinner . . ."

The phone rang, too soon. Jack wasn't finished grilling the woman yet. Irritated, he grabbed the receiver.

"Jaycee, here."

"It's Curtis. I need to see you down in the basement."

Jack dropped the phone, climbed out of bed.

"Where are you going?" Stella cried.

"Trouble on the floor," Jack grunted, buttoning up his shirt.

"Great. Just great," she moaned, rolling out of bed. "I'm gonna use your shower, okay? And by the time you've finished your business downstairs—"

Stella Hawk heard the door slam. She turned around.

Jaycee was gone.

*2:22:59 P.M. PDT*
*Microwave Tower,*
*Experimental Weapons Testing Range*
*Groom Lake Air Force Base*

Tony Almeida reached the bottom of the ladder and stepped carefully around several bundles of wire, each as thick as an overstuffed cobra. Some ran from the generator to the microwave emitter at the top of the steel skeleton. Others were connected to the control panel set up under a nearby tent. With each step, Tony felt his shoes stick to the scorching concrete.

Shading his eyes with his hand, he looked around. Dr. Megan Reed was under the open flap of the tent, discussing the logistics of today's demonstration with Corporal Stratowski. From under the brim of an oversized Air Force-blue hardhat, fluttering strands of reddish-blond hair framed her freckled face. The headgear seemed incongruous, clashing with the project head's summer suit and high heels.

Near the pair, Phil Bascomb was busy running a diagnostic on the control panel, and the others had gathered at the water station, soothing their parched throat.

Tony looked up. Steve Sable was almost finished connecting the last power cable. He'd be climbing down the ladder in a minute or so. Now was the time.

Tony casually leaned against the hot metal, right next to the ladder—really a series of metal bars screwed into the steel structure. He quickly drew a wrench out of his pouch, slipped it over one of two metal bolts that held the fifth rung from the bottom in place. The tower had been erected only a few hours ago, and Tony expected the bolt to be looser than it was. In the end, he had to use both hands to break the seal. After that, it took only a few seconds to loosen the screw enough to fail the moment it was tested.

He'd barely slipped the wrench back into its pouch when he heard Sable's boots on the ladder. Tony stepped down and waited, feigning a yawn. As a final touch, he wrapped his foot around the power cable Sable had just connected.

The moment Sable put his weight on the loose rung, it gave way with a metallic clang. Still clutching the rails, Sable's body bounced against the ladder. He grunted, the wind knocked out of him, and his grip on the rail slipped. He would have landed hard, but Tony was there to catch him. Tony eased the man to the ground in one smooth motion.

"Are you okay, Steve?" Tony said in mock alarm.

"Sure, sure," Sable wheezed. Sitting up, he pushed Tony away. "Just let me catch my breath, Alvarez . . ."

Tony looked around, satisfied it had happened so quickly, no one even noticed. Sable checked himself out. Tony yanked his foot, disconnecting the power cable at the top of the tower. It dropped down, coiling around them like a dead snake.

"Son of a bitch," Sable cursed. "Who the hell put this tower together, the Army Corps of Engineers?" Then he spied the end of the power cable he'd just attached and cursed again.

"Don't worry. I'll fix it," Tony offered.

But Sable stumbled to his feet. "I'll reconnect the damn thing. I broke it," he said, obviously trying to save face. A moment later, Sable was moving up the ladder again, the end of the fallen line strapped to his belt. This time he carefully avoided the defective rung.

Tony stepped back, watching the man climb. When Sable reached the halfway mark, Tony strolled over to his computer, sitting under the limited shade of a wooden packing crate open on one side. Pretending to check the power grid, Tony slipped his fingers into a secret compartment in the side of his PC, found the data cable stored there. He plugged the cord into a jack in the cell phone he'd lifted from Sable's pocket.

Tapping the keys, Tony called up a hidden program embedded in the computer's engineering software. Before Sable was finished reattaching the power line, Tony had completely downloaded the cell phone's memory, including all the numbers stored in the directory and calling log. As Tony saved the data in a hidden file for examination later, he smiled, remembering how he'd picked up the skill he'd practiced so well today—and it wasn't from CTU's cursory training.

During his misspent youth on the South Side of Chicago, Tony had been a devoted Cubs fan, but he never had the cash for game tickets. After riding a crowded el for an hour, however, he always had enough pilfered money to buy tickets at Wrigley Field for himself and his younger cousin, and even a few snacks. It was a smooth operation, and he was never too greedy, stealing just enough to get by and returning the wallet without his mark ever catching on.

The petty thefts were a sin, and his pious grandmother would have beaten him silly if she'd found out. She never did. By the time CTU got around to training him in the art of picking pockets, Tony discovered he could teach his class a few things.

"Okay, Tony, I'm coming down," Sable called from the top of the tower.

Tony pocketed the man's cell and sauntered back to the base of the ladder.

"Good job," Tony said, patting the man's back with one hand, while slipping the cell back into Sable's pocket with the other.

"Yeah," Sable said, squinting up at the microwave emitter. "Now let's power it up and see if this baby actually works."

*2:46:21 P.M. PDT*
*The Cha-Cha Lounge, Las Vegas*

Max Farrow lay on his back in the holding cell, his throat a jagged slit. Clotting blood pooled on the green linoleum floor, caking his hair and arching outward like an obscene halo. Mouth open, jaws slack, the man's dead eyes, wide and seemingly startled, stared at the fluorescent lights embedded in the ceiling. Farrow's left arm was twisted and lay under him, his right was bent at the elbow. In that fist, Farrow still clutched a blood-stained splinter of orange fiberglass, a shard from the shattered chair.

Farrow was alone in the room. Don Driscoll, Curtis Manning, and Jack Bauer observed the grim tableau through the two-way mirror, like it was some macabre museum display. Jack's eyes roved the scene, seeking clues. Don Driscoll stammered at his side.

"Ray Perry was supposed to be watching him, Jaycee. I gave him the orders myself. I don't know what the f—"

"Where's Perry now?" Jack asked, cutting the other man off.

Driscoll shook his head. "The guys are looking for him, but he ain't turned up yet. I . . . I think he ducked out last week to bang some chick over at Circus, Circus. Maybe that's where he is now . . ."

Driscoll's voice trailed off, his eyes still glued to the corpse on the other side of the glass. "Hell of a way to die . . ."

"What?" Jack demanded.

"I said that's a hell of a way to die," Driscoll replied. "Suicide, I mean . . ."

Jack and Curtis exchanged glances, neither convinced the death was a suicide.

"When you find Ray Perry, I want to see him. Immediately," Jack said through gritted teeth.

"You got it, Jaycee."

Then Driscoll tapped the glass. "What do we do about him."

"I'm going to seal the room for now. Nobody comes down here until I say so. Nobody . . ."

"Why don't I have the guys dump this stiff in the desert. Nobody will be the wiser—"

"No," Jack shot back. "I'll deal with the problem my way . . ."

Don Driscoll raised his arms in mock surrender. "Whatever you want, Jaycee."

In his mind, Jack had already decided to summon a CTU forensics team to examine the scene and perform an on-site autopsy, even if their arrival aroused suspicion among the staff. He'd find some way of explaining it all. Right now he only suspected Farrow's death was homicide. Before he could make his next move, he had to know what really happened, because if Max Farrow was murdered, there was a traitor in his ranks. And that traitor had to be weeded out as soon as possible, before the turncoat did more damage.

1 2 3 **4** 5 6 7 8 9
10 11 12 13 14 15 16 17
18 19 20 21 22 23 24

• • • • • • • • • • • • • • • • • • • • • • • • • • • • • •

THE FOLLOWING TAKES PLACE
BETWEEN THE HOURS OF
3 P.M. AND 4 P.M.
PACIFIC DAYLIGHT TIME

• • • • • • • • • • • • • • • • • • • • • • • • • • • • • •

*3:01:16 P.M. PDT*
*Mesa Canyon Townhouses*
*North Buffalo Drive, Las Vegas*

The streets surrounding Mesa Canyon, a sun-washed
residential development on the outskirts of Las Vegas,
were deserted. Paul Dugan parked his Dodge Sprinter
right outside the gate of Compound One, on the corner of Smoke Ranch Road and North Buffalo Drive.
He opened the truck's door, and immediately knew
why. With nothing but concrete and sand all around,
there was no shade, so the residents had taken ref-
uge from the punishing heat and relentless sun inside
the air conditioned comfort of their mock adobe
townhouses.

Fair-haired, tall and lean—despite hours of relative inactivity spent behind the wheel—Dugan retained his boyish good looks late into his third decade. That's precisely why he was hired by Fit-Chef on the very day he filed an employment application, before he even passed his background check. Ric Minelli, Fit-Chef's smooth talking Las Vegas regional manager, was a former salesman himself. Ric understood his company's clientele and realized immediately that Dugan's home-spun charm would play well with his customer base, which was ninety-six point five percent female.

Paul had been with for Fit-Chef for a year now and liked his job. Fleeing a massive layoff in the blighted northeast, he left Johnstown, Pennsylvania and his shrew of an ex-wife, hoping to relocate to Los Angeles where he had friends. But the transmission on his car failed just shy of the California border, and while Paul waited in a Las Vegas garage for repairs, he met another driver for Fit-Chef. The man told Paul that the most popular food service in Nevada was always looking for an experienced delivery driver. Now Paul was another transplant to the fastest growing urban area in the United States.

Feeling the burn on the back of his ruddy neck, Dugan unlocked the back of the white panel truck, checked the manifest on his electronic pad. "T. Baird" was his next delivery destination. Paul grinned in anticipation. Tiffany Baird played a scantily-clad vampire at the new Goth extravaganza at the Castle Casino. Though he'd never actually seen the show, Paul couldn't help but notice the ubiquitous ad campaign, in which Tiffany's figure was prominently displayed. Of course, in reality Tiffany was nothing like her showgirl persona. She was actually rather sweet.

In the shade of the truck's interior, Paul fumbled around until he located the right order. Hefting the box, he closed the truck. As an added precaution, Dugan primed the alarm system. After what happened this morning, he knew it was wise to be careful.

Whistling tunelessly, Paul carried the boxes to the gate, pressed the buzzer. The intercom crackled immediately. "Yeah? Hello . . ."

"Fit-Chef," Paul replied. The lock clicked and he pushed through the metal gate, entering a circular plaza surrounded by townhouses. In the center of the complex, the blue waters of a swimming pool shimmered invitingly, though the poolside was as deserted as the streets outside.

Tiffany's was the fourth door to the left, but Paul didn't need to press the doorbell. She stood outside, awaiting her delivery. Even without makeup, Tiffany Baird was a stunner. Today she wore a baby blue nylon kimono that ended mid-thigh. Her long legs were naked, tiny feet slipped into matching blue plastic flip-flops. Her red hair was pulled back into a ponytail that spilled down her shapely back, held in place by an elastic hair band. Once again Paul noticed the third finger of her left hand lacked a ring.

Tiffany Baird greeted him with a smile that was tempered with surprise. "What are you doing here?"

"Hello, Miss Baird," Paul replied. "I guess I got lucky."

"I thought that Mexican kid was delivering today."

Paul frowned. "If I didn't know better, I'd say you were disappointed to see me."

"Not at all," Tiffany cried, pushing an unruly lock of hair away from her face. "It's just that the delivery is coming so late and all, I figured something must have happened."

Dugan handed her the package. She set it down on a plastic lawn chair, signed the electronic manifest he presented.

"Actually, Ignacio's day turned to crap," Dugan said. "His truck got jacked a couple of hours ago. The punk who stole it pistol whipped Iggy, put him in the hospital."

Tiffany ripped the lid off the box. "Jesus. Ain't nobody safe?" she grunted.

"Apparently not," Dugan replied. "It's crazy, too. It's not like he's driving a Brinks truck, just a shit load of diet food—er, pardon my French."

Tiffany sniffed, frowning at the contents of a plastic container. "Edamame again. They call *this* protein?"

Paul watched her rummage through the box, realized she wore nothing under the thin kimono.

"If you ever get sick of that rabbit food, let me know. I'll buy you a steak at Smith and Wollensky's."

The bold invitation had come out of Paul's mouth before he realized what he was saying. Now, face flushed with embarrassment, he waited for the polite rebuff—and felt like kicking himself.

Tiffany licked teriyaki sauce off her fingers. Then she grinned. "Fit-Chef is a real full service company, huh?"

"I . . . I'm sorry," he stammered.

"Don't be," Tiffany replied, tapping his nametag with an ebony enameled finger. "In fact, you better watch yourself, Mr. Dugan. I might just take you up on your offer."

Dugan blinked. "How about this Saturday?"

Tiffany's grin broadened. "How about Sunday. I work Fridays and Saturdays."

Paul nodded, speechless.

"You've got my phone number in that little computer of yours," Tiffany said, hefting her delivery. "Give me a call on Friday and we'll set a time."

Dugan stood blinking in the sun for a full thirty seconds after Tiffany Baird closed her front door. Finally he turned and, whistling again, headed back to the truck.

Crossing the sidewalk, Paul Dugan was too distracted to notice the late-model black Ford Explorer with tinted windows parked across the street. Still lost in a fog of euphoria, he deactivated the alarm and unlocked the door.

A shadow suddenly crossed the sun, then something exploded inside Paul Dugan's head. A sharp jolt of pain roiled his spine. His knees gave out and he dropped to the hot asphalt. Seemingly in slow motion, he reached out to steady himself—only to have the truck's keys snatched out of his semi-limp fingers. Paul grunted in protest, and another blow came down on the back of his head, slamming him flat.

He moaned as someone stepped over him. Hot tar burned his cheek. The wheels right next to his head spun, squealing, as the truck roared away. A moment of throbbing silence followed. Then a red haze engulfed his vision, and Paul Dugan's world faded to black.

*3:09:26 P.M. PDT*
*North Buffalo Drive, Las Vegas*

"Big Ed's got the keys and made it away clean," said the fidgeting man in the passenger seat.

"Let's go," the driver grunted.

Toomes threw the Explorer into gear, pulled away from the curb. As they drove by, Drew peered through the tinted glass at the man on the ground.

"Jesus, I hope Big Ed didn't kill 'em," he said, one hand clinging to the dashboard.

"So what if he did?" Toomes kept his eyes on the highway, his giant hands wrapped around the steering wheel. His rubbery jowls bounced like jelly on the rough pavement.

"Goddamn construction," he cursed.

Drew dropped back into his seat. He lifted his wrist to display his plastic Seiko watch. "It's after three. We should have been back by now."

"Relax. We're done. We're gonna pick up the other trucks."

"Yeah, we're done. But was it done smart?" Drew's voice was high. His eyes were close together, and bulged a little, like fish eyes. Now they darted nervously. "Listen, Hugo told us to snatch three trucks in Reno, Toomes. Not Vegas, *Reno*. That's 'cause he doesn't want them turning up on the Metro Police stolen vehicle sheet for twenty-four hours—"

Toomes snorted. "Hugo Bix gives the cops in this town way too much credit. Why should I give up my winning seat at a high stakes table at the Bellagio, to drive to Reno in the middle of the stinking night. All that, just to jack three trucks?"

"It's what the boss wanted—"

"Bix is *getting* what he wants," Toomes replied. "He wanted three Dodge Sprinter panel trucks, and that's what we jacked. He said it would be better if they were white, and they're white." Toomes slapped the steering wheel. "Dream come true."

Drew calmed a little. "We're in the clear, as long as Big Ed don't say nothing to Hugo before we get there . . ."

"If Big Ed says anything, he won't get paid. And Big Ed likes to get paid."

Toomes braked for a traffic light. Traffic was particularly heavy along this stretch near the Lakes.

"Man, we're later and later," Drew whined.

Wheezing, Toomes glanced at his own watch. The Rolex seemed tiny on his thick wrist, the band tight around flesh and muscle.

"It's not even three-thirty," the big man wheezed. "Hugo's boys have plenty of time to prime the trucks. We'll go fetch the two we jacked this morning and drive them over to the garage. Bix will be so happy to see us he'll never know the difference."

*3:13:08 P.M. PDT*
*The Cha-Cha Lounge, Las Vegas*

Crossing the game floor to the Tiki Lounge, Jack heard his cell phone beep over the jangling slots. He slipped into an alcove near the rest rooms, an area marginally shielded from the noise.

"Jager," he answered.

"It's O'Brian."

"Where are you, Morris?"

"Up in the rafters with the rest of the bats."

Jack automatically glanced up. Somewhere behind the one way mirrors that made up the ceiling, Morris O'Brian was watching him.

"Got a call for you, Jack. It's Henderson, across the special line."

Jack tensed, sure it was more bad news. "Put him through."

A long silence. Then Jack heard a breath inhaled hundreds of miles away, at CTU, Los Angeles.

"You don't have many fans upstairs, do you Jack?" Christopher Henderson's voice was delayed a second and oddly distorted—byproducts of Morris O'Brian's audio encryption system. But at least no one could possibly intercept the call, either here or at CTU.

"What's going on?" Jack asked.

"I have a bureaucrat by the name of Alberta Green up my ass. You know the woman?"

"Yes."

"She's been questioning our operation from its inception, even though she doesn't have a clue what we're doing. Now she's talking about pulling the plug on our budget if we don't show some results."

"She can do that?"

The pause seemed overlong this time. "She can, especially with Ryan Chappelle making the same noise. Unless we show some progress, we could be shut down tomorrow."

Jack chose not to hide his impatience. "We've *made* progress. I'll put you through to Morris again. He'll update you."

Before his boss could reply, Jack put Henderson on hold and punched up Morris.

"I heard, Jack. And I might say that from up here, you don't look particularly happy."

"Morris, I want you to brief Henderson about the technology we seized today."

"Will do. Should I mention our corpse down in the basement?"

"Say nothing for now. If Henderson asks, tell him I'm still interrogating the suspect. I need to find out who killed Max Farrow before I can reveal his death."

O'Brian paused. "Gambling again, Jack?"

"Morris. Don't second guess me. Just do your job."

"Right-O, chief. I'll—"

Jack hung up, slipped the cell into his pocket. He felt an impotent rage welling up inside of him. He already knew this operation was running on borrowed time, but Jack was hoping that today's discovery of stolen technology would breathe new life into the investigation. The death of Max Farrow had thrown more than a crimp into his plans. Ironically the man's capture had been their first break, but Farrow's death—once revealed—might end the operation immediately. Before Henderson's call, Jack felt he still had a little time to maneuver. Now, with the entrance of Alberta Green into the equation, his window of opportunity had been reduced from days to hours.

A hand on his shoulder broke Jack's concentration. "Hey, Jaycee. Have you seen—?"

"What?" Jack snapped.

Lilly Sheridan took two steps backwards. "Jesus, I'm sorry I bothered you."

The woman turned away. Jack grabbed her arm.

"Whoa, Lilly. Don't go. I'm sorry I took your head off."

Lilly pulled back. "Don't, Jaycee—" Her eyes were locked on his fingers. Jack released her arm.

"Look, I didn't mean anything," Jack told her. "I'm having a rough day, that's all. You're looking for Stella, right?"

She hugged herself, nodding. "I'm supposed to give her a ride somewhere before I go to work."

Jack nodded. "Yeah, over to Hugo's garage."

The woman frowned. "I didn't want to say."

"Yeah, well . . ." Jack grunted, in character.

Lilly shrugged. "Look, I don't know what's what . . . Who knows what game Stella's playing."

"No game, so she says. Just a repair job," Jack replied.

He watched Lilly's expression, saw the skepticism there. He wondered if Lilly was lying. If she really did know something he didn't. *Was Stella still working for Hugo Bix?*

"Let's go to my table at the Tiki," Jack offered. "Stella's using the shower. She'll be down in a minute."

"I don't know, Jaycee. I have my daughter here."

"Here?" Jack said, genuinely surprised.

A girl Jack guessed was about ten years old stepped around an idle bank of slots. She met his gaze, regarding Jaycee Jager with a mixture of wariness and unconcealed interest.

"This is Pamela," Lilly said, pulling the child close.

Jack blinked. Though Pamela Sheridan was a few years younger than his own daughter, he was suddenly reminded of Kim. Jack wondered what she was doing right now. Was Kim in school, or in rehearsal for the class play—she'd won a prized role, he remembered. With a jolt he also recalled that Kim's show was staged last week, and he'd missed her performance. The realization was so hurtful that Jack immediately pushed it aside. With an effort, he smiled down at the girl, shook her tiny hand. "Hello, Pamela," he said.

Jack's flaring emotions reined, his professional instincts reasserted themselves. He noted that the resemblance between mother and daughter was obvious. Both had wide, expressive blue eyes and high cheekbones. Lilly's blond hair was a shade darker than her daughter's and cut so short it curled around her ears. While Lilly was tall and willowy, her child was skinny, all arms and legs and a neck like a gazelle's.

"Let's go to the Tiki," Jack coaxed. "The joint's

deserted this time of day. We'll sit in the back and Pamela can have a ginger ale or something."

Lilly hesitated, then nodded. Jack, mindful of their seedy surroundings, took them straight to a remote booth near an oasis of fake palm trees and a flock of plastic pink flamingoes. The waitress appeared at Jack's shoulder. She wore a bikini top, grass skirt, and sneakers.

"Nancy, the young ladies will have ginger ales . . . Make it three."

The drinks appeared in under a minute.

"How are things at the Babylon?" Jack asked.

Lilly curled her nose. "Big political event tonight. I'm doing double duty, hostess and server. It's a nice gig with extra money attached." While she spoke, Lilly fished in her tiny purse until she found her cell phone. Still talking, she checked her messages. "Sorry, Jaycee. I'm waiting to hear from my babysitter."

She slipped the cell back into her purse.

Pamela seemed intrigued by the fake flamingoes, left the booth to get a better look. Jack leaned closer to Lilly.

"So," he said softly. "You think it's wise for Stella to go over to Hugo's garage, after she dumped him for me?"

Lilly adjusted her pink blouse. "Stella and Hugo, they're friendly. I mean, I don't know what goes on between you and Hugo, but Bix seems civilized. And Stella steers business his way—"

She suddenly covered her mouth. "Oh, crap! Maybe I wasn't supposed to say anything about that."

Jack reassured her immediately. "Our relationship

is personal, not business," he said. "It's just that Hugo's been messing with me. I don't want him messing with Stella."

Lilly looked away, sipped her drink.

Jack reached into his pocket. "Here, Lilly, I want you to take this," he said, displaying one of Jager's business cards. He turned it over. On the back was another number, written in his own handwriting.

"That's my personal cell phone number," he explained. "If I don't pick up, a guy named Morris O'Brian will. If Stella gets into a jam, or if you ever get into trouble, give me a call."

Lilly accepted Jaycee's card, but her expression said it all—the last thing she felt she needed was another sympathy play from a lowlife gangster who was banging her roommate.

"There you are."

Jack and Lilly looked up. Stella had arrived. She was as put together as she'd been when she arrived. Dress in place, makeup perfect.

"Ready to go, Lil?"

"Sure," Lilly said, jumping up. "I'll just fetch Pamela."

Stella Hawk watched her roommate chase after her daughter. "She dotes on that brat," Stella said with a sigh.

"Will I see you later?" Jacked asked, wrapping his arm around Stella's waist.

"Depends," Stella replied, peeling his hand away.

Lilly appeared with Pamela in tow. "Say goodbye to Mr. Jager," Lilly prompted.

"Nice to meet you, Pamela," said Jack.

"Bye, Mr. Jager. Thank you for the soda," Pamela replied.

"Later, lover," Stella said, blowing Jack a kiss.

*3:28:58 P.M. PDT*
*Bix Automotive Center*
*Browne End Road, Las Vegas*

An industrial area sparsely populated by air conditioning contractors and electrical engineering services, Bix Automotive Center dominated this remote and sandy stretch of Browne End Road. The garage itself was the largest building on the block, and two adjacent lots on either side were ringed with twelve foot chain link fence that protected a decade's worth of auto shop debris—stripped down car frames, engine blocks, broken axles, rusty radiators, mismatched hubcaps, and old tires stacked like poker chips.

A mammoth cinderblock rectangle constructed in the late 1950s, the windowless interior of the automotive center reeked of grease, worn rubber, waste oil and hot metal. It didn't help the unsavory atmosphere that the garage doors were closed and locked tight, or that the bustling interior was crowded with five large trucks—all of them late-model Dodge Sprinters—and a dozen mechanics working them over.

Hugo Bix presided over the chaos from his office on the mezzanine—really a ramshackle wooden shack on stilts, with a flight of metal stairs leading to the only door. For the rising Vegas crime lord, this was shaping up to be the most important day of his criminal life. But if Hugo Bix was tense, he did not show it.

Surrounded by stacks of yellowing racing forms and old license plates, a large Pennzoil sign and an array of pornographic calendars highlighting sex industry beauties from the past decade, Hugo Bix was slumped in a sagging office chair. He clutched the sports page in his large, callused hands, his scuffed, size-thirteen boots resting on a battered wooden desk.

At thirty-four, Bix's hard gray eyes and pock-marked features gave him the look of a man decades older. His skin browned by the sun, chin perpetually unshaven around a natty handlebar moustache, Bix resembled a cowpoke at a local rodeo more than Las Vegas' most powerful crime lord. Bix wore his working class roots with pride. His arms were laced with prison tattoos and roped with muscle. His hair, bleached by the sun, was long and wavy.

A cell phone on the desk rang once. Bix put it to his ear but said nothing.

"It's Roman, boss. I'm at the front gate."

"Go on,"

"Big Ed's here. He said Toomes and Drew are right behind him. They got the goods."

A slight smile curled the corners of Bix's thin lips. "Any sign of our friends from down south?"

"Not yet."

"How about the Wildman and his boys?"

"They arrived last night. They're holed up at Baxter's Motel on the edge of town, and getting antsy."

Bix grinned. "They'll have plenty to do in a couple of hours. Wildman is my ace in the hole."

Bix closed the phone. He swung his big feet off the desk, rose to his full height. Swaggering like a movie cowboy, or like the outlaw biker he once was, Bix walked to the door.

"How's it going down there?" he called.

The lead mechanic looked up. "We're almost done here. The trucks we have are loaded and there's only a few stencils left to apply. We're waiting for the other trucks you promised us."

Bix nodded, turned his back on the workmen. "I reckon they'll be here any minute."

"Then what?" the mechanic called back.

"Then you'll do your jobs and stop asking questions," Bix replied before closing his door.


*3:57:19 P.M. PDT*
*The Cha-Cha Lounge, Las Vegas*

Jack waited in the Tiki Lounge, his mind still focused on Henderson's phone call.

"You wanted to see me, Jaycee?"

Jack nodded. "Sit down, Curtis. Any sign of Ray Perry?"

Curtis shook his head. "Driscoll put out some feelers. Found out Perry wasn't hiding out at Circus, Circus. Don talked to Perry's girlfriend and she hasn't seen him in two days."

Curtis leaned close. "Do you think it was really Perry who wasted Max Farrow?"

Jack smiled humorlessly. "That would be convenient, sure. Ray's gone so we don't have a spy among us. That's what someone wants us to think."

"Who do you think it is then, Jack?"

"It could be anyone. It could be Ray Perry. Or Don Driscoll. Or Chick Hoffman. Hell, it could even be Nancy over there." To Curtis Manning's surprise, Jack laughed once. "We'll know soon enough. I think Hugo's about to make his move."

"You think sending Max Farrow here was the beginning of something?"

"I think whatever Hugo's planning, it's already begun. That's why I want you to go over to Bix Automotive and keep an eye on the place."

Curtis nodded. "Can do, Jack. I've already established a reconnaissance position inside a vacant tool and die factory across the street."

"Go now. Call Morris with updates every hour. And be careful. This whole operation is already in jeopardy. One more strike and we're out."

1 2 3 4 **5** 6 7 8 9
10 11 12 13 14 15 16 17
18 19 20 21 22 23 24

. . . . . . . . . . . . . . . . . . . . . . . . . . . . . . . . .

**THE FOLLOWING TAKES PLACE
BETWEEN THE HOURS OF
4 P.M. AND 5 P.M.
PACIFIC DAYLIGHT TIME**

. . . . . . . . . . . . . . . . . . . . . . . . . . . . . . . . .

*4:00:01 P.M. PDT*
*Groom Lake Secure Terminal*
*McCarran Airport, Las Vegas*

After helping the Senator pass through the restricted terminal's extensive security protocols, which included X-ray scans, metal detectors, and a fingerprint check, Air Force Colonel Vincent DeBlasio handed David Palmer off to the scientist in charge of the Malignant Wave Project. Palmer, who understood the silent language of the military hierarchy, saw this as a sign that the Air Force was not comfortable with the direction the project had taken, and that the top brass who originally authorized the project were now maneuvering to distance themselves from the research they initially funded.

Dr. Megan Reed was unlike any research scientist Palmer had ever met. A tall, striking blond in pearls, a crisp business suit, and high heels, she boldly shook the Senator's hand when they were introduced. She immediately dismissed DeBlasio and took charge of her VIP guest. Since both of them knew it would be unwise and unlawful to discuss the Malignant Wave Program before they arrived at the secured top secret site, the Senator and the scientist talked about their destination instead. The woman proved to be an eager and determined tour guide.

"Have you ever visited Groom Lake before, Senator?"

"I haven't," Palmer replied. "But I'm impressed by the high level of security at this terminal."

Dr. Reed nodded. "I'll pass on your compliment to Beverly Chang, or you can tell her yourself. Dr. Chang is one of the researchers in the Malignant Wave program. She was also in charge of instituting the new security protocols."

Palmer looked around. The concrete interior of the restricted terminal on the northwestern edge of McCarran International Airport was unimpressive. He glanced back at the glass doors he'd passed through earlier. The Tropicana and New York New York casinos were so close to the building they seemed to border the runway.

"I understood that Groom Lake is close to being deactivated. Was I misinformed?"

"Not at all, Senator," Megan Reed replied. "Activities on the base are winding down ahead of the scheduled deactivation. Staffing is down, but several top secret research programs still continue."

Dr. Reed did not mention the fact that those research projects were also close to deactivation—or rather, de-funding—or that Malignant Wave was at the top of the Senate Defense Appropriations Committee's endangered projects list. Palmer had come to Nevada this day to assess the program as part of his duties as chairman of the committee. He took a special interest in Malignant Wave because the weapon they were developing was supposedly based on non-lethal technology. Palmer was enthusiastic about any weapon system that had the potential to minimize casualties in times of war.

Dr. Reed took the lead. "If you'll follow me out to the airplane."

They passed through another glass door. The afternoon was dazzling, the sky a clear, cloudless blue. The brightness of the day was intensified by the sun bouncing off the bleached concrete. The noise of jet engines was deafening, so conversation ceased until they crossed to the portable staircase that led into the belly of the unmarked Boeing 737–200 parked on the tarmac.

Here, the main terminal at McCarran Airport was clearly visible across a stretch of runway, and the illusion that the Las Vegas strip bordered the runway was intensified as well. The looming shadow of The MGM Grand's green "Emerald City" towers appeared to stretch across the perimeter of the landing field.

Dr. Reed led Palmer up the stairs and into the cabin. Inside the airliner, the buffeting noise of jet engines subsided, the only sound was the steady hum of the on-board climate control system. The pilot and an air steward, both in United States Air Force uniforms, greeted them inside the door.

"I'm Captain Brent, Senator Palmer. Welcome aboard Janet Three-two-three."

Palmer noted that Captain Brent was close to retirement age. He also noticed several campaign ribbons on the officer's dress uniform, including those for Operations Desert Shield and Desert Storm. Respectfully, the Senator shook the combat veteran's hand.

Megan Reed then directed the Senator to seats at the front of the craft, close to the pilot's cabin. Behind them a scattering of civilian and military workers pretended not to stare at the high-profile politician in their midst.

"I see the Air Force is in charge of transport now," Palmer noted.

"That's correct," Dr. Reed replied, fastening her seat belt. "Formerly, the defense contractor Edgerton, Germeshausen and Grier, Inc. managed transport and security around Groom Lake. But since the deactivation was announced, their contract was voided and Air Force security took over daily operations."

Palmer lifted an eyebrow. "So EG&G is out?"

"They are. But their ongoing contracts with NASA, the Department of Energy, Defense, Treasury and Homeland Security guarantees EG&G will have plenty of work to do in the foreseeable future."

Palmer realized Megan Reed had missed the motive behind his question. The Senator didn't care that EG&G was out of a contract, only that Groom Lake's legendary security was at the same levels that existed before the transition. Rather than clarify his query, Palmer let the subject drop.

The steward brought them coffee. Within a few minutes the aircraft was taxiing down the runway.

"This aircraft is fairly empty," Palmer noted. "What kind of personnel levels are we talking about these days?"

Megan Reed's pug nose curled as she considered his question.

"Well, there are flights north every half hour," she explained. "But what we call rush hour occurs weekday mornings, when our fleet of jets carry close to five hundred military personnel, contractors and civilian workers to several top secret locations in the desert. Most of these workers depart at our first stop—the main runway at Groom Lake."

She leaned back in her seat, crossed her tanned and shapely legs. "Next year I suspect those personnel numbers will be significantly curtailed due to ongoing cuts."

They hardly seemed to have left the ground when Senator Palmer heard the airplane's wheels come down again. He peered through the window, saw three concrete runways stretching whitely across the scorched brown desert terrain.

"Right now we're over Emigrant Valley in Lincoln County, Nevada," Dr. Reed told him. "Area 51 is almost below us. The experimental base is a relatively small, sixty square mile area inside of a much larger base called—"

"I know, Dr. Reed," Palmer said, cutting her short. "The Nevada Test and Training Range is about forty-six hundred square miles, Area 51 is just a tiny section of the entire complex."

She nodded, unperturbed by the Senator's apparent rudeness. "The dry lake bed is clearly visible from the air, and you can see both operating runways."

"I see three runways," Palmer replied.

"The one on our right has already been decommissioned. It's been neglected for so long it's no longer suitable for operations."

The aircraft descended then, until they were below the peaks of the Groom and Papoose Mountain ranges that surrounded the valley. Finally the wheels bumped once and the aircraft braked, engines whining shrilly. They landed in a cloud of sandy dust. The aircraft powered down and taxied to a small concrete building squatting in the sun.

"We've just arrived on the main runway, built in the 1990s," Megan Reed explained.

Palmer bit back a response. The demonstration had not even begun and already Palmer was tired of Dr. Megan Reed's endless explanations.

The "fasten seatbelt" light went off and the air steward popped the main door. Hot, dry desert air flooded the air conditioned compartment.

"Come along, Senator," Megan Reed said, rising and straightening her skirt. "Corporal Stratowski should be waiting on the tarmac with a Hummer.

He'll drive us over to Hangar Six where the demonstration will take place . . ."

*4:42:40 P.M. PDT*
*Senator Palmer's suite*
*Babylon Hotel and Casino, Las Vegas*

Sherry Palmer had just returned from an intimate luncheon with the mayor's wife and twenty-two of her closest female friends—wives of party leaders, community board members and large donors, mostly. It was an unglamorous and exhausting affair, but necessary for building useful bridges to help her husband triumph in this state's primary, and later in the national elections.

Sherry had kicked off her shoes and was rubbing her tired feet when the suite's phone rang. She nodded and Lev Cohen answered for her.

"It's Larry Bell," Lev said a moment later, his hand covering the receiver.

"Tell him David isn't taking any calls," Sherry replied.

"He doesn't want David. He wants to talk to you."

Sherry took the phone, her expression doubtful. "Hello, Larry."

"Sherry," the Congressman purred. "How was your luncheon?"

"About as charming as that impromptu press conference this morning," Sherry replied, her hackles rising at the memory.

She heard a chuckle. "What's so funny?" Sherry demanded.

"That was just a little demonstration I cooked up," Bell replied. "I thought you'd appreciate it."

"What's that supposed to mean?"

"Sherry, you and I both know your husband is running for president—"

"That hasn't been determined yet—"

"Cut the crap, woman. He hasn't announced yet, but he's caught the fever. I can see it. You forget that I've known David almost as long as you have."

"What's your point," Sherry snarled.

"Now I can be a good and loyal ally and help David reach his goal, or I can be a friendly—or even a not so friendly rival. It's really up to you."

Sherry eyes narrowed. "What are you angling for, Larry?"

"For now, I only want you to meet a friend of mine. He's a businessman with very deep pockets, who's interested in David's political career."

"And later?"

Sherry could feel Larry's smile across the wires. "The House of Representatives is a very crowded place. Very crowded," he said. "It's hard for a man of my aspirations to shine. A better fit for me would be a cabinet position in the Palmer Administration, don't you think?"

Bell fell silent for a moment. Sherry's knuckles strained as she clutched the receiver, her self control slipping.

"My friend is in the hotel. Why don't I fetch him,

bring him up to that luxury suite of yours right now, and make the introductions."

There was a long pause before Sherry replied. "I'm willing to listen," she said at last.

"Great." Bell's tone was triumphant. "See you in ten."

The line went dead and Sherry dropped the receiver into the cradle.

"What did he want?" Lev asked.

"He wants to be in David's cabinet."

Lev jumped to his feet. "What?"

Sherry shook her head, slipped her heels back on. Then she rose and, faced her husband's chief of staff. "We're going to have a visitor," she announced. "I want you to stay and listen to what this man has to say. This could work out very well for David's campaign, but only if we play our cards right."

"You're scaring me, Sherry," Lev replied, his ruddy face suddenly pale. "You can't buy and sell cabinet positions."

"Don't panic, Larry. Nothing's been decided yet," Sherry replied. "What Larry Bell wants and what he gets are two entirely different things. And if the esteemed Congressman thinks he can buy himself a cabinet position in my husband's administration, he better know that it's going to cost him and his deep pocket friend a lot of money and a lot of influence . . ."

*4:47:15 P.M. PDT*
*Tunney and Sons Quality Tool and Die*
*Browne End Road, Las Vegas*

Curtis Manning had used the abandoned factory to stake out Bix's operation several times before. A shattered front window commanded a perfect view to the entrance of Bix Automotive, just across street. Better still, because the deserted tool and die works was completely boarded up, no one suspected the building could possibly be occupied, even by a homeless vagrant.

On one of the early reconnaissance missions, Curtis found a back entrance known only to a nest of rattlesnakes he was forced to quietly eradicate before taking sole possession of the property. After he'd found the broken window with the strategic view, Curtis set up a bent steel chair behind an ancient desk and used them for his observation post.

In the beginning, Curtis Manning believed Jack's goading of Hugo Bix was both reckless and a waste of CTU resources. While it was known that Bix was a powerful player on the local crime scene, there was no evidence the man was connected with the stolen military technology. Now Curtis knew differently, and he was man enough to admit it to anyone who asked, especially his boss, Jack Bauer.

Manning had several years' experience as a member of CTU's tactical team, but this was his first real covert operation. Because of his inexperience, Curtis looked to Jack for instruction and Bauer was proving to be a *very* good teacher.

Today, Jack had provided Curtis Manning with a dangerous new challenge. Every other time he had infiltrated this property, he'd done so at night. This time Curtis would have to slip into the old factory in broad daylight, which meant taking special precautions. First he parked his car many blocks away, in an alley behind an apartment building on Pena Lane. Then Curtis crossed two yards, three empty lots, and climbed two chain link fences to get behind the abandoned factory without being spotted. Weaving his way through a gauntlet of dozens of dented and forgotten Dumpsters, Curtis finally reached the rear of the abandoned tool and die factory.

The back door was blocked by an old steel grate, but Curtis had found another way in—a hole in the wall masked by a sheet of plywood lodged in a pile of debris. He tossed the wooden panel aside and stepped through the ragged gap. Once inside the building, he used shafts of afternoon sun streaming through holes in the collapsing roof and broken windows to guide his way through the factory's gloomy interior—right to the battered desk he'd placed near a hole punched in the grease-stained front window.

Curtis had hidden some bottles of water under a pile of wooden boxes and was relieved to see they were still untouched. After checking for scorpions, he grabbed a plastic container and sat down at the desk. Curtis no sooner unscrewed the cap on the water and focused his CTU issue mini-binoculars on Bix's establishment, when a white panel truck arrived at the gate. Curtis recognized the man behind the wheel, too. It was Drew Hickam, one of Bix's goons.

Curtis dutifully recorded the event on his PDA. He noted that the truck was a Dodge Sprinter, late model, and that the vehicle was sporting dealer plates. He tapped in the numbers, sure they were fake, and noted the time in the log. A garage door opened and the truck drove through. The door immediately closed again, but before it did Curtis noticed plenty of activity inside. Yet the place was shut tight. Odd on a day like this. So many people working inside, no one drifting out for a smoke, a break. Something big was going on, big enough for Bix to hide his activities from prying eyes.

Curtis had only been at it for twenty minutes, but already the afternoon heat was oppressive. In a few hours the sun would go down and it would become cooler—maybe even cold. But for now, Curtis stripped off his jacket, then the Kevlar vest underneath, draping them both behind his rickety chair. He loosened his shirt and rolled up sleeves already damp with perspiration. He left the shoulder holster carrying the fully-loaded Glock in place.

Manning spotted another truck pulling up to the gate a few minutes later. This one was driven by Frank "Fat Frankie" Toomes, a high stakes gambler closely associated with Hugo Bix. Curiously, the white panel truck was also a current year Dodge Sprinter with dealer plates. The truck soon disappeared inside the bowels of the Bix Automotive garage. He wondered if the arrival of two trucks of the same make was some kind of weird coincidence. He doubted it. In fact, Curtis Manning was almost certain something more ominous was going on.

*4:56:40 P.M. PDT*
*Senator Palmer's suite*
*Babylon Hotel and Casino, Las Vegas*

"Mrs. Senator David Palmer, I'd like you to meet Mr. Jong Lee."

Larry Bell arrived inside of ten minutes, as promised. He wore a Fendi suit and a look of satisfied triumph. For her part, Sherry Palmer acted suitably contrite.

"A pleasure to meet you, Mr. Lee," she said graciously, extending her hand. "And please call me Sherry. Can I offer you something. Coffee or tea, perhaps a drink."

"No, no, I can only stay a moment. I do not wish to waste your valuable time"

Sherry directed her attention to the woman beside Jong Lee. "And who is this beautiful creature?"

"Her name is Yizi," Jong said. At the mention of her name, the woman bowed deeply. "Alas, she speaks no English."

"I'd like you to meet the Senator's Chief of Staff, Mr. Lev Cohen."

Cohen's handshake was perfunctory.

"A pleasure," Jong said in flawless English.

They sat around the central table. Jong with Yizi

on the couch. Sherry on the lounge chair. Lev Cohen remained standing, a drink from the bar in his hand.

"Mr. Lee is a Taiwanese chip manufacturer who holds many defense contracts with the United States military. That means Lee here has a stake in who wins the next presidential election," Bell explained.

"More than that," Jong declared. "Your government has been my nation's greatest ally, since the dark days of the Japanese invasion, since our present government was established in 1947. I and many of my compatriots know that it is only America's military might and our own resolute spirit that keeps Taiwan, the Republic of China, safe from those bandits in Beijing."

"Excuse me for being blunt," Sherry said, "but I'm not sure I understand why you're here, exactly."

"Of course," Jong said with a nod. "Senator Palmer is head of the Senate's Defense Appropriations Committee. In his position, he has made it a point of sharing American defense technology with Taiwan. I merely want to make certain your husband will continue to support my nation when he becomes president. "

"Unfortunately my husband has not yet been elected," Sherry replied.

Larry Bell threw his long arm around Jong's shoulder. The cultured man winced at the familiarity of the gesture. "Don't worry about old David," Bell said with a laugh. "He's one guy who knows how to win."

"I would like to make his victory even more certain," Jong said.

Larry Bell rose and glanced at his watch. "Look at the time," he cried with all the conviction of a high school thespian. "I really have to go. There's so much to do before tonight's gala event."

With a curt farewell, Bell departed. Sherry focused her gaze on Jong Lee.

"You were saying?" she prompted.

"I was merely suggesting that I would like to make a generous monetary contribution to Senator Palmer's presidential campaign fund." Jong said with a crooked smile.

Lev Cohen spoke up. "We have a committee for such things, Mr. Lee. Contact them and they'll tell you where to mail the check."

Sherry Palmer silenced the chief of staff with a touch of her hand.

"What Mr. Cohen means is that there are many barriers against my husband's campaign accepting foreign donations. There are limits to the amount one can give, and much scrutiny. If they wished, our political enemies could use such contributions against us."

Jong smiled again. "I understand perfectly, Mrs. Palmer—"

She raised a finger. "That's Sherry."

"Ah, yes . . . Sherry. I would, however, prefer to give much more than the allowable amount, and also avoid such scrutiny."

"Just how would you do that?" Lev Cohen demanded.

Again, Sherry silenced the man with a gesture. "I'm not sure I understand."

Jong frowned. "Then I must be even more blunt. I am prepared to contribute five million dollars cash, today, in exchange for one piece of information."

Lev Cohen paled. Sherry smiled knowingly. She'd been waiting for this shoe to drop since Jong Lee entered the suite.

"I know why your husband is here in Nevada, Mrs. Palmer," Jong continued. "I know that even as we speak, he is witnessing a demonstration of a brand new weapons system at Groom Lake Air Force Base less than fifty miles from this spot."

Lev choked on his drink.

Sherry blinked in surprise, then quickly recovered. *So that's where he went,* she mused bitterly. *And the worst part about it is that I had to hear the truth from a defense contractor from Taiwan!*

"I'm not free to discuss such things, Mr. Lee," Sherry replied coolly.

"No need to. Though the information is top secret, I know this because the chips I manufacture are vital components in the system being demonstrated."

Sherry's eyes narrowed as she studied the man.

"You see, I require information that only your husband can provide," Jong continued. "I need to know whether or not today's demonstration was a success, and whether or not the program will continue. It is a very expensive proposition to retool my factories. With this advance knowledge, I will know whether or not to proceed with the retooling process, or move on to more lucrative opportunities."

Sherry nodded. "And for that information?"

"I will pay five million dollars, cash."

Sherry's mind reeled. Five million dollars would nearly double David Palmer's campaign chest. And since it was cash, the money need never be declared on any campaign budget statement or election board. It would be a secret fund, used at her discretion, if and when the need arose.

"I am always glad to help a political ally," Sherry declared. "Therefore I accept your very generous offer, Mr. Lee. In the name of my husband."

Cohen's eyes went wide and he turned beet red. But he knew better than to speak up.

Jong rose and bowed. "Here is my card," he said. "My cell phone number is there. Call me with the information I ask for, and the money is yours."

Sherry raised a manicured eyebrow. "Oh, I'll call you, Mr. Lee. But it's Mr. Cohen here who will accept the money. You understand why I can't . . . And why this conversation never took place."

Jong grinned. "I understand completely . . ."

• • • • • • • • • • • • • • • • • • • • • • • • • • • • • • •

THE FOLLOWING TAKES PLACE
BETWEEN THE HOURS OF
5 P.M. AND 6 P.M.
PACIFIC DAYLIGHT TIME

• • • • • • • • • • • • • • • • • • • • • • • • • • • • • • •

*5:04:02 P.M. PDT*
*Hangar Six, Experimental Weapons Testing Range*
*Groom Lake Air Force Base*

Relentless in her pursuit of perfection, Dr. Reed kept
Tony Almeida and the rest of her staff hopping all
morning and into the early afternoon. Tony knew
from weeks of observation that Megan Reed had
gained her "people skills" at Donald Trump's School
of Management. Her modus operandi was to brow-
beat her staff to the point of exhaustion, but never
had her ham-handed managerial style been more evident than today.

Then, roughly at two-thirty, Dr. Reed hastily departed with Corporal Stratowski to meet and greet

today's VIP observer at the Las Vegas terminal, and the members of the Malignant Wave team visibly relaxed. The necessary tasks still got done—now under the sensible supervision of Dr. Phillip Bascomb—but the mood was much lighter, despite the crucial, make-or-break demonstration looming over their heads.

It wasn't too long after Tony downloaded the contents of Steve Sable's cell phone into his laptop that he managed to slip the phone back into the man's lab coat pocket. A simple pat on the back and Tony smoothly returned the man's phone. It was gone, then back again before the other man noticed his cell was ever missing.

That left Tony with another urgent problem. He didn't have the tools to analyze the information he'd stolen, which meant that he had to transfer the cell phone memory to Jamey Farrell at CTU, Los Angeles, as soon as possible. But every time he tried to get back to his office, some new task arose. Finally, almost ninety minutes after Dr. Reed's departure, Tony found the chance to excuse himself when Dr. Bascomb went to the cafeteria to grab a late lunch.

"Yo, Steve, I think my laptop's winking out. I'm going to switch to the backup in my office," Tony lied.

"Take your time," Dr. Sable replied, swigging from a bottle of water. He'd found a shady corner and was playing craps for pebbles with a pair of young airmen.

"I'll be back in five."

"Hey, man, no sweat," Steve said with a laugh. "The tough stuff's done and Madame de Sade won't be back for another half hour. Have yourself a party, Antonio."

Tony shut the computer down and tucked it under his arm. He left the shade of the tent, crossed the hard-packed sand to the hangar unnoticed. Dani Welles was locked in a heated debate with Dr. Alvin Toth about which television physician was the most competent. Toth opted for someone named "Marcus Welby, M.D."—then expressed dismay to learn that no one among them had ever heard of the show. Dani was pushing for George Clooney's character in *E.R.*

"I said the most competent television doctor, Dani. Not the 'the one with the tightest booty,'" the elderly doctor complained.

Only Beverly Chang seemed tense. She avoided conversation with the others while silently staring at her own computer screen. Tony knew she was obsessively running and rerunning various diagnostic programs on the hibernating transmitter atop the steel tower. He knew because he'd been monitoring her computer with his own.

As soon as he reached his cramped cubicle in a dim corner of Hangar Six, Tony kicked up the window air conditioner, then fired up his desktop PC. Then he downloaded a copy of the data from Steve's cell into his desktop. Now the real task began.

Groom Lake AFB, and especially Area 51, was the most closely watched patch of ground in America. The activities of the staff were monitored closely, both inside and outside the base. Telephones, cell phones, and Internet connections were also screened.

Tony knew that Steve had tinkered with his own cell phone, perhaps placed some sort of scrambler inside of it. Despite this precautions, Tony realized that the watchers of Area 51 still knew *someone* was using an unauthorized cell phone. They just couldn't pinpoint the phone's location or trace down the individual—yet. It was a dangerous game Steve Sable was playing. Sooner or later, he was bound to get caught.

Now Tony was about to test a theory of his own. He had to send a large package of data over the Internet to Jamey back at CTU, without that data being noticed or intercepted by the security screening software. It was much easier to monitor Internet connections than it was cell phone signals, so any misstep by Tony would result in immediate arrest by Air Force security personnel and a rough interrogation by Intelligence officers.

Before he went undercover, Tony, Milo Pressman and Jamey Farrell discussed this problem in CTU's conference room. They came up with several creative solutions. As usual, Jamey's first impulse was to try a high tech fix.

"It's simple," she'd said with a confident smirk. "We use encrypted bundles broken down and dispatched through the base's entire computer network. Air Force security protocols might detect the transmission—and I'm not saying they will—but there's no way their security software could locate which computer was the source of the transmission. Nor could the information be easily decrypted if it was intercepted, because the fragments are too small to provide enough source material to crack the digital coding."

"But wouldn't the data arrive here a mess?" Milo asked.

Jamey shrugged. "I could put it together in no time because I know the code."

"Too risky," Tony replied, shaking his head. "I might be forced to send a data package every other day, or even every day. And I want a 24/7 CTU remote camera link on any classified activity, too. With all that information streaming out of Area 51 in tiny little bundles, the Air Force would make it a point of sniffing me out."

Milo shrugged. "How about we go low-tech. Something like carrier pigeons."

Milo was taking a shot, but it got Tony to thinking. "I think I have a low tech solution," he announced.

Instead of launching into his plan, Tony talked about how the Internet was born out of research begun in the 1960s by the Advanced Research Projects Agency of the U.S. Defense Department. It was they who created the ARPANET, the first networking system consisting of just four computers, at the end of 1967. Soon after that, software and protocol research began. One development was the Network Control Program, or NCP, which provided a standard method to establish communications links between different hosts. This allowed the ARPANET to expand exponentially.

"He's right," Milo said. "According to CIA files, Area 51 had an ARPANET by 1977, if not earlier."

"Yes," Tony continued. "But in 1983, the current TCP/IP protocols replaced NCP as the principal protocol of the ARPANET. After that, the ARPANET became a small component of the then fledgling Internet, and things only got bigger from there."

Milo nodded. "Meanwhile the outmoded NCP protocols were forgotten. Your point?"

"Air Force intelligence used standard TCP/IP protocols to monitor Area 51's Internet connections, right? So I can avoid detection by sending the data to CTU using the older NCP protocols, the old ARPANET pathways."

Jamey blinked, understanding his logic. "That will work, provided I can locate some of the older pathways."

Milo shook his head. "Sounds a little far fetched. You're still transmitting data. Why won't you get caught?"

"It's like the power company trying to meter electricity that is somehow sent through natural gas lines," Tony explained. "The electric company isn't paying attention to the gas system, so it slips right past them."

Milo nodded. "Okay, I'll dig up some of those old protocols and we'll give it a try. But Tony, if I were you, I'd use that same analogy when I explained this scheme to Christopher Henderson."

Tony chuckled at the memory. He'd done just that at the pre-mission briefing and Henderson was hooked. Together, Milo and Jamey developed protocols to translate the data, and stored them in Tony's laptop so that now it took Tony only minutes to convert the data and drop it into an NCP packet. Then he sent the packet on its way. Back in Los Angeles, Jamey would download this data, along with the camera feed from the test site, by tapping into the old ARPANET routes at UCLA, and then downloading all the collected data into CTU's mainframe. And it all happened with only a few seconds' delay.

Tony closed down his computer, then glanced at his watch. In forty-five minutes the demonstration was scheduled to take place. Tony grabbed his backup laptop, and hurried back to the site. He wanted to be present for the final preparations.

*5:15:47 P.M. PDT*
*Hangar Five,*
*Experimental Weapons Testing Range*
*Groom Lake Air Force Base*

"This is certainly an impressive machine," Senator Palmer declared with genuine awe.

"The Boeing Sikorski LO–88 Blackfoot was commissioned by the Army," Dr. Megan Reed explained. "The brass were looking to procure a stealthy insertion and recovery aircraft suitable for conducting special operations. Unfortunately the Pentagon wasn't happy with the helicopter's payload limitations, and the program was cancelled shortly after this prototype was tested—successfully, I might add."

The cavernous interior of Hangar Five housed only

one aircraft, a sleek, black shape that reminded Senator Palmer of a predatory raptor. A tri-motored, rotor-controlled aircraft, the LO–88 Blackfoot resembled no helicopter Palmer had ever seen. Instead of a main rotor on top of the aircraft, the Blackfoot had two ten-bladed fans housed in engine nacelles affixed to both sides of the aircraft's fuselage. The vertical tail rotor was conventionally set on the tail fin, but was also housed in a hooded nacelle.

Apart from the propeller housings, there were no rounded edges on the Blackfoot. Viewed from the front, the fuselage was triangular—its bottom was flat, sides sloped like the body of an F–117 stealth fighter. This shape—the so-called "Hopeless Diamond" configuration—was designed to deflect radar waves. It was also clear to the head of the Defense Appropriations Committee that no metal was used in the construction of the craft's exterior—everything was fashioned from super-strong plastics or extremely-expensive radar-absorbing composite materials. Two flat-paned cockpit windows in the shark-like, pointed nose were tinted black to match the light-absorbing surface of the fuselage.

Palmer circled the high-tech stealth helicopter once. "This aircraft is quite amazing. But I have to ask, why am I here? This has nothing to do with the demonstration . . . Or does it?"

"The Blackfoot may have disappointed the Army, but it's the perfect platform to carry the Malignant Wave device to the enemy," Dr. Reed explained. "It's low observable, has a range of over a thousand miles, terrain-mapping capabilities. It can fly nap of the earth, and because of the new vortex technology that powers the main engines, the Blackfoot can also attain altitudes no other helicopter can match."

"I believe I've already expressed my amazement," Palmer replied. He crossed his arms behind his back and waited for the other shoe to drop.

"We learned during early trials that the low-observable composite material used in the Blackfoot's construction not only works to repel radar, it also deflects the waves generated by our weapon. Therefore the pilot and co-pilot can deploy Malignant Wave without risk."

Palmer nodded. "I'm impressed that you're thinking ahead, Dr. Reed. But I find it a little presumptuous, as well. Or wouldn't you agree?"

Dr. Reed frowned. "I don't think I understand, Senator."

"Your research seems to be farther along than anyone on my Committee imagined. I'm even more eager to see this non-lethal technology demonstrated." Palmer glanced at his Rolex. "Shouldn't we proceed with the demonstration?"

"Of course, Senator," Dr. Reed replied, still smiling. "I understand your eagerness and share it. I merely wanted to show you the Blackfoot, and let you know that *if* my team is given the green light, we can immediately proceed to the next level—deployment of the Malignant Wave technology under simulated battlefield conditions."

Senator Palmer frowned. "It's nearly five thirty now. Is there a problem?"

Corporal Stratowski, who'd been standing quietly

on the sidelines, stepped forward. "I'm sorry to report it's a matter of security, Senator. The Chinese have taken a special interest in Area 51 in the last few days. Their last space-based surveillance satellite of the day won't pass over Groom Lake for another ten minutes. After it's out of range, we can proceed with the demonstration."

Palmer nodded. "Sorry for my impatience, Corporal. I wasn't aware of the facts."

Then the Senator faced Megan Reed. "Well Doctor, in the mean time, perhaps you can introduce me to the rest of your team . . ."

*5:24:02 P.M. PDT*
*Mirabelle's French Dry Cleaners*
*Monitor Street, Las Vegas*

Ignoring signs that promised "guaranteed two-hour service," and proclaimed that all cleaning was "done on the premises," Yizi checked the address on the store front against the card she clutched between manicured fingers. Satisfied she'd arrived at the correct address, Yizi pushed through the glass door.

The tiny shop seemed empty, but an electronic buzzer sounded somewhere out of sight. The atmosphere inside the dry cleaners smelled of bleach. Behind the counter, hundreds of shrink-wrapped garments hung on a large circular rack.

A young Chinese man appeared at once, stepping through a curtained door in the wall. He wore nondescript pants and a crisp white shirt with a plastic nametag that identified him as Mr. Hsu. He smiled politely, though he'd never seen the woman before.

"May I help you," Mr. Hsu asked in perfect English.

"This is an urgent job. My boss wants this cleaned at once," Yizi replied, also in English. She slid the garment across the Formica table top. Then her dark eyes met his. "Jong Lee wants you to know there is a stain in the right sleeve, Mr. Hsu."

Still smiling, Hsu nodded. "I understand completely. Tell Mr. Lee that the jacket will be ready in two hours."

"Good afternoon, then," Yizi replied. Without another word, she spun on her heels and left the shop immediately.

Mr. Hsu, jacket in hand, once again stepped through the curtain. He set the garment down on a stainless steel table and began his search. It didn't take long for Hsu to locate the instructions tucked into the sleeve, exactly as the woman promised.

It took the man a few minutes to read and memorize the handwritten instructions. Then he dropped the message into a document shredder, along with his Green Card and plastic nametag.

"Yee! Uhr!" Hsu cried. Two young Chinese men with thick necks and close-cropped stubble on their heads hurried from the depths of the roaring, windy cleaning plant.

"Yes, Captain?"

"Alert the team. Make final preparations. The mission is on for tonight."

A flicker of emotion crossed their faces. "At once,"

they replied smartly. Uhr and Yee returned to the bowels of the cleaning plant, while Hsu hurried to the front of the shop and locked the door. He turned out the lights and hung the closed sign in the window. Behind him, he heard the dry cleaning machines power down and the steady whine of the dryers fall suddenly silent. For good measure, Hsu placed a fitting screen in front of the glass door, so that no curious eyes could see the activity within.

Though his US government-issue Green Card identified him as Anh Hsu, an immigrant from Hong Kong, only the name on the card was accurate, the personal history a careful fabrication devised by China's military intelligence bureau, the Second Department. In truth, Hsu had never even seen Hong Kong, even after he fled the tiny rural village in the Jiangxi Province of South-Central China where he was born. Hsu's village did not even have electricity until the mid–1980s, and Mao's modernization programs passed them by. Consequently, Hsu was raised without the education or benefits of the city-bred youth of Beijing, or even China's newest acquisition, Hong Kong. The people of Hsu's village were perpetually poor due to abysmally low agricultural prices, so poor that no one in his town—not even the town doctor—owned a bicycle or a clock, let alone a radio or television.

Because of the Communist's government's Draconian birth control laws which limited Chinese couples to two children, most female babies born in Hsu's village were placed outside to die of exposure. Girls were considered useless mouths to feed, while boys would at least grow up to work the fields. Considered too uneducated and unskilled for factory work, compared to those citizens born in the cities, Hsu faced a dull future as a subsistence farmer.

So, to escape that fate, he became a member of the two and a half million strong People's Liberation Army, the largest military on Earth, enlisting just days after his seventeenth birthday.

Through drive, diligence and hard work—and by exhibiting a cold ruthlessness that impressed his superiors—Anh Hsu moved up the ranks, until he was promoted to a level seemingly unattainable for one of such lowly birth and questionable heritage—a Captain in the Second Department's Human Intelligence Bureau. Among his newfound skills, he learned to speak English like an American. But Hsu was not content with a behind-the-scenes position analyzing data on some desk-bound general's staff. In an effort to boost his visibility, Hsu volunteered for service in the 6th Special Warfare Group, a unit that performed a variety of operational missions including counter-terrorism, long-range reconnaissance, sabotage, hostage rescue, hit-and-run strikes, and deep penetration warfare.

Captain Hsu's military achievements and fanatical drive eventually attracted the attention of Communist Chinese espionage agent Jong Lee, also a member of the Second Department. Lee, an active espionage agent who passed himself off as a Taiwanese lobbyist when spying on the West, was one of China's greatest operatives. Because of his formidable reputation, Jong Lee was permitted to recruit Captain Hsu.

For his part, Hsu admired Jong Lee because he never displayed a dearth of imagination, nor the slavish lack initiative of his peers in the PLA. Lee was not afraid to act, and act boldly.

It was Jong Lee who devised their current mission to seize America's most advanced technology from under the long noses of the United States Air Force, and it was Lee who convinced his masters in Beijing to go along with his perilous plan. Along the way, he also convinced Captain Hsu to join him, though in the end it did not take much convincing. Like Jong Lee, Captain Hsu despised the decadent Western democracies, and resented their phenomenal wealth and economic might.

*And so tonight, after months of planning and preparation, I will lead a commando raid so audacious it will shift the balance of power between the United States and China forever. Perhaps our daring strike here, in the enemy's heartland, will convince those old fools in Beijing that the time for war against America is now. . .*

*5:48:02 P.M. PDT*
*Hangar Six, Experimental Weapons Testing Range*
*Groom Lake Air Force Base*

Dr. Reed made the introductions, starting at the top of the food chain with Dr. Phillip Bascomb, then working her way down the pecking order.

When she returned to Hangar Six with the Senator in tow, the woman rudely corralled the staff, then lined them all up in the hot afternoon sun for a military-style review. Her managerial skills had never been so clumsy, and pretty much everyone was mortified by the woman's behavior—except for the oblivious Dr. Reed, of course.

What could have been a very uncomfortable few minutes was lightened considerably by Senator David Palmer's charisma and easy charm. Unlike most VIP visitors to Area 51, the Senator from Maryland seemed to take a genuine interest in the people involved in the project, not only the project itself. He spent a few minutes with each member of the Malignant Wave team, quizzing them on their tasks, their credentials—though the conversation was not always on topic. When Palmer tried to grill Bascomb about his previous experience as a microwave specialist for NASA, the scientist found a way to switch topics. While most professionals loved to talk about their work, to Palmer's surprise, Dr. Bascomb preferred to talk about his pro-basketball days.

So did Dr. Alvin Toth, who grinned up at the Senator while pumping Palmer's hand. "You and Larry Bell were a hell of a team," the paunchy pathologist said.

"We still are, Dr. Toth," Palmer replied. "I'm having dinner with Larry tonight."

Beverly Chang smiled nervously when the Senator complimented her on the efficiency of her security system. The thirty-something cyber specialist shook his hand, but seemed too shy to meet his stare.

Senator Palmer and Steve Sable spoke only briefly. Dr. Sable received a shock when the Senator cited his work on the F–22 Raptor's highly-advanced computer control system.

"I read your report last year, Dr. Sable. Seems to me the Air Force owes you a debt of gratitude for ironing out a litany of technical glitches."

"I'll be sure to remind them, Senator," the software engineer replied with a smirk.

"This is Dani Welles, the youngest member of our team," Dr. Reed said, moving quickly past the acerbic Dr. Sable.

The Senator smiled at the young woman, and offered his hand. "Delighted to meet you, Ms. Welles."

When their hands met the woman nearly gushed. "Please call me Dani, Senator."

"A pleasure . . . Dani."

"This is Antonio Alvarez," Dr. Reed said. "He's our energy specialist."

Senator Palmer hardly glanced at Tony. His attention was drawn to a sudden burst of activity a few hundred yards away, at the test site. A tow tractor appeared on the scene, dragging two wheeled carts carrying aluminum cages. In one cage, a pair of Rhesus monkeys were strapped to metal gurneys. The primates—a male and a female—had gray-brown fur and hairless pink faces. Rendered immobile, the monkeys snarled fearfully, lips curled back to reveal sharp teeth. Their dark eyes blinked against the sun's glare.

Palmer moved closer, and noticed the animals' heads were shaved. Electrodes had been implanted deep into the apes' skull, wires running to monitors attached to the bars.

In the other cage, two small pigs squealed with fright. Unfettered, they sniffed the bars of their prison with their flaring snouts.

Steve Sable turned his back on the scene, glanced at Tony. "If you're a card-carrying member of PETA, you better leave now, amigo," he muttered.

"Ah, the test animals have arrived," Dr. Toth said. "I'd better go make sure the monitors are working."

Dr. Bascomb nodded. "If you'll excuse me, Senator. I also have work to do."

Both he and Dr. Toth hurried back to their instrument panels inside the tent. Within seconds, the entire team had dispersed to complete final preparations.

"Just be patient a little longer, Senator," Dr. Reed said with a hint of pride. "Show time is just minutes away."

The Senator glanced at Megan Reed, who watched as the cages were carefully unloaded by a group of airmen. Under Beverly Chang's supervision, the cages were placed inside an invisible box bordered by four yellow poles pounded into the ground, about seventy-five yards away from the microwave tower.

"I wasn't aware lab animals would be used in this demonstration," Palmer said, unable to mask his distaste.

"I believe it's necessary, Senator Palmer," Dr. Reed replied. "In order to truly understand the power of this weapon, you must witness the Malignant Wave's effect on actual brains and central nervous systems. I don't believe a print-out of a microwave graph would be sufficient."

Palmer frowned. "I defer to your expertise, Dr. Reed."

*5:56:40 P.M. PDT*
*The Cha-Cha Lounge, Las Vegas*

Morris O'Brian led Jack Bauer to the sub basement storage room. Hands quaking, the little man unlocked the steel door, pushed it open, switched on the overhead light.

"Over there, Jack," Morris croaked, averting his eyes.

Jack stepped over two canvas bags filled with dusty Christmas decorations, moved around a row of unused roulette tables. The corpse was there, where Morris had pointed. Face down on the concrete floor, blood had oozed from the stab wound after death, staining the floor black.

"Who is it, Jack?"

Bauer crouched over the dead man, carefully turned the corpse onto its side. The skin was already spotted with purple blotches, limbs stiffening but not yet frozen by rigor mortis, so the man had been dead for several hours.

Jack used his pen flashlight to probe the floor around the body. Not enough blood on the ground, so Jack knew he didn't die here. He tossed the corpse, fishing through the man's pockets, under his belt, under the shirt and inside his pants. He'd already made a positive identification, so Jack wasn't trying to find out who the dead man was. He just wanted to see what he found—a wallet, keys, loose change, a pack of matches and a couple of chips from Circus, Circus.

"It's Ray Perry," Jack replied.

Morris swallowed loudly. "That explains why he's been missing. I guess we know it wasn't Ray who killed Max Farrow in his cell, then."

Jack lowered the corpse to the ground. "He's been stabbed a couple of times, but the neck wound finished him. I think Perry was killed in the security room, before or after Max Farrow was murdered. His blood mingled with Farrow's. I should have figured out that there was too much blood." Bauer's expression darkened. "In a scene like that, there always seems to be too much blood . . ."

Bauer stood, tucked the dead man's wallet into the back pocket of his black Levi's. "Why were you down here, Morris?"

"Blew a bank of cameras on the northeast side of the gaming room. I wanted to check the circuit breakers . . ." Morris pointed to the opposite wall. "That's the box, over there. I found the problem, corrected it. Then, as I was leaving, I saw . . . him."

"Did you tell anyone?"

Morris stared at the dead man, shook his head. "I was looking for Curtis . . . Found you instead."

"Who else has a key to this room?" Jack demanded.

Morris shrugged. "Too many people, Jack. Curtis . . . Don Driscoll . . . Chick Hoffman. That guy Manny . . . what's his name . . . The guy who works the night shift. I think the bartender has a copy, too."

"How well was the body hidden?" Jack asked, his mind categorizing the likelihood of each man's guilt.

"I wouldn't have found Ray, except that I was taking a peek at those roulette tables over there." Morris scratched his chin. "Saw his feet sticking out from behind the canvas bags."

"Nobody comes down here much, anyway," Jack said, thinking out loud. "Whoever stashed the corpse here knew it was only a matter of time before Perry was found. Which means the killer only needed to buy a few hours, maybe less . . ."

"What's that mean, Jack?"

Bauer's eyes narrowed as he stared down at the dead man. "It means our traitor is going to make his move very soon . . . and we have to be ready."

1 2 3 4 5 6 **7** 8 9
10 11 12 13 14 15 16 17
18 19 20 21 22 23 24

. . . . . . . . . . . . . . . . . . . . . . . . . . . . . . . .

**THE FOLLOWING TAKES PLACE
BETWEEN THE HOURS OF
6 P.M. AND 7 P.M.
PACIFIC DAYLIGHT TIME**

. . . . . . . . . . . . . . . . . . . . . . . . . . . . . . . .

*6:01:34 P.M. PDT*
*Hangar Six, Experimental Weapons Testing Range*
*Groom Lake Air Force Base*

Megan Reed led Palmer to the tent erected less than fifty feet from the microwave tower. As soon as he entered, he felt a cool blast of air, heard the whine of a cooling unit. While he watched, the tent flaps were lowered, completely blocking the sun's rays. Palmer's eyes were immediately drawn to a bank of six high definition screens. One screen focused on the microwave tower. Four other screens displayed close up, real time images of the animals inside their cages. The last screen projected four fluctuating lines resembling the scribbles made on paper by a seismograph.

"Those are the electroencephalograms of the male and female Rhesus Macaque," Dr. Reed explained.

Dr. Toth jumped into the conversation, sounding like a college professor. "You see, Senator, the resulting EEG will allow us to gross correlate brain activity. Through the electrodes implanted in the monkeys skulls, we can detect changes in electrical activity in the brain very accurately—on a millisecond level, in fact."

"Power levels?" Dr. Bascomb called from behind his control station.

"Stabilized on maximum output," Tony replied.

"Then we're ready," Bascomb announced. "Prepare for two, one-second bursts at the count of ten."

"Should I brace myself or something?" Senator Palmer asked, eyeing the canvas walls nervously. "This tent isn't exactly a bomb shelter."

Megan Reed chuckled. "The microwaves are invisible, so there's nothing to feel or hear. And the beams are directed to strike the animal cages within the target perimeter." She tapped the screen with a manicured fingernail. "Only the ground inside that staked out square will be affected. Within these yellow markers you see here . . ."

Palmer watched Bascomb grip a switch. "Burst one," he cried, flipping the switch, then immediately turning it again.

"Second burst in ten seconds," Bascomb warned. At the count of ten he flipped the switch again—on, then off.

"Power down," Bascomb commanded. "Demonstration concluded at eighteen hundred hours, four minutes . . ."

Tony tapped the keys on his laptop and disengaged the power generator from the microwave emitter. Steve Sable pulled a tent flap aside and disconnected the power coupler—a move that was like throwing the safety on a handgun. There was no way the microwave emitter could discharge now—even accidentally.

The Senator only realized the demonstration was over when he found himself in the middle of a sudden crush, as everyone inside the cramped tent moved forward to peer at the images on the high definition screens. Palmer got a good look at one of the display screens—a close up shot of a Rhesus monkey. The creature's eyes were wide, but seemed unfocused—almost cross-eyed. When the primate shook its head to clear its vision, violent tremors wracked its body. Breathing became rapid, then erratic. Foam flecked the ape's pink lips and drool rolled down the side of its mouth.

Megan Reed stepped in front of the display. Blocking his view, she directed Palmer's attention to the waves running horizontally across the EEG monitor.

"You can see that the Gamma rays are off the chart," the woman said over the excited voices of her staff members. "We're seeing sharp waves, spikes. . . . The female is especially affected. She's exhibiting the same spike-and-wave complexes we observe in cases of human epilepsy. Both primates are completely immobilized. Released from their bonds, they would be unable to stand or even sit up without support."

"What exactly happened?" Palmer asked.

"It's very simple to put in laymen's terms," Dr. Toth said. "The motor cortex is a general term that describes several regions of the cerebral cortex. The motor cortex is that part of our brains involved in the planning, control and execution of voluntary motor functions."

"Yes," Bascomb said, nodding. "The primary motor cortex is responsible for generating neural impulses that control movement. Then there's the premotor cortex and the supplementary motor area—"

"Too technical, Phillip," Toth protested. "In laymen's terms, we know that electrical impulses generated by the motor cortex control voluntary movement. What the Malignant Wave device does is scramble those electronic signals, throwing the entire brain into chaos—"

"You see, the Malignant Wave induces a kind of instantaneous multiple sclerosis in those exposed to its waves, but without the multiple scars—or scleroses—found on the myelin sheaths of the victims," Dr. Reed declared. "In fact, there is no visible physical trauma caused by the wave device, even on a microscopic level. Only the electrical functions are scrambled."

Palmer glanced at another monitor, this one displaying the pigs in their cage. The creatures twitched and rolled in their own feces. When they attempted to stand, their flanks twitched and their limbs shook violently.

"The pigs have fouled their cages," Palmer noted.

Dr. Reed nodded, smiling. "Bowel and bladder

control is *voluntary*, Senator. The animals have lost the ability control those functions."

Dr. Toth lifted a tent flap and gestured to a pair of men in spotless white lab coats. As one, the duo moved toward the cages. Palmer noticed the technicians were carrying hypodermic injector guns.

"Those two men?" he asked. "Are they going to administer some sort of sedative, or perhaps the antidote? When do the waves' effects wear off?"

Dr. Bascomb looked away. Dr. Reed cleared her throat, then spoke. "Senator, those men are going to euthanize the animals. There is no antidote to the Malignant Wave effect, nor does it wear off."

Palmer turned away from the ghastly scene, faced the woman. He seemed to tremble with barely contained anger. When he spoke, Palmer's voice was a low, threatening rumble.

"Malignant Wave is supposed to be a non-lethal weapon system, Dr. Reed. That's what the committee was promised."

"Yes . . . Well," she stammered. "As I said, there is no physical trauma induced by the waves . . . Only—"

"Only you render the victim helpless. Unable to control its most basic bodily functions—forever."

Megan Reed blinked. "Of course, Senator. Think of the disruption to the enemy's ranks on the battlefield, as medics try to administer care to hundreds, perhaps thousands of soldiers so afflicted. The drain on the enemy's resources would be catastrophic. In the end, they would be forced to resort to euthanasia, if only to be merciful. The enemy would have to kill their own troops! Think of the effect such dire measures would have on their morale. "

Senator Palmer shook his head.

"No," he declared. "I refuse to consider your logic. It is too terrible to contemplate. Malignant Wave is not non-lethal technology, despite what you say, Dr. Reed. In truth your team's invention is one of the most vile and hateful methods of execution I've ever witnessed."

Dr. Bascomb rose, faced the Senator. "But, surely you see the value of such technology?"

"Value! In this, this . . . abomination?" Palmer cried. "We asked for a new type of non-lethal technology. Instead, you've invented nothing more than a diabolical new weapon of mass destruction. Can you imagine this weapon in enemy hands? If we allowed this program to go forward to deployment, we would unleash a new arms race."

Once again, Senator Palmer shook his head. "If you think I or anyone on my committee will endorse such a weapon, you are sorely mistaken."

Palmer spied Corporal Stratowski lurking in a corner. "Corporal, I need to get back to Las Vegas at once. Take me to the airfield," he commanded.

"Right away, Senator. The Hummer is parked outside."

As Palmer crossed the tent, Megan Reed caught his arm.

"Senator, please let me accompany you back to the city," she pleaded. "I'm sure you've gotten the wrong impression of our work here. I think I can change your mind . . . Convince you to see things our way . . ."

Palmer glanced at the high definition screens a final time. He watched a man injecting one of the monkeys with poison, looked away immediately.

"Don't bother, Dr. Reed," Palmer replied. "Nothing you say could ever change my mind. As of this moment, consider the Malignant Wave Project cancelled."

*6:23:41 P.M. PDT*
*Las Vegas Boulevard*
*At the corner of Tropicana Avenue*
*The Las Vegas Strip*

From behind mirrored sunglasses, Pizarro Rojas placidly observed the Las Vegas strip as it rolled past his windshield. The MGM lion blazed rose gold in the fading light, the sun a radiant ball of fire in the fast purpling sky.

In the seat beside him, his twin brother Balboa snored quietly. But Balboa had been in America for months now. The Las Vegas strip was nothing new to him. In fact, his brother showed very little appreciation of America, or perhaps he merely missed his wife and family back in Colombia.

For Pizarro this place was astonishing, a revelation. Though he'd heard about such luxury, never in his wildest imaginings did he envision the spectacle.

Pizarro Rojas reclined his seat, stretched his short,

powerful legs. The middle row of the sports utility vehicle was roomy and comfortable, the air conditioner flooded the compartment with cool filtered air, enough to stir his long, curly hair. In all respects, he decided this was a much better ride than the steel box he and his two bodyguards had ridden in across the U.S./Mexican border.

"What do you think, Carlos?" Pizarro called to the driver. "Does this vulgar display of capitalistic excess offend your socialist sensibilities?"

Carlos Boca, an ex-Cuban special forces commando, glanced at his young boss's reflection in the rear view mirror.

"What offends me is that Fidel was such an ass," Boca replied with a sneer. "After the Revolution, in 1960, casinos like this . . . All this money . . . It could have belonged to Cuba. If Castro had nationalized the resorts, modernized them, then he could have used the jobs and the influx of foreign capital to benefit the Cuban people."

"If he catered to foreign economic interests, then our beloved Fidel would have been no different than that pig Batista." As he spoke, Roland Arrias ran his fingers along the jagged scar that ripped a canal down the right side of his face. Like the driver, Roland had a powerful build, thick neck and a shaved head.

"You are wrong, my brother," Carlos replied. "Vietnam and China are models for the future. Not the economic cesspool Cuba has become."

Pizarro Rojas knew the two men were as close as

brothers—with their powerful physiques and army haircuts, they even resembled one another. Only Roland's grotesque scar set the men apart. The pair bickered constantly, usually over Cuban politics. Somewhere along the line, Carlos had lost faith in his Supreme Leader and the Communist Revolution, while his fellow Cuban remained a committed ideologue. The pair looked to be in their forties, but Pizarro didn't know which was older, which the younger. All he cared about was the fact that both men were ex-Cuban Special Forces and trustworthy allies.

Back at Big Dean's Truck Farm, the Cubans had traded their dusty denims and work boots for dark suits and black silk shirts. Under the jackets, in shoulder holsters, each man carried a Russian-made Makarov PM. Carlos also had a long Spanish steel stiletto strapped to his leg. Stashed in a secret compartment hidden under the floor mats were their AK–47s, along with hundreds of rounds of ammunition. Somewhere along this route, another SUV with six other military trained Cuban expatriates was moving toward the same rendezvous—Bix Automotive.

Roland Arrias snorted. "You are the fool, my friend. Russia lost the courage of their convictions, turned to Western-style democracy—which there is no such thing. Now the Russian people live in a gangster state."

Listening to these men, Pizarro was reminded of the conversations he and Balboa shared with their youngest brother, Francesco. Little Franco never cared for politics. He loved music and women. Always a hothead, Francesco was beloved by their mother and doted on by their father. As leader of the cartel's hit team, Francesco was also respected by the men under his command, some much older than he was. And young women could not resist his charms, either. When he was gunned down by an unknown American agent in Nicaragua, Francesco left two bastard children behind, from two separate mothers. At least his children would live on, under the care of their paternal grandparents.

It was those same American agents that stole back the technology his family had paid dearly for—in money *and* blood. The loss of prestige they suffered at the hands of these Americans shook the foundations of the Rojas' once-powerful drug empire, made them appear weak and vulnerable to friends and enemies alike.

Behind his sunglasses, Pizarro's expression darkened. Ahead of them stood the many tiered tower of the Babylon Hotel and Casino. A banner fluttered from the building's mammoth portico, proclaiming the resort as the site of the Pan-Latin Anti-Drug Conference. The Cubans also fell silent as they passed the target of their impending operation.

In just a few hours Pizarro Rojas would return, along with his brother Balboa, and his team of Cuban assassins. He would return to this majestic place to exact a measure of vengeance for the crimes committed against his family—not just vengeance against America, but against other Latin American governments and law enforcement agencies who dared to oppose the Rojas cartel.

After the daring assault and the multiple assassinations to come, the defeats of the past would be forgotten. With their honor and respect fully restored, the other cartels would clamor to join a new alliance forged and ruled by the Rojas clan. Soon his family would control all of the cocaine production and distribution in the Northern Hemisphere, just as the Saudi Arabian sheiks controlled the oil flowing out of the Middle East. Even America, with all of her military might, would be paralyzed with the dread of another cartel attack. Their leaders would make speeches, promise to wage yet another war against drugs, while sitting on their pristine, perfectly-manicured hands and doing nothing. . .

*6:48:17 P.M. PDT*
*Tunney and Sons Quality Tool and Die*
*Browne End Road, Las Vegas*

For nearly an hour, Curtis Manning saw no one enter or leave the multiple-block compound of Bix Automotive, though the mysterious activity inside the garage clearly continued. Occasionally Curtis would see the flash of a welder's torch visible behind the garage's oily windows, or someone would step outside for a smoke or a breath of fresh air, only to be ordered back into the enormous garage by Roman Vine, Bix's strong-arm man. Manning noted that today Vine was carrying an illegal sawed-off shotgun, and he wasn't shy about flashing it.

Curtis was about to report in when he observed a Saturn minivan roll up to the garage door. Roman Vine spied the car and waved it forward. Curtis quickly counted four men inside the car before they drove into the garage. He didn't get a good look at the faces, though he did notice that one man wore reflecting sunglasses. Curtis noticed this because the man stared directly at the abandoned Tool and Die factory as if he were looking right at Curtis.

Dutifully, Curtis snapped a digital image of the men with his PDA, then forwarded it to Morris O'Brian at the Cha-Cha Lounge. While he performed that task, another SUV—this one a Chrysler—pulled onto the Bix lot. Curtis had no time to snap digital pictures of the men inside that vehicle. They all appeared to be Hispanic males in their late twenties or early thirties. Curtis counted six men in the car.

Curtis had just pulled the cell phone out of his pocket when his PDA sounded. He checked the display and discovered his data drop to Morris had not gone through.

Suddenly alarmed, Curtis then checked his cell phone and found he could not get a signal, no matter how hard he tried. That should have been impossible, because he'd used the cell phone when he last checked in with Morris, less than thirty minutes before.

Someone was jamming the signals in the area, which meant that Bix or his men probably suspected someone was in the vicinity, spying on them. Curtis tucked the devices into his pocket, then reached for his jacket. It was time to go. . .

*6:55:57 P.M. PDT*
*Bix Automotive Center*
*Browne End Road, Las Vegas*

Carlos Boca looked up from the liquid crystal display screen. "You were correct, Pizarro. There was someone in that building across the street. I believe they are still there."

Pizarro stood in the middle of the crowded garage. Hugo Bix had come down from his tattered office to greet the Colombian brothers and their Cuban allies, only to be silenced by an angry Pizarro Rojas. Chewing his lip, Pizarro waited for the results of Boca's transmission scan.

"You're certain there is a watcher?" Balboa asked, glancing at his brother, then at the Cubans.

"You're the jamming expert, Balboa. What do you think?" Carlos stared at the Rojas brother. Balboa nodded.

"Whoever's spying, they have attempted to send a data transmission, either from a PDA or a laptop computer. Then, just now, the observer also tried to make a phone call. I blocked both signals with the jamming system," Carlos explained.

Pizarro Rojas faced Hugo Bix. The American cowboy was over a head taller than the squat, wide Colombian. "Have your men checked that abandoned building across the street?" Pizarro demanded.

Bix pursed his lips and scratched his stubbled chin under the handlebar moustache. Then he glanced at his partner. "I reckon Roman here will know," Bix replied.

"No one's been in there, man. What's the point. Not even bums will sleep there 'cause the building's full of rattlers," Roman told the Colombian.

Pizarro frowned. "There are more than snakes around. My man says you are being watched, which means that someone is inside that building across the street."

"If that's true, then Roman here can deal with the situation," Bix replied smoothly.

Roman nervously wiped his upper lips. He hated snakes.

Carlos Boca set the black box on the hood of a car. "My brother and I will take care of this."

"No," Pizarro Rojas countered. "I need you both here, to examine the quality of the American's work. We can't afford any mistakes."

Carlos nodded, gestured to three men from the other SUV. He gave them terse instructions in Spanish, and the men retrieved AK–47s from their vehicle. Then they headed for the back door of the garage.

"What if the intruder gets away?" Bix asked. "Out of range of that do-hickey of yours?"

Carlos watched as the trio slipped outside, then split up. "Don't worry. He won't," Boca vowed.

Inside the garage, Pizarro Rojas peered at the sprinters lined up in a neat row. "The trucks are prepared, I see."

"Six of them, just like you ordered," Bix replied. "They've all been stolen hundreds of miles from here, and we've supplied phony license plates and electronic key cards with the proper vendor codes. Each of these trucks has been customized to breeze right through the Babylon's security without arousing suspicion.

"Behind the wheels of these babies—" Bix thumped the hood with the flat of his callused hand, "—you and your boys can roll right into the underground delivery area and park where you want."

Bix's homespun smile broadened. "Best of all, every one of those damn trucks is loaded for bear."

*6:59:55 P.M. PDT*
*Babylon Hotel and Casino, Las Vegas*

The bell rang and the doors opened. Lilly Sheridan's daughter Pamela looked up, blinking with astonishment at the man stepping into the elevator.

The new passenger was perhaps the largest man Lilly had ever seen. Not only tall—this man's shoulders were as wide as the refrigerator back at her crummy rent-a-house. He wore a tailored suit that Lilly just knew cost more than she earned in a month, even counting her tips.

*He must be a pro-basketball star*, she concluded. *Or maybe a football player*. But a closer inspection changed her mind. *He's too old to be a pro anything*.

The man's face was a mask of concentration. Brows furrowed, he rubbed his chin. Suddenly, he seemed to realize she was there. The man's face relaxed, his brown eyes met hers.

"Hi," Lilly said shyly.

"Hello."

The man's voice was deep, almost a rumble. He noticed Pamela then, and his smile became dazzling. "Do you like the ride?" he asked.

Pamela nodded. "Makes me queasy, though."

He nodded. "Me too."

The elevator slowed. "Have a good evening," the man said.

"Enjoy your stay at the Babylon," Lilly replied.

He turned and smiled. "Thank you," he said, and the doors closed again.

"Mom, who was that man?"

"I don't know," Lilly replied, distracted. She was worried the banquet manager would be waiting at the entrance to the ball room. Evelyn did that sometimes, to make sure everyone had dressed properly. She didn't want the woman to see Pamela. Too much to explain, and Evelyn would figure out her scam.

"No babysitter, no job," she'd say, sending Lilly home rather than letting her stash her daughter in the dressing room for a couple of hours, where the child wouldn't do any harm.

The bell rang again and the doors opened. The ballroom doors were open wide, but there was no sign of Evelyn or her assistant Janet.

"Hurry, let's go," Lilly hissed, pushing her daughter toward the glittering banquet room.

1 2 3 4 5 6 7 **8** 9
10 11 12 13 14 15 16 17
18 19 20 21 22 23 24

· · · · · · · · · · · · · · · · · · · · · · · · · · · · · · · ·

THE FOLLOWING TAKES PLACE
BETWEEN THE HOURS OF
7 P.M. AND 8 P.M.
PACIFIC DAYLIGHT TIME

· · · · · · · · · · · · · · · · · · · · · · · · · · · · · · · ·

*7:02:11 P.M. PDT*
*Tunney and Sons Quality Tool and Die*
*Browne End Road, Las Vegas*

Curtis spotted the gunman approaching the tool and die factory the moment he slipped through the hole in the back wall. It was a close call for the CTU agent, with Curtis emerging into the fading afternoon just as his stalker rounded the corner. Fortunately the man's eyes were fixed on the sand at his feet—most likely wary of rattlesnakes—so Curtis managed to slip around the building without being seen.

Using the forgotten collection of Dumpsters for cover, Curtis kept glancing over his shoulder, trying to get a better look at his pursuer. A quick glimpse convinced him the man was one of six who'd arrived in the second SUV. All of those men had the same spare, hardened look of ex-military types, and the man certainly carried his assault rifle with assured familiarity.

Curtis paused in a narrow gap between two rusty steel containers, to stare up at the purpling sky. The sun was low on the horizon, but it would be over an hour before it was truly dark. Unfortunately, with at least one man on his trail and possibly more, Curtis could not afford to wait for night to hide his movements—he had to get out of here now.

On his knees, peering out from between two dented containers, Curtis watched as the armed man discovered the hole in the wall, then carefully crouched low and crawled through it.

The moment his stalker disappeared inside the factory, Curtis was moving. He had about thirty feet of barren, sand-swept concrete to cross before reaching the cover of a lone Dumpster set apart from the rest. He'd use it to boost himself over the eight-foot fence, then he'd cross three vacant lots beyond the fence to reach Pena Lane, where he'd parked his car.

Feet pumping, Curtis traversed the stretch of concrete in under three seconds—only to be stopped in his tracks when another man stepped out from behind the Dumpster, his AK–47 leveled at Agent Manning's stomach. Immediately, Curtis threw his hands over his head.

"Don't shoot," he cried, resorting to Plan B. "I know I was trespassing. I lost all my money at the craps table and was lookin' to find a place to crash, that's all."

The man was young, Curtis guessed in his early twenties. By haircut and physique, the CTU agent pegged him as ex-military. But this man was clearly a private in some socialist state's army, because he was clearly not accustomed to thinking or acting independently. Curtis saw the man's confused expression, knew he was wondering if he'd cornered the wrong guy, and if the real culprit was getting away.

"Get on the ground and take out your weapon," he commanded in a thick Cuban accent.

"Chill man! I don't have any weapons," Curtis cried, adding a touch of hysteria to his performance while remaining on his feet.

"Get on the ground," the man roared, moving perilously close. But still the gunman didn't fire. Either he was reluctant to pull the trigger on the wrong man, or he feared alerting his prey. In any case, the youth stood there, eyes darting left and right, wondering what he should do next.

"I know . . . You're looking for the *other* guy," Curtis stammered, he hoped convincingly. "I saw him in the factory. He took off before I did. The dude had a phone in his hand, maybe a gun too . . ."

The gunman blinked, lowered the assault rifle's muzzle, just a little.

"He went that way," Curtis said. He kept his left hand over his head while he moved his right arm across his body, moving as if he were going to point. While the gunman was focused on the action over his left shoulder, Curtis dipped his hand into his jacket.

The Cuban spotted the move too late. Curtis

whipped out the Glock, slapped the rifle barrel aside with his hand. The man jerked the trigger and the AK–47 chattered, blowing out chunks of concrete. Before he could recover, Curtis shoved the muzzle of his Glock into the man's chest and fired twice.

Blown backwards by the impact, the gunman slammed into the steel trash container, then slid to the pavement. The man's heart and lungs poured out of the basketball sized exit wound in his back, splattered to the ground. Curtis was more concerned with the assault rifle, which clattered to the ground a few feet away.

Spitting dust and concrete shards, Curtis lunged for the fallen rifle. But a sudden burst from an automatic weapon peppered the ground around the AK–47, denting the barrel and splintering the stock.

Unable to locate the direction of the fire, Curtis abandoned the now-useless rifle, rolled across the pitted concrete and onto his feet. More tracers tore the air around him as he took off in a run. He had no choice but to head right back to the forest of Dumpsters. Another burst struck the ground around his pounding feet, then punched holes into the steel containers.

Curtis hit the ground on his belly, used his elbows to drag himself forward, deeper into the tangle of steel boxes. Bullets ricocheted over his head, occasionally striking concrete. He felt hot pain and realized a piece of shrapnel had torn a hole in his leg.

Gasping, Curtis touched the wound, satisfied it was not life threatening. With the shooters' location uncertain, he decided to wait a few minutes before moving again. While listening intently for any sound, he rolled onto his back and yanked the PDA out of his pocket. He checked the display, silently cursing the continuing lack of signal. Then he activated the homing beacon inside the device and stuffed the personal digital assistant into a rust hole eaten into the side of a dirty Dumpster. He thrust his cell phone there, too. Curtis knew that if he was killed or captured, Morris or Jack, or another CTU agent could locate and retrieve these items and the data they contained, once the jamming was lifted.

Curtis heard angry voices. Two men. They'd found the corpse of their comrade. He strained to hear the instructions quietly issued by the leader. From what he could understand, the men were circling the Dumpsters to flank him. Keeping his head, Agent Manning noted that the leader spoke Spanish with refined Castillian accent—another Cuban, Curtis guessed.

When he'd counted to a hundred, Curtis adjusted his grip on the Glock. Then he rolled over onto his belly again and slithered among the Dumpsters until he found a place where he could stand.

With two eight-foot fences to climb and long, empty stretches to cross, Curtis knew that the gunmen would easily cut him down before he ever reached Pena Lane. Since that escape was blocked, Curtis decided to surprise his hunters and head right back where he came from—the factory. If he reached the building, which was right on Browne End Road, he could probably hold off a siege until help arrived.

Not that he was expecting to be rescued. Neither Jack nor Morris knew he was in trouble. But an explosion of automatic rifle fire, even in such a remote section of town, would probably attract someone's attention, even if it was only the junkies at crack houses along Pena Lane.

Counting on the timely arrival of a Metro Police squad car was a flimsy plan at best, but it was the only one he had. Cautiously, Curtis rose to a crouch and moved back to the factory. He made it all the way to the hole in the back wall before shots rang out. Shells smacked the bricks above his head as Curtis dived across the threshold.

Without sunlight pouring through broken windows and holes in the roof, the factory's interior was nearly pitch black. Fortunately, Curtis knew his way around the building, and he stumbled blindly forward, waiting for his eyes to adjust to the gloom. Behind him, he heard a crash, then a burst of fire raked the room he'd just fled.

At least one of the gunmen was inside the building, too.

Clutching the Glock, Curtis groped for the door to the next room. He found the doorway, slipped through it—and the butt of a rifle slammed into his guts.

Curtis doubled over, the breath dashed from his lungs. Dimly, through a haze, he saw the dark silhouette in the darker void as the man loomed over him. He raised his Glock feebly, and another sharp blow set it flying from his stunned hand.

To avoid a third strike, Curtis rolled onto his side,

kicked out with the last of his strength. He heard a satisfying grunt as his booted foot connected with flesh. Curtis kicked again—this time with both legs— and his timing was perfect. His attacker was falling forward, kneecap shattered, when Curtis' boots sunk into his midriff. Helpless, the man was lifted up and thrown backwards by the powerful double-kick. He crashed through the front window, plunged onto the curb of Browne End Road.

Curtis clutched the battered desk and hauled himself to his feet. He heard heavy footsteps behind him. With nowhere else to go, Curtis followed the man through the window. His victim, sprawled on the ground, clutched at Curtis as he tried to limp away. Agent Manning smashed the man's throat with a booted foot, felt bone and cartilage snap under his heel. The groping hands fell away. Stumbling forward, Curtis searched vainly for the dead man's AK–47.

Across the street, at Bix Automotive, men were streaming out of the garage, a few of them armed. Curtis turned and loped down the street, one leg stiffening from the still bleeding wound. He knew running was useless, but he wasn't ready to give up yet. He glanced over his shoulder. Already his pursuers were in the street. In another few seconds, they'd start shooting and it would be over. Only a miracle could save him now.

Amid shouts of surprise, Curtis heard the roar of a high-performance engine, the squeal of tires. The men in the street scattered as the vehicle raced through them, threatening to run down anyone who didn't get out of the way. Then the custom painted cherry red BMW skidded to a halt between Curtis and his pursuers. The passenger side door opened.

"Hurry up, get in," a familiar voice called.

Crouching, Curtis dashed to the car, dived into the seat. The woman reached her arm over him, slammed the door. Still half-sprawled across the front seat, Curtis was slammed backwards by the sudden acceleration. Hand against the dashboard, he pulled himself up. Out the windows, Browne End Road was speeding by. Bix Automotive and the men chasing him shrank in the rear view mirror.

Curtis faced the woman behind the wheel. "Thanks, Stella . . . I don't know what you were doing here, but you saved my life."

Stella Hawk said nothing, her eyes on the road. Finally she peeked at Curtis through long eyelashes. "You're bleeding on my leather upholstery."

Curtis looked down. Blood seeped from the bullet graze in his leg. He'd also gashed his side on jagged glass when he jumped through the window.

"Sorry," he grunted. "I'll have it cleaned for you."

Curtis stared at the road, orienting himself. "Make the next right," he told the woman. "I need to get back to the Cha-Cha Lounge as soon as possible."

Tires howled again as Stella negotiated the turn without slowing down. Sniffling, she reached a manicured hand into her purse.

"I'm not kidding, Stella," Curtis said, touching his guts gingerly. "You really pulled my ass out of the fire back there."

Curtis blinked in surprise when he saw the thing in her hand. Before he had time to react, Stella Hawk raised the .38 and shot him in the chest.

*7:33:12 P.M. PDT*
*Babylon Hotel and Casino, Las Vegas*

Sherry Palmer returned from her pre-banquet appointment at the Babylon's beauty spa, to find her husband standing alone on the balcony. Motionless, he watched the neon of the Las Vegas Strip blot out the stars under in the early evening sky. Sherry dropped her purse on the glass coffee table, and went out to greet him.

"David, I was worried you wouldn't get back in time for the event."

His stare remained fixated on the streets below. For a moment, Sherry thought he hadn't heard her. Then her husband spoke.

"Did you ever wonder what would have happened if there was someone at the Manhattan Project who realized the horror of what they were creating, and warned them against developing the first atomic bomb?"

Sherry frowned. "I think Oppenheimer did just that, David. It didn't matter. There was a war on. The bomb was created to end it."

David nodded. "But I wonder if there might have been another way."

Sherry touched his arm. She knew she had to be

careful now. Ask the right questions without sounding like she was asking anything. If she pushed too hard, he would only pull back.

"You saw something today, didn't you David?" she probed gently.

Her husband's frown deepened. "You worried that I might make a decision that will come to haunt me?" he said. "That I'll do something to jeopardize my run for the White House."

"David, you know I just want what's best for both of us—"

He raised a hand to silence her. "I stopped something today," he told her. "Something so terrible that if I never do anything else, I've already performed a service to humanity."

Sherry shook her head. "I don't understand."

He faced her then, and smiled. "No you don't," he replied. "Consider yourself blessed that you don't."

"What happened, David?" she asked.

"Nothing, thank God," he replied. "In my capacity as head of the Senate Defense Appropriations Committee, I cancelled a research program that did not bear the results the Pentagon was expecting . . ."

"But David—"

"Let's leave it at that," Palmer said, wrapping his wife in his arms.

"All right," Sherry purred. "I know better than to push you for answers you're not willing to give."

"You smell nice," Palmer observed.

"It's the shampoo. I had my hair done for the banquet tonight. Or hadn't you noticed?"

"I noticed," he lied.

Sherry gave him a doubtful look. "You'd better get dressed yourself—after you take a shower. You smell like you just played the second half all by yourself."

David chuckled. "Maybe you'll be more receptive to my advances after I've cleaned up my act?"

Sherry slapped his butt. "Get in that shower right now. If we're late, Larry Bell will only use the time to upstage you again."

"I'm going," David replied, heading for the bathroom. A moment later, Sherry heard the water running. When she was sure her husband was in the shower, she lifted the phone and dialed Jong Lee's room. He answered on the first ring.

"This is Lee," he said.

"Mr. Lee, I have rather bad news for you. Whatever it was your company was working on, I'm afraid the project is about to be cancelled."

There was a pause. "You're sure, Mrs. Palmer?"

"Absolutely certain, Mr. Lee. I guess you won't have to retool your factories after all."

"Yes, that is true." Another pause. "Mrs. Palmer . . . Do you know if the demonstration was a success?"

Sherry frowned. "I believe it was, Mr. Lee. But the project is cancelled nevertheless."

"Good to know," Lee replied, hardly able to contain his glee.

"And that other matter we discussed?"

"Of course, Mrs. Palmer. Send Mr. Cohen to my suite in two hours to collect the funds. I shall have the package ready for him."

"Thank you, Mr. Lee. My husband's campaign appreciates your support."

Sherry hung up before the man could reply. Shaking with excitement, she went to the bar and poured herself a scotch. She swallowed it in a single gulp. She had to be careful tonight, hide her emotions. It was difficult, however. The thought of all that money in a secret fund made Sherry Palmer feel giddy. With five million dollars at her disposal, she could buy a lot of favors, and destroy a host of political rivals, too.

*7:46:35 P.M. PDT*
*Bix Automotive Center*
*Browne End Road, Las Vegas*

Men scattered as the cherry-red BMW swung into the lot. The automatic garage door had barely opened enough to admit the vehicle when it roared right through. Skidding on the greasy concrete, Stella Hawk braked inches from the line of white Dodge Sprinter trucks.

She popped the passenger side door and kicked the groaning man with her Roger Vivier heels. "Get out before you ruin my goddamn upholstery," she screamed. Standing near the trucks, Pizarro Rojas watched her performance with interest. His brother Balboa, who had been examining Hugo Bix's silver Jaguar, frowned at the woman's vulgar display.

Curtis Manning tumbled out of the front seat, into a puddle of grease. Hugo Bix stepped forward, looming over the semi-conscious man.

"Hell," he said with a crooked grin. "Look what the cat dragged in."

Lilly was not amused. She climbed out of the car, slammed the door. "You dumb bastards almost lost him," she cried, eyes flashing. "Jesus Christ! Don't you know that if Curtis got away, he'd have warned Jaycee something was going on over here."

"We had it under control, honey," Bix replied in a reasonable tone.

A sneering Stella scanned the faces around her, then glared a challenge at Carlos and Roland. "Next time, don't send a bunch of taco benders and tamale stuffers to do your job, Hugo."

Roland turned his back on the woman, walked back to the Jaguar parked in the corner to speak with Balboa and Pizarro Rojas. Together, the three men moved to the line of panel trucks, opened the door to one of them and climbed inside.

Carlos set Curtis Manning's PDA and cell phone on the hood of Stella's car, under Hugo's nose.

"This man who was spying on you is not a gangster," the Cuban announced. "I can't crack the codes, but this device—" he touched the PDA. "This belongs to a federal agent. FBI, perhaps DEA. I was lucky to be able to hone in on the tracking beam."

Hugo snorted, then threw back his head and laughed. "That dumb som' bitch of a bastard Jager has a snake on his own damn team. This guy here's probably working to bust his whole crew."

Fat Frankie Toomes' expression soured. "Too bad we stopped him."

Bix peered at the man on the ground. Curtis hadn't

stirred. He looked to be dying, or dead already. "Yeah, maybe . . ." Bix grunted, glancing in Roman Vine's direction.

Roland Arrias returned to speak with his partner Carlos. Pizarro and Balboa remained with the trucks. The brothers seemed reluctant to get involved with Bix's business.

"The charges are set. A very professional job," Roland reported. "There is more C4 than we asked for. More than enough to do the job. The Rojas boys are quite happy with the arrangement, despite the presence of this pig—" He spit on Curtis.

Bix smirked. Carlos faced the American. "You have fulfilled your part of the bargain."

A Cuban stepped forward, opened a leather attaché case. It was stuffed with cash. Stella's eyes narrowed when she saw the money. She licked her lips.

"Five million dollars," Carlos said. "You've already received the shipment of cocaine. Count the cash if you wish."

Bix grinned. "I trust you, amigo." He reached out, closed the case himself. Roman Vine took it from the Cuban.

"What do you want me to do with this here *federale*?" Bix asked, his booted foot prodding Curtis's kidney.

"Throw him in one of the trucks. He killed two of my men, he can die with the others in the first blast."

While a pair of Cubans grabbed Curtis under the arms and dragged him to one of the trucks, Carlos faced Bix.

"We have only one problem now," he said. "One of the men this American agent killed was the brother of a waiter at the Babylon. He was to take his brother's place this night, in order to plant the final bomb in the banquet hall."

Bix frowned. "Spot of bad luck there, eh, amigo?" He rubbed his chin. "Look, I can provide you with a driver or two—for a price. But I can't get you close to the VIPs, not without advance planning. I reckon nobody can. Not now . . ."

"I can."

Carlos and Roland turned to face Stella Hawk. Head cocked, hands on her hips, she nodded. "Yeah, you heard right. I can get one or two of you in, anyway. I'm a performer at *Risque*, which is inside the Babylon, and my roommate is a waitress at tonight's shindig. I'll get you past security, or around it."

Pizarro Rojas, who'd only been listening up to now, stepped forward. "How much is the services of this . . . this *puta descarada* going to cost?"

The insult rolled off her back. "Five hundred thousand dollars," Stella replied, extending her hand, palm up. "Payable right now."

Pizarro glanced at his brother. "Pay her."

Bix studied the man. For a guy who'd been forced to cough up an extra half million dollars, Pizarro Rojas seemed pretty calm. His brother Balboa didn't look nearly so happy. Sour faced, he rummaged through the scuffed and dirty canvas bag that he'd carried across the border, came up with a stack of thousand-dollar bills.

"You better deliver what we've paid for, or you will

not leave the hotel alive," he grunted as he handed her the money.

Stella flashed him a smile. "Don't worry, Pedro. Satisfaction's guaranteed." She climbed into her car, stashed the money in a secret compartment behind the dash.

Finally, Pizarro Rojas moved toward Hugo Bix, until the two men stood toe to toe. Rojas, a head shorter than the American, looked up to meet his eye.

"In a few minutes we will drive away from here in these trucks," Rojas said. "But I will always remember the service you and your men provided for me, for my family. In times of trouble, when the other gangs turned on us, you remained loyal." Pizarro touched his head. "A Rojas never forgets his friends, as you shall soon discover."

Turning his back on Bix, he headed back to the trucks. On the way, he took Stella's arm, pushed her toward the first vehicle. Despite the rough handling, Stella smirked. Heels clicking, she obediently followed her new, high-paying boss.

"*Adios, amigo*," Bix called as he walked to his office. "And good luck . . ."

By the time Bix reached his cluttered desk upstairs, the trucks were rolling out of the garage. Carlos Boca stood at the door, directing the deployment. He spaced each departure a few minutes apart—a wise move, Bix realized. It would look odd if six identical Sunflower Gardens Florist trucks rolled out of a garage nowhere near the location of the real shop on the other side of town.

Watching the last of the trucks roll on to their target, Bix lifted his phone, pressed a button.

Downstairs, Roman Vine answered the phone on the wall. "Yeah, boss."

"Time to call the Wildman. Tell them it's a go."

Bix slumped down in the battered office chair and propped his feet on the desk. While the Rojas boys were having their fun, Hugo Bix had been planning a private party of his own. He'd just passed the order along to the out-of-towner gunmen Roman Vine hired from the El Paso mob. While the authorities' attention was diverted to the big blowout at the Babylon, Bix was going to light his own kind of fire at the Cha-Cha Lounge, and Jaycee Jager and his crew were going to burn.

. . . . . . . . . . . . . . . . . . . . . . . . . . . . . . . . . . . .

THE FOLLOWING TAKES PLACE
BETWEEN THE HOURS OF
8 P.M. AND 9 P.M.
PACIFIC DAYLIGHT TIME

. . . . . . . . . . . . . . . . . . . . . . . . . . . . . . . . . . . .

*8:05:11 P.M. PDT*
*Babylon Hotel and Casino, Las Vegas*

Jong Lee answered the door to his own suite. Lev Cohen blinked in surprise, expecting the woman Yizi to
greet him. The Asian man was dressed casually and
appeared relaxed, so Palmer's Chief of Staff recovered quickly. Lev greeted the man, but did not extend
his hand. Nor did Jong Lee offer his.

Pale under his red-brown beard, Lev shifted uncomfortably. Adjusting, then re-adjusting his tie. He
didn't like this part of the job, but he was well aware
that this *was* part of his job, the sordid under-the-

table dealings that made the machine of politics run.

At least, after years of struggling, he'd latched on to a star that was going to take him all the way to the top. He'd help David Palmer get elected President of the United States, then Lev Cohen would be a name. After a successful stint in the White House, he'd launch his own consulting firm, maybe do a little lobbying on the side, or even a job with big media.

Lev had made the decision long ago to play along, do what was necessary to succeed—even if it meant playing the bag man and handling dirty money. Best to just get it over with as quickly as possible. Unlike the previous chief of staff, Cohen had survived two campaigns with Senator Palmer not only because he was very good at his job, but also because he understood something his predecessor did not—it was Sherry Palmer who called the shots with David Palmer's political career, not the Senator.

Oh, sure, when Senator Palmer spoke, Lev nodded politely, always took the man's suggestions under serious consideration. But he always did what Sherry wanted, when she wanted it done. That's what made Lev a survivor.

"If you will please be seated, Mr. Cohen."

"I really don't have time . . ."

Jong Lee took his arm, guided Lev to the suite's living room. Though fresh desert air filled the suite, the curtains were drawn on the balcony. The spacious room was lit by a single lamp. A leather case sat, lid open, in the middle of the glass coffee table. Its interior was filled with neat stacks of thousand dollar bills. Cohen slumped down in a straight backed chair. Behind him the curtains stirred with the breeze.

"It is all there, Mr. Cohen," Jong Lee said, sitting in an armchair on the opposite side of the coffee table. "I insist you count it."

"That's really not necessary, Mr. Lee—"

"Indulge me," Lee said, crossing his legs.

Lev shrugged. "All right, if you insist."

He reached for a stack of bills, but his hand never touched the paper. Instead, a sudden burst of wind tickled his neck—then his mind exploded with black jets of agony as sharp blades plunged into his throat. As a red haze clouded his vision, Lev tried to cry out but no sound could possibly emerge from the ravaged larynx. He tried to raise his hands to clutch at his neck, but the tendons in his shoulders had been pierced or severed, his arms paralyzed. Finally, he tried to stand, but his assassin pressed the three-pronged blades farther downward, until they sunk deeper into his abdomen, to pierce arteries, scrape bones. Finally his lungs were punctured and collapsed like deflated balloons. Mouth open, eyes wide but unseeing, Lev Cohen's world ended.

When she was sure Palmer's man was dead, Yizi yanked the twin sai out of his shoulders, stared at the blood staining the long silver prongs. Standing behind the corpse, the woman's eyes narrowed and she trembled like a cold kitten.

Yizi blinked, snapping out of her short trance. Slowly she lifted her chin. She wiped the bloody sai on the dead man's clothing, slipped them into her belt. Unlike traditional sai, which are not sharpened, the prongs of uneven length, Yizi's weapons had three twelve-inch prongs, each as sharp and the point of a diamond.

"You are calm now?" he asked in Chinese, using the metaphor.

"Yes. Thank you for the opportunity to indulge myself."

Jong nodded once. "From now on you must kill with detached precision, quickly and without hesitation. Then move on to the next target. There will be nothing elegant about this operation. This is not wushu, it is slaughter."

"I understand."


*8:17:48 P.M. PDT*
*Tiki Room*
*The Cha-Cha Lounge, Las Vegas*


Jack's phone buzzed. "Jaycee."

"It's Morris. Heard from our girl in Los Angeles, Little Jamey . . ."

Jack raised an eyebrow. "And?"

"Our friend Tony, out at Area 51, he uncovered the traitor. A fellow named Dr. Steven Sable."

"What's the proof?"

Morris chuckled. "Tony picked his pocket, stole the man's cell phone and downloaded its contents. What a bunch of secret agents we are. Pickpockets, gambling cheats, loan sharks, torturers—"

"Enough editorializing, Morris. I need real information." Jack's tone was icy.

"Jamey traced the stored phone numbers," a contrite Morris replied. "Turns out that in the past six months, our distinguished researcher made seventy-three calls to one Hugo Bix. The last call Dr. Sable made today, just before Tony grabbed his phone, was traced to a number at Bix Automotive."

"Have you alerted Tony?"

"We sent him the message. Don't know if he's retrieved it yet. His movements are carefully monitored at Groom Lake, so he isn't always available to us . . ."

Jack checked his wristwatch. "What about Curtis?"

"Curtis hasn't reported in yet. He's ordered radio silence so I'm not supposed to contact him." Morris paused. "Can't say I'm worried yet, but I will be if I don't here from Mr. Manning soon."

"Patch Curtis through to this phone as soon as he calls in," Bauer commanded.

Jack ended the call, tucked the cell into the pocket of his leather jacket. Stretching his legs, Jack glanced again at his watch. He still had a turncoat at his casino. Someone had murdered the Midnight Cowboy Max Farrow, the guy with the Area 51 technology. And that same someone likely murdered the Cha-Cha Lounge's security guard Ray Perry too.

Though he knew it was best to wait until Bix made the first move before he took action against the traitor in his midst, Jack also realized there were several precautions he could take. He didn't want to be surprised by a premature move on the turncoat's part.

One of those precautions involved returning to the subbasement storeroom where Morris had found Ray Perry's corpse. For a long time Jack wondered why the killer had stashed the body there. Jack believed he'd finally solved that riddle. If he was right, then it was time to set a little booby trap, a simple snare that would help Jack unmask the traitor before more damage was done . . .

*8:21:06 P.M. PDT*
*Babylon Hotel and Casino, Las Vegas*

Jong Lee had observed the execution, and the joy Yizi took from the act, with impassive detachment. Legs crossed, chin resting on his hand, he assessed the woman's performance while he waited for her to finish the task of moving Lev Cohen's corpse.

When Yizi appeared behind the man, the sharp sai in her hands, the demure servant who bowed obsequiously at every man, who subserviently anticipated every wish, was gone, the true Yizi revealed.

Small and lean, with her raven-black tresses pulled back into a bun. Her white skin contrasted with the form-fitting black jumpsuit that hugged her lithe body from neck to toe. Made from a super-elastic microfiber, the suit was snug enough to reveal the woman's hip bones under her taut flesh. Indeed, Jong Lee could count the woman's ribs. Her pale flesh and skeletal appearance, coupled with the way she clutched her sai—a weapon that resembled the pitchfork so common in colorful depictions of the Western devil—were the reasons Jong Lee had assigned her with the code name "Reaper."

Yizi was one of the unintended consequences of the People's Republic of China's misguided effort to control its burgeoning population. Another, far more dire consequence, was the wholesale abortion of generations of female babies. Now, over two decades after the failed policies were initiated, China was paying the price—a large majority of the nation's male population would never have a Chinese wife because of the gender imbalance.

But not all of the female babies proved useless. In time the State established a secret bureau inside the PLA. This unit was charged with the recruitment and training of young girls from a very early age. Those females who exhibited promise were selected for "special combat reeducation," a lifetime of training which included combat tactics, espionage tradecraft, techniques of terrorism, and modes of assassination. Only girls who passed dozens of rigorous intelligence and physical screening were accepted, and they could be dropped from the program at any time. Rejection meant instant execution, for the females were considered expendable. During their indoctrination and training, every aspect of these women's lives was regulated, their bodies and minds completely controlled.

Yizi had begun her training at the age of six. Now she was twenty-two, a woman, though Jong Lee knew that in almost no sense of the word was Yizi a true woman. Like her sisters in the "special program," Yizi's menstrual cycle had been curtailed—a consequence of the rigorous training, as well as the hormones and steroids she'd been injected with.

It did not matter in the end. Yizi possessed all the charms of a woman, and could use them to seduce and corrupt a man if so ordered. Though Yizi was a skilled espionage agent, Jong learned she was a superb assassin—efficient, cool under pressure, and pathologically addicted to her vocation.

Yizi appeared at his side. "It is done." It was true, Where Lev Cohen died, there was only blood.

Jong Lee nodded, then spoke. "You know the plan. Go back to the dry cleaners. Captain Hsu is awaiting your instructions. Use the phrase you have memorized. I will meet you at the airport at the appointed time . . ."

Jong watched as Yizi slipped a raincoat over her ebony jumpsuit, draped the purse over her shoulder and left the suite without a backward glance.

With a contented sigh, Jong Lee settled deeper into his chair and pondered the possibilities of success or failure in the next phase of his operation. Jong knew he was in control of Yizi and of his commandos. They would behave within the bounds of their training and his expectations. What Lee could not control were the Rojas brothers.

Jong Lee had helped facilitate the attack on the Pan Latin Anti-Drug Conference because it fit in with his own plans. The Rojas desired revenge against America, and against the law enforcement agencies that had targeted his family, interfered with their schemes and murdered Francesco Rojas, the youngest son in the family.

All Jong Lee wanted was a diversion—one so dramatic and violent that it would keep the American authorities too busy to figure out Lee's real goal, until it was too late to stop him.

In a few minutes, Jong Lee would leave this place, never to return. But before he fled the conflagration to come, he had to make one final phone call to set the last wheels of his elaborate plan in motion.

Glancing at his watch, Lee lifted the receiver and dialed the secret cell phone number of the traitor he controlled, a member of the research contingent inside of Groom Lake Air Force Base.

*8:38:13 P.M. PDT*
*Nebuchadnezzar Ballroom*
*Babylon Hotel and Casino, Las Vegas*

The massive, three-story tiered ballroom was bathed in radiant light. The chamber's golden glow was rivaled only by the glittering array of guests, a mingling of international political figures, media barons, celebrities, literati, law enforcement officials, wealthy philanthropists and social activists.

The Babylon Hotel was built to resemble a Middle Eastern ziggurat—a circular tower ringed by a sloping ramp that descended from the rooftop ballroom all the way down to the atrium on the third floor. The

ramp contained the hotel's famed hanging gardens—
an amazing array of ecological-systems made up of
thousands of trees, ferns, plants and flowers from all
over the world. The gardens were separated by glass
walls. Some of the gardens were open to the desert air.
Others were enclosed in glass and climate-controlled.

The elegant décor in the ballroom repeated the ziggurat motif, with swirling ramps instead of staircases
leading up to tiered dining areas and bars that over-
looked the main ballroom far below. Crystal chandeliers in circular swirls dangled from a high roof that
loomed a hundred feet over the revelers' heads. Most
of the walls were made of glass—tall windows with
striking views of the Las Vegas Strip.

Sherry Palmer watched her husband near one of
those massive windows. Looking distinguished in
his evening clothes, the Senator from Maryland was
huddled with the ambassador from Nicaragua, and
a military man from Peru, along with their jewel-
bedecked wives. He must have been charming them,
because the men were laughing, the woman gazing
up at him with rapt attention.

She noted that her husband's mood had improved
considerably, most likely because David was in
his element now. As much as he hated impromptu
speechmaking, David Palmer loved to be around
people. He seemed to feed off their energy, and he
took a genuine interest in those he met. David was
able to instantly connect with someone on a person-
to-person level. Even when he spoke to a crowd,
many people who answered Lev's questions in focus

groups conducted later all said the same thing—David Palmer seemed to be talking directly to them, that they felt the same connection with him as he felt for them.

Whether his was a skill learned early in life or a trait embedded in his DNA, Sherry didn't know. She only knew that David's affability was an invaluable campaign tool that, if harnessed properly, would carry him all the way to the Oval Office.

Sherry did not share her husband's considerable people skills. She was a good manager—cool under pressure, efficient, detail-oriented. She possessed plenty of business savvy and a political horse-sense, too. Sherry was adept at *handling* people, at manipulating them into giving her what she needed. But she could never win the loyalty, the respect, or the genuine love and friendship accorded her husband. David didn't manage people, he seduced them, and under the spell of his undeniable charisma, they willingly followed his lead.

Sherry glanced at the delicate, jeweled Rolex on her wrist. She should have heard from Lev by now.

*How long can the meeting take?* she wondered.

Jong Lee was supposed to hand off the cash, and Lev was supposed to take it back to his suite, and call her immediately. Once again, Sherry squeezed her tiny handbag to make sure the cell phone was inside, that she hadn't misplaced it somewhere.

Becoming more concerned by the minute, she turned away from her husband, walked to a line of dining tables along the glass wall. She saw a seating card marked "Mr. Jong Lee," at a table designated for businessmen concerned with the detrimental effects of the drug epidemic. Though most of the seats were filled with stuffy men and their plump wives, Lee's chair remained vacant.

If Lev didn't call her in the next fifteen minutes, Sherry resolved to go searching for him. *You can't trust anyone these days*, she mused bitterly. *Not when it came to five million dollars. . .*

### 8:57:56 P.M. PDT
### Las Vegas Boulevard

Curtis awoke to the smell of flowers. Then he felt the floor bump under him. He tried to open his eyes, but only one eye actually opened. The left side of his face was swollen, the eye glued shut, His head throbbed. He tried to touch the wound and found his wrists were bound together with thin steel wires that bit into his flesh. He felt another bump and realized he was riding on the floor in back of a truck.

Finally Curtis remembered it all—the identical white trucks, the Cuban hit team, the presence of the feared Rojas brothers in Las Vegas, the plot to blow up the anti-drug conference and its VIP guests at the Babylon.

Curtis studied the ferns and flowering plants around him, sniffed again. Underneath the cloying scent of flowers was another ominous smell, one he was familiar with. Curtis was definitely detecting the distinctive lemon-citrus odor given off by the plastic explosive Composition 4. Eyes darting, Curtis' intense gaze moved beyond those plants, to rows of plastic garbage cans hidden behind them—each one filled with C4 explosives and rigged to a timer with bright blue detonation cords.

This truck had five others just like it. More than enough to bring down one of Las Vegas' most glittering casinos, and murder everyone inside.

When Stella Hawk shot him in the chest with the police special, the relatively small .38 caliber bullet hadn't penetrated the Kevlar vest Curtis wore under his jacket, but the impact stunned him, knocking him out cold for a few minutes. He finally came around when Stella kicked him out of her car, onto the floor of Bix's garage. Fortunately, the wound on his leg and the deep gash in his side caused by a shard of glass, provided enough blood to fool Stella, Hugo Bix, even the Cubans. No one took the trouble to examine him because they all believed he was dead or close to it.

While the conspirators talked over him, Curtis feigned unconsciousness. It hadn't been easy to remain motionless during repeated jabs from Bix's cowboy boot, or the rough treatment he'd received from the Cubans, who'd tossed him into the back of this truck and tied him up.

Resorting to a trick of his trade, Curtis had tensed his muscles while his wrists were tied. But he must have seemed too tense, because the hit man became suspicious and used the butt of his Makarov PM to knock Curtis into unconsciousness.

Still disoriented, Curtis wondered how long he'd

been out. This truck had not yet arrived at the Babylon, but what about the other five?

Curtis was trussed up and helpless, he'd been chased, dragged, beaten and shot, but he still had a job to do. If he didn't stop these terrorists, they would blow up a major American hotel and claim untold lives. He had to free himself, stop this truck, and warn the authorities before it was too late . . .

1 2 3 4 5 6 7 8 9
**10** 11 12 13 14 15 16 17
18 19 20 21 22 23 24

• • • • • • • • • • • • • • • • • • • • • • • • • • • • • • •

**THE FOLLOWING TAKES PLACE
BETWEEN THE HOURS OF
9 P.M. AND 10 P.M.
PACIFIC DAYLIGHT TIME**

• • • • • • • • • • • • • • • • • • • • • • • • • • • • • • •

*9:06:19 P.M. PDT*
*Montana Burger, Home of Real Montana Beef*
*Tropicana Boulevard, Las Vegas*

"Catch!"

Metro Police Sergeant Philip Locklear tossed the colorful bag at his partner. "Scoot over, Dallas. You eat your Montana burgers. I'll drive."

The younger man stepped out from behind the steering wheel, circled the white Metro Police car. Climbing back inside, he opened the bag and rummaged through it.

"Hey, you didn't get anything for yourself."

The sergeant shook his head, threw his hat on the

dashboard, and ran his knobby fingers through his salt and pepper hair.

"I can't eat that fast food crap. It bothers my stomach."

Sergeant Locklear was in his mid-forties, but looked ten years older. Skin like leather, his blue eyes were frozen in a perpetual squint from too many decades of exposure to the desert sun. Though he was never in danger of failing his annual department physical, Locklear had a rounded belly from too much beer and too much couch surfing.

"What bothers your stomach are those ten cups of coffee you drink a shift. That stuff will kill you."

Officer Brad Dallas was the former second-string quarterback of the Las Vegas High School football team. Ex-military and still sporting the same haircut he had in boot camp, Dallas was too gung-ho for his own good—and his partner's. Still buff at twenty-nine, he was a health and fitness nut, except for the cholesterol-heavy Montana burgers he ate two at a time.

"What stuff will kill me?" Locklear asked, starting the engine.

"Caffeine, man. Coffee is the devil's brew."

The sergeant nodded. "Yeah. I heard that some-where."

They rolled out of the Montana Burger parking lot a moment later, swung onto the road that took them to their patrol zone along the Strip.

"How about you take a gander at tonight's SVR. Shout out anything that catches your eye."

Chewing a mouthful of burger, Officer Dallas thumbed through the three page printout on blue paper. The Stolen Vehicle Report was information so new it hadn't reached the LVMP database yet. Such intelligence was the purview of the select few members of Metro's Repeat Auto Theft Squad, RATS for short. Las Vegas ranked third in total car thefts for the past five years running. The RATS patrol was formed to lower that statistic.

Because a minority of car thieves steal the majority of cars—usually to use the pilfered vehicle to commit yet another crime—the Metro Police RATS was formed to target those nefarious individuals. Of the twenty to thirty Metro Police cars prowling the Strip on a given night, one or two of them belonged to the RATS patrol, though no one but the officers in question were aware of that fact. RATS patrol cars were not specially marked, and the RATS members wore the same uniforms and performed the same duties as other patrolmen. But they were also specially trained to recognize and arrest repeat offending car thieves, and to spot the telltale signs of car-theft related activity.

When the pair began their shift, the big case was a car jacking in North Las Vegas so violent it landed the victim in the morgue. That suspect was captured by the Nevada Highway Patrol an hour ago—the news had just come across their radio when the all-points was called off.

Without a special target for tonight's patrol, Sergeant Locklear was fishing for an interesting angle.

"Not much here," Dallas noted. "There was an assault and truck jacking this morning, out at Mesa Canyon, corner of Smoke Ranch Road and North Buffalo. The truck was a late model Dodge Sprinter, white with commercial plates. It was a Fit-Chef delivery van."

The sergeant made a face. "My ex-wife ate that crap all the time. Shit cost an arm and a leg, but she never lost an ounce from that fat ass of hers."

Brad Dallas had met his partner's ex-wife. She was an attractive woman with nice legs and a biting sense of humor, and he didn't think she had a particularly fat ass, either. Officer Dallas wasn't going to argue the point, however.

"Hey, this is weird," Dallas said a minute later. "Someone else jacked a Dodge Sprinter this morning. Over near Mulberry Mall. It was white, too . . . Same model year."

He flipped through the pages. "Damn. Here's another one. Nine AM, a uniform supply company van in front of a Dunkin' Donut."

"Okay, so you're thinking that somebody's planning a big heist using a trio of Dodge Sprinters? How likely is that?"

"I didn't say that," Dallas replied. "I was just saying I thought it was interesting, that's all. Anyway, if you're thinking about it, why stop with three?"

"Okay, partner. I'm hooked," Sergeant Locklear declared. "I think it's time you check the police data banks in Reno and see if they're losing Dodge Sprinters, too."

They turned onto Las Vegas Boulevard. Traffic was moving, but the streets were already packed with cars.

Washing down the last bite with a gulp of Diet Coke, Dallas put his greasy burger wrapper on the seat and swung the dashboard computer so it faced him. The young policeman wiped his fingers with a napkin, then cracked his knuckles. The RATS patrol had special access to up-to-the-minute car theft data from all over the state, not just Vegas. In a moment, Brad Dallas was exploring the state's law enforcement database, city by city.

*9:18:19 P.M. PDT*
*Las Vegas Boulevard*

With each swerve and bump, Curtis managed to shift position, until he could observe the two men in the front seat. The driver was grizzled and well into middle-age, with sagging eyes and a blubbery neck. Curtis recognized that one—the fellow who beat him into unconsciousness and tied him up.

The man in the passenger seat was young, with dark, excited eyes under bushy eyebrows and close-cropped hair. His name was Hector and he seemed nervous and jumpy. While Curtis watched, the man swallowed an amphetamine without water. Both men wore nondescript navy blue uniform-type overalls that appeared black in the gloom of the truck's interior.

Right now Curtis was helpless to do more than watch. There was no way he could free himself from the wires binding his wrists. They were firmly embedded in his ravaged and swollen flesh. Fortunately, after the older guy had beaten him down, he did a sloppy job of wiring Curtis' legs. By twisting around for several minutes—and ignoring a considerable amount of pain—he'd managed to loosen the wires enough so that he could sit up, maybe get to his knees or even his feet, when the time came.

"You missed the turn, Salazar. The Babylon is on the other side of the boulevard," Hector cried.

The young man suddenly turned his head around, to peer over the back of his seat. Curtis froze, but the man's gaze passed right over him, to the view out of the rear windows. After a glance, he turned around again. Curtis relaxed enough to breathe.

"You have to circle around now, old man. Try making a U-turn and be quick about it. Come on, come on, do it man. we're running behind schedule."

The younger man's voice was laced with adrenaline. He trembled with nervous impatience.

The older man frowned, rubbed his hairy neck. Then Salazar jerked the steering wheel into a sharp turn. Hector grunted in surprise, clutched the dashboard. Curtis, still on his back, used the vehicle's momentum to help him roll to his knees. Fighting to remain upright, the steel truck bed digging into his kneecaps, Curtis heard tires squeal and the angry blare of a horn.

"Watch out, *estupido*," Hector warned. "You're cutting across traffic, man! You want to get us killed?"

*9:24:03 P.M. PDT*
*Las Vegas Boulevard*

"Would you look at that," quipped Sergeant Locklear. Still behind the wheel, he stared down his nose at a white van swerving none too safely across two lanes of traffic.

"Dude. That's a white Dodge Sprinter!"

Still staring, Officer Dallas read the stenciled letters on the side of the panel truck. "Sunflower Gardens Florist."

"I know the joint," Locklear said. "It's over near the University. A little late to be delivering flowers, though."

Officer Dallas grinned in anticipation. "What are you gonna do, Sarge?"

A thin smile crossed Locklear's worn face. He sped up, weaving through traffic to catch up with the white truck. They just made it through two traffic lights and ran a third, until the Metro squad car was finally tailing the rear bumper of the truck. Locklear flipped on the bubble lights, blasted the siren.

To both officers' surprise, the vehicle slowed down immediately. But it still rolled for half a block, along a fairly deserted stretch of road bordering on the newly built Wynn Hotel. Finally the truck turned off Las Vegas Boulevard, onto a service road made of uneven concrete, that led to a fenced-in construction site. The truck halted at the locked gate, perhaps fifty yards away from the busy boulevard.

Locklear rolled to a halt bumper to bumper with

the Sprinter so the truck could not flee the scene, threw the police car into neutral.

"Check the plates. I'm going to talk to this guy."

Before Dallas could reply, Sergeant Locklear was out of the car and approaching the truck, one hand on his holstered gun. The younger man entered the plate numbers and waited for the computer to spit out a report.

"I told you not to pull over, man," Hector hissed, a drop of saliva flecking his sweating lip.

"What was I supposed to do, drive away, have him chase me? This truck is full of explosives." Salazar clutched at Hector's arm. "Calm down, *hermano*. I can talk us out of this . . ." He reached down to clutch the handle of his own weapon. "Or I can shoot if I have to."

"Too late for talk." Quivering, Hector pulled the MP5K automatic from under the seat.

"No, Hector," Salazar cried.

Sergeant Locklear appeared at the driver's open window at just that moment. "Okay, step out of the car—"

Hector squeezed the trigger and the shot cut the Sergeant's command short. The burst blew past Salazar's face and the man howled. The policeman's head exploded, and the torso dropped from view.

Curtis made a desperate lunge over the seat, too late to save the officer. He looped his arms around Hector's neck and yanked the man backwards. The *Maschinenpistole K* continued to chatter until the

9mm magazine was spent. The shots went wild, firing into the seat, the dashboard. At least two bullets slammed into Salazar's abdomen. Face scorched by powder burns and gut shot, the man behind the wheel fumbled with the handle and opened the door—only to tumble to the pavement, his own weapon clattering to the ground.

Clicking on an empty chamber, Hector let the gun fall and clawed at the suffocating arms coiled around his throat. Curtis groaned as the wires around his wrists dug deeper, but he did not let up on the pressure. Bracing his knees against the back of the seat, he pulled until he heard Hector's neck snap. The fingers raking his arms went limp, and Curtis let the dead man slide out of his grip.

The passenger door opened. "Out with your hands up!" Officer Dallas shouted in a voice tinged with panic.

Curtis immediately raised his hands to show us the wires binding his wrist. "I'm not armed!" he cried. "I was a prisoner of these men. I'm a federal agent—"

"Shut up," Dallas screamed. "Shut the fuck up and get down on the ground."

Curtis could hardly move. The wires still bound his ankles as well as his arms. Instead of arguing with the cop, Curtis stumbled through the door, landed on the pavement.

The policeman loomed over him, gun waving in Curtis' face.

"I can't hurt you, but you have to listen to me," Curtis said in a reasonable tone.

The policeman saw the wires around Curtis' arms and legs. But instead of freeing him, Officer Dallas circled the front of the Sprinter to the driver's side. Curtis heard the cop moan.

"Jesus, oh shit Jesus, Sarge . . ." he whimpered.

Officer Dallas appeared a minute later. "Listen to me," Curtis said. "I'm a federal agent. These men are terrorists . . ."

"I have to call for an ambulance—"

"You have to set me free first," Curtis said in a firm voice. This time his words, or his tone, seemed to penetrate the policeman's shock. Officer Dallas fumbled at his belt, pulled some kind of cutting tool free of its holster. He attempted to cut the wires binding Curtis' wrist. The policeman hesitated when he drew blood.

"Just cut it, man," Curtis commanded. He swallowed the pain while Officer Dallas probed the flesh to cut the final loop. When his hands were free, Curtis snatched the Teflon cutter out of the cop's trembling hand and cut the wires on his ankles.

Dallas helped Curtis to his feet. "My partner's dead . . ." he said.

"You and your partner may have saved countless lives. There's a bomb in this truck. More on the way to the Babylon. We've got to put in a call to your department, warn them—"

"What are you talking about," Dallas demanded.

"This truck is full of explosives," Curtis repeated. "There are five other trucks just like it at the Babylon. Terrorists are going to blow up the hotel."

Curtis opened the back of the truck, showed the

policeman the barrels of C4. Curtis also yanked the detonation cords. This truck bomb wasn't going off—but there were five others out there just like it. That message finally got through to Officer Dallas.

"I'm gonna call this in," he declared.

The officer raced back to his squad car. Curtis limped to catch up.

He counted it a miracle that he was able to convince the policeman, but Curtis envisioned another time-consuming conversation just like it when detectives arrived. It would be better if he could alert CTU. They could issue an immediate Code Red.

Officer Dallas sat down behind the wheel and lifted the radio handset. Curtis stepped around the open squad car door. "After you call in, I need you to patch me in to the Counter Terrorist Unit at frequency—"

Curtis was interrupted by a hail of automatic weapon fire. The police car windshield exploded in a million little pieces. Officer Dallas jerked in the seat as bullets tore through his body. More shots struck the hood, the door, inching toward Curtis. He reeled backwards before he was hit.

Down on one knee, Curtis faced the white truck. Salazar was stumbling forward in a pained crouch. Arm extended, he squeezed the trigger on an empty MP5K. Salazar's other arm clutched his abdomen, which bubbled black blood that dribbled onto the pitted concrete.

Curtis lurched to his feet, struck the man across the face with a bunched right fist. Salazar's jaw shattered, the automatic tumbled from his hand. Salazar dropped to his knees, but before he tumbled to the ground, Curtis snatched the man's head in his hands and twisted, snapping the Cuban's hairy neck. Curtis released him, and Salazar's dead face bounced off the pavement.

With a groan, Manning limped back to the police car. Officer Dallas was finished, his body slumped over the steering wheel, dead eyes wide with surprise. The radio handset was shattered, and several shots hit the engine block. The squad car was as dead as its former occupants.

Manning bit back a curse and pondered his next move. Desperately he searched the bodies, but came up empty. Without a radio or cell phone, his options were strictly limited. He could wait for the police to show up and try to explain what happened all over again—an absurd waste of time, and dangerous if the cops were trigger happy or didn't buy his story. He could drive to the Babylon and try to put a stop to the terrorists, maybe get in touch with CTU from a pay phone. Or he could drive the truck back to the Cha-Cha Lounge, get Jack and Morris involved, and alert CTU of the danger from there.

His mind made up, Curtis reached across the dead policeman and snatched the shotgun off the rack, along with spare ammunition. He took the dead officer's pistol, too. Then Curtis limped back to the Dodge Sprinter, climbed behind the wheel. There were bullet holes in the dashboard, and the windshield was cracked, but in the first break Curtis got all day the truck started up immediately. He threw it into gear, backed up, pushing the disabled police cruiser car out of the way.

When he had enough room to maneuver, Curtis made a fast U-turn and rolled onto Las Vegas Boulevard.

*9:53:00 P.M. PDT*
*Babylon Hotel and Casino, Las Vegas*

Pizarro Rojas couldn't believe how easily it was to get around hotel security and into the underground garage. The counterfeit electronic card glued to the windshield, another gift from Hugo Bix, worked perfectly. A hidden electronic eye automatically scanned the card, and the gate rose to admit them. With Balboa behind the wheel, Stella and Pizarro Rojas hiding in the rear of the truck among the flowers and explosives, they rolled unchallenged and undetected into the supposedly secure area. A uniformed guard even waved to Balboa as he sped past the glass-enclosed security booth.

They found a parking space close enough to one of the central support struts to blow it apart when the truck bomb detonated. There were six struts supporting the hotel's main tower, and six truck bombs to take them out—or at least that was the plan. The Rojas brothers didn't have time to circle the entire garage and see if they other trucks were parked in their designated spots. They would find out how many men reached the hotel and planted their explosives when the Cubans rendezvoused at the airport later. They did check the timer on the bomb. It was working perfectly.

Then Balboa activated a second timer, this one on a device Hugo Bix had procured for them from his secret source inside the U.S. military. The electromagnetic jamming device was about the size of a microwave oven, and Hugo's men had installed two automobile batteries to power the machine. Bix had guaranteed that this advanced, military-style jamming device would effectively cut all communications in and out of the Babylon.

Pizarro frowned. Hugo Bix had proved himself to be a valuable ally. Pizarro would be sorry to lose him.

"At ten forty-five the timer will activate the jamming mechanism," Roland told his brother. "At that moment, all the hotel's phones and computers will fail. Satellite communications will be jammed, too. No information will get in or go out."

"Then what happens?" Stella asked.

"The keynote address is scheduled to begin at approximately eleven o'clock. The truck bombs will detonate fifteen minutes later, right in the middle of the gringo Senator's speech to the conference."

For the first time since she'd met him, Stella Hawk saw Balboa Rojas smile. "Everyone will die," he gloated. "Everyone."

When they left the truck, Balboa locked the doors, then broke the keys off inside the locks, one by one. Before they'd left Bix's garage, he'd instructed the other drivers to do the same thing.

Stella Hawk led them through the underground

parking garage, to an exit door that took them out-side, along a sidewalk made of flat desert stones that wound through a manicured lawn. Both men carried potted plants that concealed bricks of C4 and two detonators—the explosives destined for the main ball-room. Once again, Pizarro marveled at the luxury of the hotel. Even a remote spot such as this, a forgotten corner of this grand hotel, had an expensive sidewalk, glowing footlights, a perfect lawn.

"That's the Babylonian Theater up ahead," Stella informed them, her heels clicking on the stones. "In the *Risqué* show we use real fire on stage, so the city's fire code required the theater to have a bunch of emergency exits. These doors are never guarded, and one of them has a broken lock. The dancers all know about the busted door. They use it to step outside for air, to smoke, snort coke or shoot up."

"*Puta* heroin junkies," Balboa sneered.

Tossing a sidelong glance at Pizarro, Stella's full lips curled into a smirk. "Some girls have a problem dancing nude six nights a week in front of a packed house. I'm not one of them."

They reached a steel door. Stella halted. "Here we are."

There were no handles, no way to open the door that the Rojas brothers could see. Without comment, Stella reached into her bag, pulled out a wire coat hanger than had been spun into a tight loop. She un-bent the end, slid it into the crack between the door and the doorjamb. The men heard a click.

"Open sesame," Stella chirped.

She held the door open and the men slipped inside. Pizarro locked eyes with her as he crossed the threshold and Stella could see his attitude was softening. His face wore the same sneer as his brother's, but she could see admiration behind his stare, too. Stella gently closed the metal doors, faced the brothers.

"How close are we to the ballroom?" Pizarro asked.

"Top floor," Stella replied. "And I'm sure the guest elevators are well guarded. I know where the service elevators are located however."

Pizarro stepped aside to allow Stella to pass. "Lead on," he said, almost civilly.

1 2 3 4 5 6 7 8 9
10 **11** 12 13 14 15 16 17
18 19 20 21 22 23 24

. . . . . . . . . . . . . . . . . . . . . . . . . . . . . . . . . . .

THE FOLLOWING TAKES PLACE
BETWEEN THE HOURS OF
10 P.M. AND 11 P.M.
PACIFIC DAYLIGHT TIME

. . . . . . . . . . . . . . . . . . . . . . . . . . . . . . . . . . .

*10:07:07 P.M. PDT*
*The Cha-Cha Lounge, Las Vegas*

The call Don Driscoll had been waiting for came near
the end of the evening shift. He reached his meaty
hand into the orange jacket, then placed a cell phone
to his ear.

"This is Driscoll."

"It's Wildman. We're outside. You ready to rumble?"

"Go to the back of the casino. Follow the building until you find a steel door marked High Voltage.
I'll be there in five minutes to let you in. Be ready to
go . . ."

Driscoll slipped the phone into his pocket. The
pit boss looked for someone to spell him, spotted

Chick Hoffman closing his roulette table. Like the big casinos, dealers at the Cha-Cha worked twenty minutes, then had twenty minutes off. While that was a lot of break time, casino management had learned that an inattentive dealer could cost the casino a lot of money. Since the crowd was so light, Driscoll had given the okay for Chick Hoffman, Frank Ross and Bud Langer to close down their tables for the break. Now he approached Chick.

"Play pit boss for fifteen minutes," Driscoll asked. "I need to take a dump."

"Will do," Chick replied, cooperating for once instead of giving him lip. Driscoll figured Hoffman was still jazzed about the vig Jaycee was slipping him for collaring the cheat.

Instead of heading for the employee break area, Driscoll went behind the bar and hopped into the freight elevator. He rode it down two floors to the beverage room. Passing stacks of untapped kegs, cases of the hard stuff, he entered the dingy hall.

The click of his leather heels bounced off the cinderblock walls as he walked to the remote storage room. The place seemed undisturbed, the air musty. Just to be safe, Driscoll checked on the corpse.

Ray Perry was right where he left him. Driscoll had stabbed Ray to death in the security cell where he'd killed Max Farrow, then rolled the body here on a freight handler. He knew he'd have to come back to this room, to the circuit box to cut the alarm on the back door. It was as good a place as any to stash a corpse.

Driscoll approached the steel circuit box, opened the hatch and threw several switches. He deactivated the alarms at the back door, and cut the juice to all the security cameras in the basement.

Driscoll pulled out his cell phone, dialed the number to the observation booth.

"Morris here," O'Brian answered.

"It's Driscoll. Where's Jaycee?"

"He's downstairs, in the security cell," Morris replied. "Seeking clues about the unexpected demise of our guest, I suspect. Do you need to talk to him?"

"Nah," Driscoll replied. "It's nothing."

In the hidden catwalks over the dealer rooms, Morris O'Brian hung up the phone at his security control station.

"Over here, Jack," he called.

Jack Bauer peered over his shoulder.

Morris flipped a switch and a security screen came to life. They were looking at a view of the subbasement hallway. While they watched, Don Driscoll stepped through the storage room door.

"You were right, Jack. Driscoll's the turncoat. He sold you out to Hugo Bix. Poor slob doesn't know I bypassed the camera control system. Thinks we can't see him."

Bauer nodded. "I knew it had to be Driscoll, or Chick Hoffman. I would have bet on Don, though, and I would have been right." Jack paused. "What did you tell him?"

"What you told me to tell him," Morris replied.

"That you were in the security room. Look, there he goes. He's heading for the back door."

"What's outside?" Jack asked.

Morris threw another switch, and a third television screen sprang to life. Jack saw six men on the screen. They didn't look like truck drivers, cowboys, housewives or military personnel on leave—the Cha-Cha's usual clientele. They looked more like gang bangers from South Central, with dark, oversized hip hop clothes and plenty of bling.

One man, sporting cornrows, clutched a sawed-off shotgun. Another with an Oakland Raiders cap pulled low over his eyes, reached into his hooded sweatshirt. Morris adjusted the camera and a close-up revealed his hand resting on the stock of the Uzi tucked into his stretch pants.

Morris whistled. "Those guys are gunning for bear." He looked at Jack. "How's that make you feel, Smoky?"

Bauer frowned. "I'm going to be busy for a while."

While Morris watched, he stripped down to his black Levis and charcoal gray undershirt. With cold, calculating precision, Jack slipped the Glock out of his shoulder holster, fed a fresh clip into the handle.

"Cut the power to the freight elevator right now. I've already locked the other doors. The only way in or out of the basement is the door Driscoll is going to open. Let the hit team enter the building. Let them go down the stairs. When I give the signal, cut the electricity to the subbasement."

O'Brian nodded. "What's the plan, Jack?"

Bauer slipped the Glock back into its holster. "I'm going to do to them what they want to do to me."

*10:19:47 P.M. PDT*
*Babylon Hotel and Casino, Las Vegas*

"You can page Mrs. Ankers if you want to," Stella Hawk told the security guard. "But if these floral arrangements aren't on the dessert table in five minutes, Evelyn is going to raise holy hell—and somebody is going to pay."

The guard, mid-twenties and pimply-faced, chewed his lower lip. He'd stopped the trio at the restaurant's service elevator, demanded to see their employee identification cards. Stella produced hers—then challenged the man.

"Look," Stella said in a reasonable tone. "Evelyn sent me down here to find the guys with the flowers. I found them. Now unless you want to help me carry these arrangements upstairs, I suggest you let them pass. You don't want to make Mrs. Ankers angry . . ."

The security man was new to the job, but even he'd heard about the banquet manager's legendary temper. The guard weighed his options and stepped aside to allow the men with the flower pots to pass. Stella, Pizarro and Balboa moved into the elevator. As the doors closed, Stella flashed the guard a flirtatious smile.

"See you later, Tiger," she purred.

The car began to rise, Stella faced the brothers.

"This elevator is express to the banquet floor. We'll exit near the kitchens. Follow me and keep your mouths shut."

"Watch you tone, *puta*—"

"Enough," Pizarro cried, silencing his brother. "This woman has helped us so far. She has earned our respect."

Balboa sneered, but said nothing. A moment later the doors opened onto a long hallway. At the end of the corridor, an open door revealed the restaurant's busy kitchen. They heard voices, the clatter of pots and pans.

"Come on," Stella whispered. "And be quick about it."

She led them to door marked EMPLOYEES ONLY. They entered an empty break room, and an adjacent room with a coffee pot, microwave oven, and vending machines lining the wall. Stella took them to another door. Seemingly unused, it was blocked by a row of fiberglass chairs.

"It's a dead end," Balboa grunted.

"Wrong, amigo," Stella said. She slid the chairs aside with her dainty foot and pushed the door open, just a crack. The room beyond was small, filled with white starched chef and wait staff uniforms hanging on metal racks.

"Why are we here?" Pizarro asked.

"To see her," Stella whispered, pushing the door wider.

Alone in the uniform room, a ten year old girl sat at a metal table, her back to the open door. She did not notice their presence because music from an MP3 filled her ears. Humming along with a tune by Hilary Duff, Pamela Sheridan scribbled in a coloring book, crayons littering the table top.

"What is this about, woman?" Pizarro said doubtfully.

"I told you. My roommate, Lilly, is a waitress at the banquet tonight. She gave me a ride to Bix's garage earlier today, told me some sob story about how she was stuck for a babysitter and planned to stash the kid in this closet for the evening . . ."

"And this helps us how?" Balboa demanded.

Stella rolled her eyes. "Hold the rug rat hostage, and I guarantee you Lilly Sheridan will do anything you ask. To save that kid, she'll plant those bombs herself if she has to."

*10:28:04 P.M. PDT*
*The Cha-Cha Lounge, Las Vegas*

Morris O'Brian was glued to the television screen. Five minutes before, he'd watched Don Driscoll open the back door to admit the six-man hit team. Once inside, Driscoll led the urban punks down three flights of stairs to the subbasement.

Now Morris watched as Jack Bauer, a Glock cradled in his right hand, slipped through that same door and locked it behind him. Driscoll and the hit team were trapped in the cellar. Morris knew those men wouldn't be leaving, unless it was feet first.

Switching to the security camera in the stairwell,

Morris watched as Bauer crept down the steps, paused on a landing. To Morris, Jack seemed to be listening to the whispered words of the hit team as they moved toward the security room.

Bauer glanced up at the camera, then reached around a thick pipe to retrieve the device he'd hidden there earlier. Jack slipped the AN/PVS–14 night vision goggles over his head, adjusted the straps, then fitted the monocular image intensifying unit over his left eye.

When Jack looked up again, his elaborate night vision gear reminded Morris of a half-human cyborg from a science fiction novel.

In his right he still clutched the Glock. Jack raised his left, palm open.

At the prearranged signal, O'Brian cut the electricity. Regretfully, his television screen went dark, too. He reasoned the cameras wouldn't pick up much without the lights anyway. Morris sighed. He might be blind, but so was the hit team.

"Good luck, Jacko," he muttered.

Immediately, Morris felt a hand on his shoulder. He looked up, blinked in surprise.

A woman loomed over him, her complexion bone white, with a foamy crown of blacker-than-black hair topping her high forehead. Sharp cheekbones accentuated large eyes, but her face was dominated by a wide, scarlet mouth. In her ubiquitous black blouse and slacks, Nina Myers reminded O'Brian of the Angel of Death from the stories about the 1918 influenza epidemic his grand mum told him.

"What are you doing here?" Morris demanded. His

tone was sharp—he was still rattled by the drama unfolding in the basement.

"Nice to see you too, Morris," Nina replied, hand on her hip.

"How . . . How did you get here?"

"Actually, I took a cab from the airport."

"I . . . I didn't mean to ask how you got here," Morris stammered. "I meant to ask why you're here."

Nina's scarlet lips dipped into a pout. "Alberta Green sent me. She's shutting down the operation. This investigation is over, effective immediately. I'm here to supervise the deactivation . . ."

Morris slumped in the chair, absorbing the news.

Nina pushed her hair back. "Look, I need to see Jack right away."

"Sorry, love, you'll have to wait," Morris replied with a crooked grin. "I'm afraid Agent Bauer's rather busy right now."


*10:37:30 P.M. PDT*
*Babylon Hotel and Casino, Las Vegas*

The desserts were dished up, the coffee served. The second round of after dinner speeches, including the keynote address by Senator David Palmer, was about to begin.

Evelyn Ankers interrupted Lilly Sheridan at table six and send her to the beverage pantry to fetch pitchers of distilled ice water for the speaker's podium.

As she crossed the crowded banquet hall, the cell

phone in Lilly's skirt pocket vibrated. She waited until she was in the wings and out of sight to before answering, lest the authoritarian banquet manager catch her on a personal call. Finally Lilly reached a quiet alcove near the rest rooms and reached for the phone. Along with the cell she pulled someone's business card out of her pocket. Lilly immediately checked the caller's number. As she feared, the call came from her daughter.

"Pamela, I told you not to call me unless—"

"Shut up and listen for once, Lilly. I have a gentleman here who wants to speak with you."

"Stella? Is that you? Where's Pamela? What's the mat—"

A man's accented voice interrupted her. "Lilly Sheridan, listen carefully. We have your daughter. She's safe as long as you follow our instructions."

Icy hands seemed to squeeze the breath out of Lilly's lungs. "I don't understand. Is this some kind of sick joke—"

"It's no joke, honey." Stella again. "We're here in the uniform storage room where you stashed your kid. Pamela's safe. It's up to you to see that she stays that way. Here, talk to your mom, cuddle bunny."

Lilly strained to hear over the noisy crowd. "Mom. I'm scared. Aunt Stella is acting weird and—"

"That's enough," Stella Hawk interrupted. "In a couple of minutes, a guy's going to show up in front of the kitchen door. He'll be pushing a serving cart with flowers on it. That's Carlos. He'll tell you what to do."

"Stella, why are you doing this?"

"Shut up, Lil. I can't stand it when you whine."

Stella hung up.

Trembling, Lilly lowered the phone, leaned against a pillar to keep from falling down. She twisted her head to face the kitchen door, but saw no one pushing a flower cart. Fumbling to put away her phone, Lilly realized she was clutching something in her left hand—Jaycee Jager's business card. She stared at the number scrawled on the back, her mind racing. Jager was Stella's boyfriend. Could he have something to do with what was happening? Somehow she didn't think so, but Lilly realized Jaycee might know something.

Crouching out of sight behind the coffee station, Lilly quickly punched in Jaycee's number.

*10:41:00 P.M. PDT*
*The Cha-Cha Lounge, Las Vegas*

When the lights went out, Jack heard the gang's cries of alarm. He listened while Don Driscoll tried to calm them, insisting the power failure was just a glitch.

But it was their leader, the man called Wildman, who finally restored order. Despite his outlandish appearance, Wildman seemed to know what he was doing. That was unfortunate. Jack assumed that when the lights failed, the gang would panic, maybe scatter. He could easily gun them down one by one. But since they stuck together, the hit team had a better chance of stopping Jack before he got them all.

Bauer crept down the remaining steps. With the night vision equipment, he could clearly see the men in the corridor—white blobs in a field of green, twenty feet away. Their guns were drawn, and they had formed a defensive circle. Jack was willing to wait for a better shot, because it would be difficult to take them down now.

Then Jack saw Don Driscoll reach into his pocket. When his hand came out again, the man was clutching a flashlight pointed in Jack's direction. Like it or not, the time for Jack to strike had come.

Aiming with both hands, Jack stepped away from the wall and fired. The first shot took out the man with the shotgun. He tumbled to the concrete floor. The second shot slammed into the man with the Raiders cap, threw him backwards in a gush of blood. His fall left a man in a hooded jacket exposed, and Jack shot him next. The man reeled but didn't go down, so Jack shot him again.

The man with the cornrows stepped behind Don Driscoll. Jack paused, unwilling to risk hitting his pit boss. He shifted his aim and took down the other three hit men in quick succession, each with a tap to the head.

A flash exploded in Jack's night vision goggles as Wildman opened fire. Tracers lit the walls as they tore down the corridor. Silhouetted in the muzzle flash, Jack saw Don Driscoll drop. The leader of the hit team was exposed now, and Jack fired his last round. Wildman slammed into the wall and slid to the floor, the top of his head blown away.

Jack stepped over a dead man to reach Don Driscoll. He didn't have to check the body to know the man was dead. Wildman's random shots had cut Don Driscoll's body in half.

Jack cursed. He'd hoped to grill the man about Hugo Bix's next move. Holstering the Glock, Jack reached into his back pocket for his cell, pressed speed dial.

"O'Brian," Morris answered.

"It's over," Jack announced. "Give me some lights down here . . ."

The lights sprang on a moment later. The grotesque scene was not improved by the harsh fluorescent glare.

"Jack, could you come upstairs. We have another development," said Morris.

Jack touched his forehead, looked away from the dead men sprawled on the floor. "I'll be right up."

Jack closed the cell phone—and it chirped immediately. He checked the display, didn't recognize the number.

"Jaycee," he answered.

"Jaycee! What is Stella doing? Why is she threatening to hurt my daughter?"

"Lilly, is that you? Slow down. What's going on?"

"Some man, with Stella. They're here at the Babylon. They've got my daughter, Jaycee! They say they'll hurt her if I don't do what they want . . ."

Jack's mind raced. There was something at the Babylon tonight . . . He'd seen it in the daily threat report. An anti-drug conference with VIP guests.

"Where are you right now?" Jack cried.

"I'm in the ballroom, the speeches are about to start. I—"

Suddenly the line went dead. Jack tried for a signal, got one immediately. He hit redial and after three rings, was transferred to Lilly's voice mail. Jack raced down the corridor and took the stairs two at a time.

*10:46:01 P.M. PDT*
*Babylon Hotel and Casino, Las Vegas*

Curtis stomped on the gas pedal, crashed the Dodge Sprinter through the security gate at the entrance to the hotel's underground parking garage. Over the squeal of tires, Curtis heard the guard's shouted commands to halt.

*Good*, he thought. *That got their attention.*

He circled the first level of the parking garage, looking for the other truck bombs. He realized only then that there were six levels to this parking garage, enough space for thousands of cars, light trucks, and SUVs. He could never find the bombs in time. Not without help.

Curtis skidded to a halt, snatched the shotgun off the seat and jumped out of the truck. He'd spied a fire alarm box near the elevators. Curtis broke the glass with the butt of the shotgun and pressed the red button.

The teeth rattling sound of a dozen alarm bells filled the garage. Covering his ears, Curtis moved on to another alarm box and smashed it open.

He knew that triggering the fire alarms was an act of desperation. Curtis did it because he'd run out of options. For the last hour, he'd experienced the déjà vu feeling he was trapped in one of those nightmares he'd experienced as a child, dreams where you try to make an important phone call but keep messing up the numbers, or you try to yell for help and can't find your voice. Curtis had never felt more ineffectual or more isolated.

The irony was that ten minutes after he left the dead cops, Curtis believed his problems were solved. He steered the truck into a strip mall where he'd spotted an all night liquor store with a pay phone under its sign. Standing in the neon's glare, Curtis punched in the ten digit emergency phone number to CTU, a number unique to this current operation. He hoped to reach Jamey Farrell or Milo Pressman, convince them to issue a Code Red and dispatch emergency teams to the Babylon.

Instead, Curtis was connected to an electronic voice telling him the number he called was no longer in service. He hung up and called again, fearing he'd erred in the dialing. Curtis nearly smashed the receiver when he got the same taped message a second time.

He cursed loudly, causing the winos on the corner to give him a wide berth. Curtis realized something bad had happened. Someone back at CTU headquarters—Ryan Chappelle, George Mason, Alberta Green, or maybe Richard Walsh or Henderson himself—had shut them down with extreme prejudice. The Vegas operation was in the throes of deactivation, a bureaucratic mess that left Curtis without any access to CTU. It was a Draconian move usually reserved for missions that had been compromised: when an agent broke the law, or leaked intelligence, or there was a catastrophic threat and the field agents had to be recalled.

*What could have happened?* Curtis wondered. *Did headquarters learn about Max Farrow's death, and the fact that Jack was hiding the murder from his superiors?*

Curtis realized that might be enough to warrant deactivation, but who would talk? He didn't, and he was damn sure Morris could keep a secret, too.

But there was no use speculating. Whatever happened to trigger deactivation, Curtis was now effectively on his own. CTU wouldn't recognize his operational codes, even if he called the number listed in the phone book and tried to explain who he was and what was happening. As far as his superiors were concerned, he, Jack, Morris, and probably Tony Almeida at Groom Lake, were all compromised. They would have to be thoroughly debriefed by their superiors before they were reinstated and their security clearances restored.

Clutching the receiver in a death grip, Curtis dialed O'Brian's number at the Cha-Cha. He was shocked to get the man's voice mail. What could Morris be doing that was more important than monitoring the activities of the field agents?

Probably establishing deactivation protocols with whoever showed up to shut us down, Curtis mused bitterly. He left a message outlining what was going on, then hung up.

Curtis considered calling 911 and reporting an anonymous bomb threat. But in the end he vetoed the idea. It would only cause more chaos. Better if he was on the scene, Curtis decided. He could do more at the hotel.

After that he drove directly to the Babylon and began setting off the fire alarms, hoping to bring the authorities. But as he sprinted toward the elevator, Curtis stopped in his tracks. Three armed men in security uniforms blocked his path. Someone shouted. Even over the shrill, constant clang of the alarm bells, Curtis heard the words clearly.

"Drop the shotgun or we'll shoot."

*10:55:21 P.M. PDT*
*Hanging Gardens Ballroom*
*Babylon Hotel and Casino, Las Vegas*

All eyes were on the podium. In the glare of a spotlight, Congressman Larry Bell commenced his introduction of the keynote speaker with a rambling account of a moment the two men shared back when they were both pro basketball players.

Lilly tried to call Jaycee Jager again, but she could not get a signal. She tried a pay phone next, but it seemed to be out of order. There was no tone, and all she heard was white noise.

Approaching the kitchen, Lilly spotted a man in

a waiter's uniform standing beside a wheeled cart strewn with flowers. She approached the stranger warily, intimidated by his intense gaze. When Lilly was within arm's length, he seized her wrist.

"Do you wish to see your daughter again?" he hissed, his hot breath on her face.

Lilly nodded and the man released her.

"Wheel this cart to a spot behind the speaker's podium, there—" he gestured with a jerk of his head. "In front of that row of flags."

"Why do you want me to do this?" Lilly demanded.

"Do as you are told," the man snapped. "Leave the cart and come back here. Then I will take you to your daughter."

Balboa Rojas slid the cart in front of her. Numb, Lilly gripped the handles.

"Hurry," he commanded. "You are running out of time."

She stumbled forward. As she pushed the wheeled cart in front of her, Lilly's mind was racing.

*There must be a bomb on this cart*, she reasoned.

Lilly looked down at the mass of flowers. There was nowhere to hide an explosive that she could see. But then, Lilly realized she didn't know what to look for, really. She reckoned that three sticks of dynamite attached to an alarm clock was probably not how bombs looked these days.

She realized the bomb was hidden under the table cloth. Weaving around a knot of women heading for the powder room, Lilly crouched low as if tying her shoe. She attempted to lift the pristine white table-cloth, but it was fastened to the cart. Lilly glanced in the direction of the kitchen, saw the man called Carlos gesturing her forward. She stood and wheeled the cart closer to the podium.

As she circled the main table, Lilly spied the man she and Pamela saw in the elevator earlier in the day. He was obviously a politician because he sat at the VIP table.

*Is he the target of an assassination? Am I an accessory to murder?* she wondered.

Circling the VIP table, Lilly approached a man standing near the row of flags, a headset in his ear. He was obviously a security man—a bodyguard, or maybe Secret Service.

*What will I do if he stops me?* Lilly wondered, half-hoping he would. But as she came closer, the man stepped aside to let her pass, and Lilly kept on walking.

She'd almost reached the designated spot when the fire alarm went off, filling the room with noise. The house lights went up, blinding her for a moment. Guests rose, milled about as the alarm bell continued. Then Evelyn Ankers raced to the podium and stepped in front of the surprised speaker.

"Yes, that is the fire alarm, ladies and gentlemen. But don't panic," the woman shouted over the rising tide of hysterical voices. "This is probably a false alarm, or a smoke condition. I'm waiting for more information now . . ."

Lilly looked around, uncertain what to do next.

Finally she left the cart and hurried back to Carlos. She had obeyed the man's command, now she wanted him to take her to Pamela.

But when Lilly reached the kitchen, the man with the flowers, the one person who could lead her to her daughter, was gone. . .

1 2 3 4 5 6 7 8 9
10 11 **12** 13 14 15 16 17
18 19 20 21 22 23 24

. . . . . . . . . . . . . . . . . . . . . . . . . . . . . . . . . . . . . .

THE FOLLOWING TAKES PLACE
BETWEEN THE HOURS OF
11 P.M. AND 12 A.M.
PACIFIC DAYLIGHT TIME

. . . . . . . . . . . . . . . . . . . . . . . . . . . . . . . . . . . . . .

*11:03:51 P.M. PDT*
*Babylon Hotel and Casino, Las Vegas*

Two big men hauled a battered Curtis into the Babylon's security center, slammed him into a chair. Adjusting their ties, the men watched every move, waiting for another chance to manhandle the CTU agent.

Curtis took in his surroundings. The elaborate hotel security center was the equal of CTU's war room, only much smaller. Men in suits were running around, or clustered in knots, their talk animated. Dozens of monitors that should have been displaying feed from security cameras were filled with hissing snow. Something was happening, and it wasn't good. No wonder the security staff was so touchy.

"You have to listen to me," Curtis said through bruised lips. "There are five truck bombs in the garage right now. They're going to go off in a couple of minutes—"

"Shut up," snarled one of the men looming over him. "We don't have time to listen to your bull—"

"Just call the police. Call the bomb squad. If I'm lying they can arrest me."

"You're already busted, asshole," said one of the uniformed guards.

"Listen. Lives are at stake. That's why I set off the fire alarms. The fire department should respond, right? When they get here, let me talk to them—"

Another man approached them, tall and thin in a charcoal suit. He had receding gray hair on a high forehead, a small mouth and dead gray eyes.

"What has this man done?" the gray man asked.

"We found him in the garage. He was armed, setting the fire alarms off," one of the suited men said deferentially.

The gray man nodded. "Then it wasn't the system that triggered the alarms?"

"No, sir. Apparently not."

"Listen," Curtis said. "My name is Manning and I'm an agent for CTU. There are five truck bombs in your garage right now, set to go off. The truck I came in, it also has a bomb in it. I deactivated it, but you can check yourself."

The gray man glanced at one of the guards. "He told us that story on the way up here," the man said. "I sent a couple of guys to check it out."

"Look, the fire department is on the way," Curtis said. "Let me speak to the chief when he gets here."

The gray man sighed heavily. "There will be no firemen, Mr. Manning of CTU. You made a lot of noise, but that's all. Some glitch has shut down our entire system. Phones. Intercoms. Cell phones. Radio and television signals. The computers that control most of the hotel's functions are down, too. Needless to say, the fire alarm never made it to the station house."

Curtis remembered how his cell phone had been jammed at the tool and die factory. What they used then could be bought at any high end electronics shop. This time, Curtis guessed they were using powerful microwave transmitter to jam everything within a mile's radius. It was advanced technology, something Bix might have gotten from his connection at Area 51.

"That's part of the plot," Curtis explained. "The terrorists who did this have used jamming technology in the past. They want to isolate the hotel before they destroy it."

Curtis could see the lingering doubt on the gray man's face. "You have to believe me. Check the truck I drove here—"

Just then, a uniformed officer burst through the glass doors. "He wasn't lying," the man cried. "The truck he was driving was loaded with explosives. The detonation cords have been ripped out, so it's not going off, but we found a truck just like it next to elevator shaft seven. The keys have been broken off inside the locks. We shined a light inside, saw the explosives—"

"That's only *one* of the trucks!" Curtis cried. "You have to start evacuating the building immediately."

The gray man faced his security contingent. "Do what you can. Clear the casino, the restaurants, right away—"

"Sir, there's a VIP event in the ballroom."

The gray man's hand fluttered. "Send a uniformed officer up to warn them. He'll have to climb the stairs. In the meantime I want one of you to take the radio car, get out on the highway until you're out of range of this, this jamming device. Then call for help."

"You don't have time," Curtis warned. "You have to evacuate the tower."

The gray man shook his head, sighed again. "That will be very difficult, Mr. Manning of CTU. Even if we get word to the people upstairs, the elevators are not working, and it would take an hour to get everyone out on the stairs . . ."

*11:04:07 P.M. PDT*
*Bix Automotive Center*
*Browne End Road, Las Vegas*

Bix looked up from the new issue of *Barely Legal* when Roman Vine burst into his office. Eli Blumenthal, the syndicate's plump, middle-aged accountant at his side. Vine tossed an attaché case onto the desk, scattering thousand dollar bills.

Bix sat up. "What the hell has gotten into you, partner?"

"The cash the Colombians paid us—the five million dollars. Eli says it's funny money. Counterfeit!"

"Son of a bitch," Bix roared. "All of it?"

"Most of it is phony, Mr. Bix," Blumenthal explained, sweat beading his lip. "The Colombians put real bills on top of each stack. You've got maybe a hundred grand, kosher. The rest is *bupkis*. Toilet paper."

Bix reached for the phone. "Amigo, huh? Loyal forever? That greasy south-of-the-border piece of shit. I'm gonna call that bastard Rojas right now—"

Down in the garage, the first of two bombs Balboa had planted detonated. This one was close to Hugo Bix's Jaguar. When he was holed up in the garage before the attack, Balboa pretended to admire the vehicle while he placed the explosive charge—not a large one, just big enough to blow the pipe on the garage's massive oil tank. Stored under pressure, the oil gushed into the garage in a black tide.

Bix heard the blast, stood up. "What the f—"

At that moment the second bomb went off. This explosive—planted under the Jaguar itself—was an incendiary device. When the hot jet of burning plasma met the flowing oil, a roiling ball of fire instantly engulfed the interior of the garage, incinerating everything in its path. The fireball was quickly followed by an explosion so large it not only leveled Bix Automotive, it also destroyed the abandoned tool and die factory across the street.

*11:08:20 P.M. PDT*
*Babylon Hotel and Casino, Las Vegas*

Balboa burst into the uniform storage room, stripped off his waiter's apron and jacket while he spoke in hushed tones with his brother. Stella sat at the table, buffing her polished fingernails. The little girl Pamela cowered on the floor, hugging the coloring book to her chest.

"What happened?" Pizarro demanded.

"I gave the woman the cart. She followed my command." Balboa bunched up the uniform and tossed it into a corner. "The alarms went off and I returned here."

"Why triggered the bells?"

"I don't know," Balboa replied. "Perhaps someone found one of the truck bombs. It doesn't matter. They could not have found them all. It's too late to stop us now."

Pizarro glanced nervously at his watch. "We must go, move on to the rendezvous."

Stella rose, straightened her dress. "What about the kid?"

"Take her," Pizarro commanded. "We'll use her as a hostage if we need to. Once we're clear of the hotel, we can release her—"

"Then I'm coming with you, back to the old country, or wherever the hell you're from," Stella insisted. "No way I'm staying in the USA. Not with a kidnapping rap hanging over my head."

Pizarro thin lips parted in a toothy grin. "Very well," he said.

His brother Balboa frowned, turned his back on the pair. "I will fetch the elevator," he said, stepping through the door.

"We're leaving, kid," Stella said, yanking Pamela's arm.

"I don't want to go," the girl sobbed.

Stella smacked Pamela across the face. The unexpected blow stunned the girl to silence.

"If you stay here, you'll get blown up just like your mother," Stella yelled. "Now come on, the elevator's right outside."

"Hurry," Pizarro cried. "We're running out of time."

*11:12:03 P.M. PDT*
*Babylon Hotel and Casino, Las Vegas*

Two uniformed officers of the Babylon's security staff took it upon themselves to break into the white Sprinter and defuse the bomb they'd discovered inside. Neither had knowledge or experience with explosives, let alone deactivating bombs, but they figured if they yanked out the detonation cords it might be enough to save hundreds of lives.

The doors were locked, the keys snapped off, so Gus Fellows used a fire extinguisher to smash the windshield. "Cub" Tanner, the smaller partner in the team, climbed through the shattered window to the front seat, then clambered into the back of the panel truck.

It was quieter inside, shielded from the shrill fire alarms booming through the garage. But peace of mind was short lived. Behind rows of potted flowers, Tanner spied the detonation cords, the barrels of C4, the timer clock ticking down. He wanted to run, right then and there. Instead, Cub grabbed detonation cords with both hands and yanked them loose.

"Am I still alive?" he asked, wires dangling from his hands.

His partner's head was thrust through the broken windshield. The man was all smiles.

"You did it," Fellows hooted. "You're a goddamn real life super hero."

*11:15:00 P.M. PDT*
*Babylon Hotel and Casino, Las Vegas*

At that moment, the other four trucks exploded—four bombs detonating at precisely the same moment, each with the force of tons of TNT.

Contained inside the parking garage, the explosive power of the multiple blasts was magnified many times. Cars were tossed like leaves in a windstorm. Mimicking water seeking its own level, the force of the blast flowed up elevator shafts, through air conditioning ducts and exhaust vents, along corridors and hallways. The main tower of the Babylon Hotel and Casino trembled as if subjected to an earthquake.

The parking garage collapsed instantly, the top floors crashing down onto the lower levels, the concrete slabs stacking up like pancakes, obliterating those unfortunates who were in their cars, or moving through the parking garage when the blast occurred.

In the ballroom, Senator David Palmer felt the floor tremble, then the entire building seemed to lurch. Screaming, people were thrown to the ground. Tall windows shattered, raining cutting death down onto partygoers buried by the torrent of crystal shards.

Amid the chaos, Senator Palmer searched for his wife. She'd excused herself to go to the powder room, promising to return before he began his speech. But Sherry had been gone a long time. Now he had to find her.

Before he took a step, David felt a tug on his arm. He looked down to see a young waitress, face pale, eyes wide with fright. She pointed to a cart covered with flowers.

"It's a bomb," she cried. "A man brought it in here."

David pushed her aside, reached the cart in two steps. He scattered the flowers, saw only a smooth, white tablecloth.

"Underneath," Lilly Sheridan said with a frightened sob.

Palmer ripped the cloth away, saw the blocks of C4 tapped to the underside of the cart. He lifted the wheeled carrier with both hands, held it over his head.

"Out of the way!" he shouted. Stumbling to the broken window, then outside to the glass-strewn balcony, Palmer ran to the edge of the building and tossed the cart over the side.

The bomb went off, knocking him backwards. Blinking away the flash motes in his eye, he crawled to his feet and went back inside the ballroom. The woman who'd warned him about the bomb was gone, and Palmer didn't really care. What happened was a mystery to sort out later. Right now, he had to find his wife.

Sherry Palmer was six floors below the ballroom when the bombs detonated. She'd gone searching for Lev Cohen, who was missing with her five million dollars. As soon as she got out of the elevator, Sherry heard the first alarms going off. She didn't panic, figuring if there was a real emergency, fire marshals would show up and order everyone out of the building. For all she knew, the alarm resulted from nothing more than an elevator that was stuck.

She went to Lev's room first, pounded on the door, then finally used her own pass key to enter. Lev wasn't there, and there was no sign he'd even returned from the meeting with Jong Lee.

Sherry decided to visit Jong Lee next. She waited five minutes for the elevator, then gave up and used the stairs to go down two floors, to Lee's room. She'd just knocked on the man's door when she felt the explosions under her feet. Then the entire building seemed to teeter on its foundations, tossing Sherry against the wall, then down to the carpeted floor. Behind closed doors, she heard screams, shattering glass, the sound of furniture breaking. The trembling subsided quickly, but the hall began to fill with a white haze.

Sherry pounded the door again. "Mr. Lee? Are you all right?"

A figure emerged from the smoke, a member of the housekeeping staff who was racing for the stairs. Sherry snagged her arm.

"My friend is in there. He's hurt. Please open the door," Sherry pleaded. The woman muttered something in Spanish while she fumbled in her pocket. Finally she produced a universal card key and slid it through the slot. The green light went on and Sherry pushed the door open.

"Thank you," she said. But the housekeeper was already gone.

Lee's suite had been battered by the blast, but there was no sign of occupation. The lamps were down, so Sherry tried the overhead light. The lights seemed dim, and Sherry deduced the power was low.

She searched the suite, found Lev Cohen in the bedroom. He'd been stabbed to death. The murderer had placed him on the bed, folded his arms across his chest, but had not bothered to close his dead staring eyes. Sherry stepped closer to examine the corpse, then stumbled backwards, choking back a sob. More smoke filled the hallway, and she coughed.

*I have to get out of here.*

Turning, Sherry fled the grisly scene, praying that the fire would engulf this suite, and obliterate any evidence of what really happened to David Palmer's Chief of Staff.

*       *       *

Outside, panicked patrons fled the hotel, to spill out through the shattered portico, onto sidewalks littered with broken furniture and shards of glass. Those fleeing the rear doors had to climb over a huge section of the famous Hanging Garden balcony that came crashing to earth in the explosion. Debris continued to rain down, along with tons of soil, trees, flowers and shrubs, as the balcony continued to crumble.

Smoke filled the air around the hotel, most of it pouring out of the underground garage. More smoke, funneled through the tower as if it were a chimney, emerge through the shattered glass walls of the rooftop ballroom.

The area jamming ended with the destruction of the transmitter in the explosions. People on the grounds around the hotel, and passersby on Las Vegas Boulevard bombarded 911 operators. Soon sirens wailed in the distance.

Underneath the Babylon, secondary explosions rumbled as gas tanks from hundreds of cars began to cook off.

. . . . . . . . . . . . . . . . . . . . . . . . . . . . .

**THE FOLLOWING TAKES PLACE
BETWEEN THE HOURS OF
12 A.M. AND 1 A.M.
PACIFIC DAYLIGHT TIME**

. . . . . . . . . . . . . . . . . . . . . . . . . . . . .

*12:00:00 A.M. PDT*
*Babylon Hotel and Casino, Las Vegas*

The fire alarm wailed, a deafening sound. Jack Bauer and Nina Myers entered the Babylon's chaotic security center, stepping over the shattered remains of the glass doors. A uniformed security officer moved to stop them. Nina flashed her CTU badge and the man backed off.

Unruffled amid the room's frenzied activity, a lanky, gray-haired man in a charcoal suit approached them. "I suspect you're looking for your agent," the gray man said. "Mr. Manning is over there."

Curtis stood at a work station, phone to his ear. He nodded to Jack, then returned to his conversation. Agent Manning was bruised and battered, but alive.

"What's the situation?" Jack asked.

"The Babylon is still standing, but I don't know for how long," the man replied grimly. "The balcony has mostly collapsed. The underground garage has caved in. There's a fire down there, too. More smoke than anything else, but the fire department reports that the chance of finding survivors is . . . minimal."

The gray man adjusted his tie with a long-fingered hand.

"You have electricity," Jack observed.

The gray man nodded. "Emergency generators are located in an outbuilding, so they were undamaged. We've even gotten some of the computers up and running and we're hoping to restore one or more of the elevators soon. That is our top priority."

"How many people have you evacuated?" Nina asked.

"Thanks to Mr. Manning's early warning, we managed to clear the casino and all of the clubs and restaurants. Some of the lower guest floors were cleared as well. But people are still trapped in the upper suites and in the ballroom at the top of the building."

Nina pushed her hair back. "What kind of numbers are we looking at?"

"Several hundred, at least," the gray man replied. "There was an event upstairs. The guest list says three hundred, but there's also the wait staff, bartenders, support—there may be as many as four hundred people trapped up there."

Jack nodded, a tight grin on his face. "Then no one's gotten out of the ballroom?"

The gray man shook his head. "Not since ten or fifteen minutes before the blast. That's when the elevators failed. The device that jammed our phones also interfered with the computers that ran the elevators."

"How about the stairs?"

"Since the explosions, the lower portions of the stairwells—the areas closest to the blast—have been blocked. Two stairwells have collapsed entirely. A third may be intact, but it's also filled with toxic smoke, deadly enough to suffocate anyone who inhales it."

The gray man paused, his hands fluttering around his tie. "I'm told the fire department sent two men up that stairwell, but carrying oxygen and all the other bits of fireproof gear, it will take them a while to reach the ballroom."

Nina faced Jack, comprehension dawning on her face. "You think the bombers are still up there, don't you?"

Jack nodded. "Lilly Sheridan was on the phone with me, waiting for instructions from the man who held her daughter hostage, when the jamming device kicked in and ended our conversation."

Bauer faced the gray man. "Curtis, Nina and I are going to be on the first elevator to go up," Jack declared.

Grim faced, Curtis appeared at Jack's shoulder. "I just spoke with Morris O'Brian," he whispered. "There was an explosion at Bix Automotive. It looks like Hugo and his gang have been wiped out . . ."

*12:39:15 A.M. PDT*
*Hanging Garden Ballroom*
*Babylon Hotel and Casino, Las Vegas*

Banquet Manager Evelyn Ankers, with help from Congressman Larry Bell and Senator Palmer, had gathered everyone trapped on the upper floors inside the main ballroom. It was a wise strategy. With most windows broken the ballroom offered plenty of fresh air, a welcome reprieve from the smoke filled lower levels. Several people were injured, and Sherry Palmer had appeared to supervise their care. Seven victims had been killed. Their bodies were covered by blood-stained table cloths.

Lilly had scanned all the faces in the room, but did not see the man she was searching for. As soon as she had the chance, Lilly ducked out of the ballroom to search for her daughter. She was sure Pamela and her kidnappers were still on this floor, even though she hadn't seen them.

Searching, she moved through the empty kitchen, to the corridor that led to the elevators. She was walking so fast she passed by the open door. It was the sound of voices that stopped her.

"Someone must have defused one or two of the bombs," a man's voice said.

"Lucky thing, my brother. We would all be dead now if things had gone as planned," said another voice, one Lilly recognized.

She peered through the open door, nearly gasped. Stella Hawk was there, hands clutching her daughter's shoulders. Then Lilly saw the others. Two men, both armed. One was the man who'd given her the bomb.

Lilly began to tremble, uncertain what to do next. She ducked back into the kitchen, grabbed a carving knife from a steam table.

Then the cell phone vibrated in her pocket and she fumbled for the phone. "Hello."

"It's Jaycee."

"Where are you?"

"I'm near the service elevator. It will be working soon, in ten or fifteen minutes. Then I'm coming up."

"Oh, god, Jaycee. They're here. They have Pamela—"

"Who? Where?"

"Stella and two other guys. They're real close, Jaycee, just down the hall."

"Can you reach the service elevator without being seen? If you lead me to these men, I'll get your daughter back."

"Yes," Lilly cried. "I'll go now."

As she raced for the elevator, Lilly heard two shots. . .

Balboa killed the firemen as they emerged from the smoky stairwell. He regretted not having a silencer on his Makarov, but reasoned there was no one around to hear the shots anyway.

He and Pizarro dragged the corpses to a maintenance room, then removed the dead men's oxygen masks and tanks, along with their fire-resistant overalls.

Stella Hawk stood watch in the corridor, her fingers bruising Pamela Sheridan's tender flesh. Silently, the girl sobbed.

"The stairs are filled with smoke, and there are only two protective suits," Pizarro said.

Balboa glanced at the woman in the hall, then back at his brother. "Take them. You and the woman. And do it quick. I am sure the authorities will be here soon."

"And the child?"

Balboa frowned. "I will keep her as a bargaining chip."

To Pizarro's surprise, his brother chuckled. "This *is* Las Vegas, no?"

"But how will you get out, elude the *policia*?"

Balboa handed his brother the oxygen masks, overalls.

"I'll manage," he replied. "In any case, someone must continue on with the next part of this operation. Better that someone is you."

"But—"

Balboa silenced his brother with a gesture. "I see how you look at that woman, Pizarro. I've known you all your life and you never looked at any woman that way before. So I want you to escape, and take her with you! I will provide a diversion, then join you at the rendezvous."

· · · · · · · · · · · · · · · · · · · · · · · · · · · · · · ·

THE FOLLOWING TAKES PLACE
BETWEEN THE HOURS OF
1 A.M. AND 2 A.M.
PACIFIC DAYLIGHT TIME

· · · · · · · · · · · · · · · · · · · · · · · · · · · · · · ·

*1:01:09 A.M. PDT*
*Dormitory B, Experimental Weapons Testing Range*
*Groom Lake Air Force Base*

Tony Almeida returned to his cramped quarters in
Dormitory B, stripped off his sweat-stained shirt and
lobbed it in the general direction of the overflowing
hamper in the corner. He wanted nothing more than
to grab a hot shower and a good night's sleep, but
could do neither until he checked in with CTU.

Still in his sweatpants and sneakers, Tony powered
up the laptop on the desk. Waiting for the system to
boot, he stretched sore muscles.

His day should have ended hours ago, after Senator

David Palmer cancelled the Malignant Wave program on the spot. But instead of dismantling the device and storing it in Hangar Six, Dr. Megan Reed ordered the crew to install the Malignant Wave engine in the Blackfoot stealth helicopter in Hangar Five, ahead of the scheduled Tuesday morning deployment test.

It was, Tony felt, an exercise in reality denial. When Dr. Reed delivered news of Palmer's cancellation to the rest of the staff, it was Dr. Phillip Bascomb who reacted most strongly.

"I've dedicated my professional life, since my days at Berkeley, to develop non-lethal technology as a means to render war less odious," he'd said. "Sure, the wave causes permanent brain damage *now*, but with more time and research, I'm convinced we could improve the device, make the effects less debilitating—or even temporary."

"Sorry, Phillip," Dr. Reed replied, turning her perfectionist streak on herself. "I didn't make a cogent argument. I let you all down."

But it was Beverly Chang's reaction that surprised them all.

"No one has officially notified us that the project has been cancelled," she said. "Senator Palmer is only one member of a committee. The other members may have a different view. We should proceed with our test schedule until ordered to do otherwise."

Dr. Reed agreed, and set them all to work immediately. They lowered the device from the tower, moved it to Hangar Five and loaded it into the bay of the experimental helicopter. Then they began work on the electronics. It was close to eleven o'clock before the device was finally installed, along with a temporary weapons panel mounted in the cockpit.

Steve Sable wanted to knock off at that point, but Dr. Chang pushed them to conduct diagnostic tests on the control panel. It was after midnight when Tony and Steve finished, and Dr. Sable headed off to bed while Tony shut down the computers and stowed the equipment.

Now Tony stifled a yawn, wearily tapped in a code that switched him over to the secret ARPANET pathways, where he could safely retrieve the intelligence Jamey sent him. Tony was shocked back to wakefulness when he read the analysis of the data taken from Dr. Steve Sable's phone. His suspicions had been correct. Sable *was* the traitor. He'd made too many calls to Hugo Bix for him to claim innocence.

Tony also learned that one of Bix's henchmen had been caught with top secret Area 51 technology earlier that day. The evidence seemed incontrovertible now. It was clear he would have to move against Dr. Steve Sable in the next twenty-four hours, before the man had a chance to pass more top secret research technology to Hugo Bix.

Fingers poised over the keyboard, Tony was about to send an update to Jamey when he heard a sound behind him, saw the shadow fall across the desk. Tony looked up, saw the wrench in the intruder's upraised hand. He tried to cover his head with his arms as the first blow descended.

*1:03:51 A.M. PDT*
*Babylon Hotel and Casino, Las Vegas*

Lilly rushed to the man she knew as Jaycee as soon as the elevator doors opened. She ignored the woman with him, and the big man from the Cha-Cha Lounge named Curtis.

"They're gone," she cried. "I heard shots a minute ago. I went back to the corridor, and they were gone."

That's when they heard another shot, this one aimed at them. The crack of the Russian handgun echoed off the walls. The bullet missed Nina's head by an inch, punched a hole in the plaster.

"Lock the elevator so no one can use it, then fan out," Jack commanded. He stared down the barrel of his Glock as he methodically checked the corridors around him.

The woman moved to the right, Curtis to the left. Lilly led Jaycee back to the hall. They moved slowly, wary of ambush.

"There were three of them, right here," Lilly said when they reached the corridor outside the maintenance room. "Stella had my daughter. When I came back, they were gone."

Jack was about to check to see if the door was unlocked. He was interrupted by a child's scream.

"That's Pamela," Lilly cried.

Jack believed the noise came from the kitchen. The girl's voice had an echoing quality that made him think of tile walls and hard, bare floors. He searched the kitchen for five minutes and came up empty.

Of Curtis and Nina, there was no sign. Perhaps they had picked up the man's trail. Jack was about to complete a wide circle of the ballroom when he heard shouts—then another shot.

Jack burst through the kitchen's double doors, Glock clutched in his fist. The ballroom was in shambles, broken glass and shattered shards from fallen chandeliers littered the floor. The room was packed, too, though the crowd seemed to be parting, as people scattered to escape the armed man carrying a little girl slung over his shoulders.

Jack stepped into the middle of the debris strewn floor, aimed the Glock. "Halt or I'll shoot!" he cried.

Lilly stumbled through the kitchen doors, saw her daughter and cried out. "Please let my daughter go!"

The man turned, squeezed a shot off in Jack's general direction. People screamed and dived for cover. Bauer didn't even flinch as the bullet ripped past his ear.

"Stop now or I *will* shoot," Jack cried. Arms outstretched, he corrected his aim.

But Balboa Rojas refused to stop. He ran through the broken window frame, onto the crumbling balcony. Jack cursed, lowered his weapon and chased the man.

When he reached the balcony, Balboa turned, held the girl in front of him like a human shield. He pointed the muzzle of his Makarov PM at her head.

"If you do not drop your weapon, I will shoot," Rojas declared.

Jack saw movement out of the corner of his eye,

but his vision remained fixed on Balboa Rojas. He crouched low and set the Glock on the ground, inching closer to the man.

"You don't have to die up here," Jack said reasonably, talking another step. "We can talk this through. If you have demands, I'm authorized by my government to listen to them."

Another step. He was in arm's reach now. Balboa's eyes were wide, nostrils flared. Jack could see he was panicking. "Move again and I'll—"

The gunshot shattered the tense stillness. Balboa's head jerked backwards in a fountain of blood. Jack lunged, snatched the girl out of his limp arms, clutched her tightly. The Makarov clattered to the balcony as the dead man pitched backwards, over the edge.

Jack turned to see Lilly racing toward her daughter. He released the girl and Pamela ran into her mother's arms.

Nina stepped out from behind the curtains. The Glock seemed huge in her dainty hand.

"Good shot," said Jack. "What about the others."

Nina frowned. "I think the man I shot was meant to be a diversion. Curtis and I found two dead men in the janitor's closet. Firemen. Their gear was missing. We called downstairs to have the stairs guarded, but we were too late. Whoever killed the firemen managed to slip past the cordon."

1 2 3 4 5 6 7 8 9
10 11 12 13 14 **15** 16 17
18 19 20 21 22 23 24

· · · · · · · · · · · · · · · · · · · · · · · · · · · · · · ·

THE FOLLOWING TAKES PLACE
BETWEEN THE HOURS OF
2 A.M. AND 3 A.M.
PACIFIC DAYLIGHT TIME

· · · · · · · · · · · · · · · · · · · · · · · · · · · · · · ·

*2:17:07 A.M. PDT*
*Groom Lake Secure Terminal*
*McCarran Airport, Las Vegas*

Gripping Stella Hawk's hand in his own, Pizarro Rojas dragged the woman across the deserted airport parking lot, toward a fence surrounding the private military terminal. The lights of the Vegas Strip blazed, but it was the sound of emergency sirens that dominated the night. In the distance, Pizarro could see plumes of smoke rising above the skyline, police and press helicopters circling the smoldering Babylon Hotel.

The Colombian was surprised to find the guardhouse empty. He led Stella around the roadblock and into the restricted aread. Crouching behind a row of parked cars near the terminal building, Pizarro spied Carlos Boca. The Cuban waved them forward.

"You made it, Senor Rojas. Congratulations. By the noise on the streets, I would guess the bombs went off on schedule," Carlos said.

Pizarro nodded. "How many others are here?"

"Eight, counting Roland and I."

"Who is missing?"

Boca frowned. "Salazar and young Hector. I don't know what happened to them. And your brother?"

Pizarro shook his head. "He helped me escape the hotel, but I'm not sure he got out himself."

Carlos Boca sighed. "Two men lost to that spy at Bix's Garage. Now Salazar and Hector—*and* your brother. I do not like these losses. I hope our goal is worth it."

"The stealth device that was stolen from us was only the beginning. If all goes well, we will have technology to match anything our enemies possess. Machines that will erase national borders. We will control the cocaine market as never before," Pizarro declared.

Roland Arrias joined them. Like Boca, he carried a metal toolbox in his hand. "There is no sign of the Chinaman," he said.

"You're wrong," Pizarro hissed. "Look."

Jong Lee stood at the terminal's front door. At his side a woman in a black jumpsuit clutched an AK–47. With a casual gesture, he waved them forward. Hesitantly, the Cuban commandos rose from their hiding places among the cars.

"Move," Roland barked, and the men sprinted to the terminal entrance. Moaning impatiently, Stella rose and followed Pizarro, heels clicking on the pavement.

"You are early," Jong Lee said.

"You didn't require our assistance, I see," Rojas replied.

"Yizi, with my commandos, secured this building—" He glanced at his Rolex. "Twenty-one minutes ago."

Jong Lee glanced at the box clutched in Roland's hand, then the one held by Carlos Boca. "You have both devices?"

Carlos nodded. "Here and operational."

"Good," Jong said. "Then let us board the airplane."

Lee led them through the silent, windowless terminal. The harsh glare of overhead fluorescent lights cast ghastly shadows across the corpses sprawled on the floor, draped over chairs and desktops. Men and women. Air Force security personnel in blue uniforms, terminal employees, and over a dozen civilian workers who had reported for the late shift had been cut down in a hail of gunfire.

"How did you manage this without attracting attention?" Pizarro asked, clearly impressed.

"Yizi, Captain Hsu and my commandos, they are all highly trained," Jong replied. "They infiltrated the terminal using current security codes and a valid card key. Their weapons were equipped with noise suppression devices, and they killed without hesitation.

It took only a few minutes to wrest control of this facility from the American military."

"Where are your commandos now?" Roland asked, stroking his scar with his free hand.

"They are waiting for us inside the plane. Hurry, now. We must take off precisely on time so we do not attract the attention of McCarran Airport's air traffic control personnel."

A moment later, the commandos exited the terminal on the opposite side of the building. In a long line they crossed the tarmac and climbed stairs that led into the passenger compartment of an unmarked Boeing 737–200, its engines idling on the tarmac.

Three minutes later JANET 9—the call sign for the two forty-five AM flight to Groom Lake Air Force Base—lifted off from McCarran on schedule. Captain Hsu was at the controls, Yizi in the co-pilot's seat.

The trip was a short one. They would reach their destination in approximately twenty-two minutes.

*2:50:12 A.M. PDT*
*Flight Control Tower*
*Groom Lake Air Force Base*

Airman Trudi Hwang was the only air traffic controller on duty that night. Since the process of base deactivation had begun, the pace of the flights had diminished, and so had the work load. With all but one of the dormitories unoccupied, the full-time staff cut to less that a hundred, there was less and less to do.

In the old days, a minimum of two controllers were required on every shift. Nowadays, it was two guys in the morning, two in the afternoon, and one lonely and bored controller on the graveyard shift.

Trudi sat up in her chair and stared out of the tall windows. The night sky was black and strewn with stars. Not even the brilliant lights of Las Vegas interfered with the star shine here in the desert. She sighed and reached for her tea, to find it ice cold.

*A desert it may be*, Trudi mused, *but it's still damn cold in the middle of the night.*

She glanced at the clock. JANET 9, the next flight of the evening, arrived in less than ten minutes. She'd already verified the IFF signal, and the pilot had radioed in. If she bothered to look, Airman Hwang could watch the blip approaching the base on her radar. Instead she headed for the tiny kitchenette to brew more tea.

Feeling lonely, she considered calling Tom, the night officer downstairs, just to hear a human voice. But the man on security detail in the tiny terminal building would only think she was interested in him and hit on her. The military was different than the real world. A girl had to watch how she presented herself, lest the men around her neglect to take her seriously.

She was filling the tea pot at the sink when a silhouette loomed in the doorway. Startled, Trudi yelped.

"Whoa. Calm down. It's me . . . Beverly."

The woman stepped into the light and Trudi breathed a sigh of relief. "Dr. Chang. You scared the heck out of me."

Beverly Chang smiled, displayed a plastic bound folder. "Sorry. I was delivering the new security protocol codes."

"You could have left them in the box," Trudi replied, moving the pot to the hot plate. "Or you could have delivered them tomorrow."

"I was awake. Big demonstration today, another experiment Tuesday. Lots to do . . ."

Turning away from the woman, Trudi shook her head. "I don't know how you scientist types do it, I mean—"

The silenced gun coughed twice. Trudi tried to cry out. Instead she dropped the tea pot and pitched forward.

Beverly Chang gripped the gun in her trembling hand, stared down at the corpse at her feet. She dropped the weapon and ran out of the tower and down the stairs. Another body sprawled on the terminal's linoleum floor. She stepped over the murdered duty officer, burst through the door.

1 2 3 4 5 6 7 8 9
10 11 12 13 14 15 **16** 17
18 19 20 21 22 23 24

• • • • • • • • • • • • • • • • • • • • • • • • • • • • • • •

THE FOLLOWING TAKES PLACE
BETWEEN THE HOURS OF
3 A.M. AND 4 A.M.
PACIFIC DAYLIGHT TIME

• • • • • • • • • • • • • • • • • • • • • • • • • • • • • • •

*3:02:51 A.M. PDT*
*Runway 33R/15L*
*Groom Lake Air Force Base*

Beverly Chang listened for the sound of jet engines. After a seemingly interminable wait, she heard a distant whine. Minutes passed. Finally blinking lights appeared in the black night sky. The lights dipped, dropping below the mountain range, plunging into Emigrant Valley.

Finally, Dr. Chang watched the Boeing 737 touch down in a cloud of desert dust, then taxi along Runway 33R/15L until it reached the tiny terminal building.

Covering her ears against the noise, Beverly rushed

to the airplane the moment the passenger door opened. Two men—Chinese—jumped out and ran to retrieve the portable steps. It took them only a moment to roll the stairs to the aircraft. The first man to emerge at the top of the stairs was Jong Lee, an armed woman behind him.

"Jong Lee. I must speak with you," Beverly cried.

Lee descended the steps. Ignoring her, he moved aside while armed men poured out of the airplane. Guns drawn, boots pounding on the concrete, they fanned out across the facility. Beverly counted thirty men, most, but not all of them Asians.

"Jong Lee, don't ignore me," she demanded. "I have done everything you've asked of me."

Finally, the tall man faced her. "Everything?"

Beverly Chang nodded. "I've given you the security codes. I killed the people in the tower."

He raised an eyebrow. "And Malignant Wave?"

"The device has been installed in a prototype helicopter in Hangar Five. The aircraft is ready to fly."

Beverly reached out to clutch his arm. Yizi pushed her away.

"My sister. Her family," Dr. Chang cried. "You promised me they would be set free in exchange for what I've done."

Jong Lee well knew, and exploited, Beverly Chang's tragic family history. While Beverly and her family immigrated to America in the 1970s, the woman's infant sister remained with her grandparents. The young woman became an outspoken member of the Falun Gong movement, and she and her family were among the first to be arrested when the People's Republic of China began to suppress the quasi-religious movement in the 1990s. As far as Lee was concerned, they'd earned their fate, as Beverly Chang would now earn hers.

"They *have* been freed, Dr. Chang. Join them."

Yizi stepped forward, sai raised.

Pizarro Rojas exited the plane at that moment. Beside him an unruffled Stella Hawk, her makeup and hair painstakingly restored to their former glory, paused at the top of the stairs.

The pair watched as Yizi thrust her razor-sharp sai into Dr. Beverly Chang's throat. With a gargling cry, the woman grabbed Yizi's wrists in a death grip, while she twitched and bucked on the end of the three-pronged blade like a speared fish. Finally, Dr. Chang died, and Yizi let the corpse slide to the ground. The assassin stepped back, trembling, her glassy eyes staring in fascination at the bloodied blades.

Stella Hawk observed the woman's bizarre behavior, shook her head sadly. "Man, that chick's got a *lot* of issues."

*3:13:54 A.M. PDT*
*Hangar Five,*
*Experimental Weapons Testing Range*
*Groom Lake Air Force Base*

Cold water dashed Tony's face. He tried to open his eyes, blinked against the harsh fluorescent light.

"Come on, Alvarez, wake up. We need to talk."

A hand slapped Tony's cheek. He winced, opened his eyes. Tony realized he was sitting up, but when he tried to stand he found he'd been strapped to a metal chair.

"Sorry, pal," Sable said with a smirk. "You've got to stay put while I arrange a little industrial accident."

The left side of Tony's face throbbed and he shook his head to clear it.

"Sorry about the beat down, buddy. You look pretty good, all things considered. I wrapped the wrench with cloth. Didn't want to leave too many marks. Might look suspicious."

"You want my death to look like an accident." Tony said, his voice hoarse.

Sable tossed one end of a long length of electrical cable on the floor, then hooked the other end to a large generator. "Yeah. Something like that."

Tony twisted his head to look around. He wasn't in the dorm anymore. Sable had brought him to Hangar Five, just a few dozen feet away from the Blackfoot helicopter prototype.

Sable touched the frayed end of the cable to the tip of a power meter, grinned in satisfaction.

"Smooth move, the way you swiped my phone, then put it back," Sable said. "I wouldn't have known, except I added my own feature to the software—a download log that I check every time I use the phone."

Tony groaned, pulled on the electric cables binding his hands and feet.

Steve Sable slipped an insulated glove over his hand.

"Now we're going to have a little talk, Tony . . . If that's your name—"

"Go to hell."

"What are you? Air Force Intelligence? DEA? The Swiss Guard?"

Tony refused to answer, so Sable touched his knee with the frayed end of the electrical cable. A blue flash, and Tony cried out. The smell of scorched flesh wafted into his nostrils.

"What do you know?" Sable asked. He held the electrified cable in the gloved hand, twirled it like a lasso. Then he whipped it across Tony's chest. Another flash, more acrid smoke rose. The tendons stood out on Tony's neck and arms.

"It's what do *we* know, Sable," Tony replied, sweat streaming down his naked torso. "*We* know you've been selling advanced technology to criminal gangs through Hugo Bix. *We* know you sold a stealth device to the Rojas Cartel. *We* know enough to put you away for life, no matter what you do to me."

"What I'll do to you will look like an accident—"

"You won't fool anyone," Tony cried.

"I will, just long enough to board the six AM flight out of here. By the time they find your corpse, I'll be heading South."

Tony stared at the man.

"Oh, yeah, Tony. Don't act so surprised." Sable smirk was reason enough to kill him. Tony strained at his bonds.

"You're looking at a man with a plan. I made Bix a pair of military style jamming systems like none before. I also made another stealth device—this one my

2.0 model. Very much improved. Delivered them last week. In return, Bix promised me a ticket out of the U.S. of A. and a comfy job with the cartels."

Sable laughed. "I did a little vocational research and guess what? Technical advisors working for drug cartels have a much better lifestyle than slobs who work for the federal government. We're talking seaside villas. A mistress or three. Fancy cars and a hefty bank account. I don't know about you, but to me a seaside villa sounds a whole lot better than some trailer park in Pahrump—"

Sable's rant was interrupted by the a burst of machine gun fire and a woman's scream.

*3:42:31 A.M. PDT*
*Groom Lake Air Force Base*

The strike had been decisive and Jong Lee had reason to rejoice. Stepping over the machine-gunned woman sprawled on the tarmac—a civilian worker reporting early for the next flight home—Jong's face remained impassive, even as he reviewed his successes.

The late Dr. Chang had paved the way for their undetected landing. The communications jamming device supplied to the Colombians through Hugo Bix was working perfectly. The scarred man, Roland Arrias, was inside the Boeing 737, monitoring the device to ensure that all communications in and out of Groom Lake were cut off.

Meanwhile Captain Hsu's strike team had stormed the puny garrison and slaughtered the security staff.

While the Cubans searched the hangars for fugitive Air Force personnel or cowering researchers, Jong Lee issued new orders to Captain Hsu.

"Go to Dormitory B. It is the only one that is occupied," Jong said. "I want you to capture all the scientists and researchers staying there, bring them back here. I will decide who is useful, and we will take them with us. The others will be executed."

"Yes, sir."

"I want you to place two guards around the airplane, and have it refueled. We will depart within the hour. With the stealth device the Cubans installed, the 737 will be invisible to American radar. We will cross the border and land at our base in Mexico three hours from now."

Hsu nodded.

"And after you've brought the prisoners here, you must make preparations for your solo flight in the Blackfoot, Captain Hsu."

· · · · · · · · · · · · · · · · · · · · · · · · · · · · · ·

**THE FOLLOWING TAKES PLACE
BETWEEN THE HOURS OF
4 A.M. AND 5 A.M.
PACIFIC DAYLIGHT TIME**

· · · · · · · · · · · · · · · · · · · · · · · · · · · · · ·

*4:08:05 A.M. PDT*
*Hangar Five,*
*Experimental Weapons Testing Range*
*Groom Lake Air Force Base*

Face tense, eyes wide, Steve Sable peered through a gap in the hangar door. Another gunshot echoed in the night.

"Son of a—they shot somebody else," Sable cried. "A mechanic, I think. Guys in black BDUs pulled him out of the big hangar . . . shot him in the back of the head, execution-style."

Tony, still bound, twisted his head to face his captor.

"They're after the technology in Hangar 18. Lots of equipment there. They got a taste for high-tech from the stuff you peddled. Now they're here for the rest."

Tony paused to listen as another burst was unleashed.

"They're getting close, Sable. They're going to be here soon. What do you think they're going to do to you?"

Sable heard cries outside, backed away from the door.

"Listen," Tony said. "You were right. I'm an agent for the Counter Terrorist Unit. Cut me loose and I can deal with these guys. Send an SOS—"

"You can't send shit!" Sable cried. He slammed his cell phone down on the workbench. "Everything is jammed. The cell phone is worthless."

"I have weapons," Tony said. "Stashed in Hangar Six. Cut me loose and I can protect you."

Eyes shifting like a frightened animal, Sable hovered over Tony.

"Yeah, how can I trust you?" he asked.

"You have no choice," Tony replied, staring straight ahead.

Tony felt cold steel against his wrists. "You've got to understand this was nothing personal, Tony. What I did to you I did to survive. Now we're on the same side, right?"

While Sable babbled, he cut away the cables until Tony was free. Groaning, the CTU agent reached down and rubbed his legs where the wires chafed him. Then he reached for something lying on the floor.

"You're free, Tony. Buddies again, right? Don't forget to tell the feds how I helped you. After this is over, I want to cut some kind of a deal."

"Sure," Tony replied. "Let's shake on it."

Sable extended his arm, and Tony thrust the live wire into his open hand. Sable jerked as if struck, reeled against the workbench. He wagged his arm to free his hand, but the circuit would not be broken. Like a poisonous serpent that sank its fangs deep into flesh, the cable pumped thousands of volts through Steve Sable's twitching body. Tony crossed to the generator and turned up the juice.

He waited until Sable was on his back, and smoke was coming out of the man's ears, eyes and nostrils before he cut the power.

"Yeah, there's your deal, old buddy," snarled Tony.

Legs numb, Tony stumbled to the hangar door, peered through the crack. He saw the Boeing 737 squatting on the tarmac, two men guarding it, both armed with assault rifles. A third man was pumping jet fuel into the aircraft. It was clear the enemy—whoever they were—was planning to escape in the same aircraft that brought them.

Tony grinned mirthlessly. *Not if I can help it.*

Shirtless, Tony was clad in light gray sweat pants and white sneakers that practically glowed in the dark—no match for the black camouflaged BDUs the bad guys were wearing. After he stashed Dr. Sable's still smoldering corpse in a storage bin, Tony raced to the grease pit behind the helicopter.

Dipping his hand in the muck, Tony smeared the

brackish tar all over his pants, his shoes, then his hard-muscled arms and torso. Finally, he streaked oil across his forehead, his cheeks, under his eyes.

Tony moved to the rear of the hanger. On the way he grabbed Sable's cell phone and tucked it into his sweats.

*Who knows, I might get to use it yet*, he thought.

Cautiously, Tony slipped out the back door and vanished in the fast fading night. . .

*4:49:14 A.M. PDT*
*Hangar Six, Experimental Weapons Testing Range*
*Groom Lake Air Force Base*

Jong Lee's commandos had corralled their hostages in Hangar Six. The doors were open and the massive interior of the hangar blazed with light.

The hostages, mostly scientists, engineers and researchers, had been rousted out of their beds and marched to this place. Many still wore robes, pajamas, sweats or underwear, and walked in bare feet or slippers. The few airmen and officers spared immediate execution were in uniform or work clothes. Now everyone was huddled on the concrete floor, hands on their heads, and their armed captors silently watched over them.

Captain Hsu's men had stormed the dormitory and captured its occupants in an efficient and methodical manner. But the prisoners soon learned that their captors were prone to casual violence if their authority was challenged in the smallest way.

As they were herded out of the dorm at the start of their march, Dr. Megan Reed—ridiculously clad in a pink Meow, Meow Kitty teddy and little else—refused to obey one of the soldier's commands quickly enough, and was knocked to the ground by the butt of his rifle. Corporal Stratowski moved to defend the woman and was executed on the spot, in front of everyone.

After that, the hostages were cowed, though Dr. Bascomb had to be restrained by Alvin Toth, or the middle-aged, pony-tailed scientist would have been murdered, too.

Gunfire could be heard all over the base. While Captain Hsu grabbed the prisoners, the bulk of the raiders descended on the hangars, stripping them of everything of value.

When the hostages were led past a 737 parked on the runway near Hangar 18, they saw men in black BDUs packing the cargo bays with everything from computers to prototypes of advanced weapons systems, test missiles, even bits of random machinery. Like technology-starved locusts, the raiders stripped advanced avionics systems out of the cockpit of experimental aircraft, looted file cabinets, ripped the hard drives out of every computer.

From her spot on the floor, Dr. Reed observed the activity swirling around the airplane. She also used her time to study their captors, listen to their words. Some of the men spoke Spanish, but most were Asians and spoke a dialect of Chinese. If Dr. Chang were here, she could translate. Megan wondered what had happened to her friend, Beverly. Perhaps she got away.

Dani Welles sidled a little closer to her boss. "How's the jaw?" she whispered.

Megan Reed frowned. She'd done everything she could to forget the pain. It only reminded her of Corporal Stratowski's sacrifice and filled her with guilt. She'd counted the hostages in the hangar—twenty-two. She busied her highly-trained brain a dozen different ways, yet nothing worked. The image of Corporal Stratowski's final seconds would suddenly flood her mind. The memory was impossible to ignore.

"They just shot him," she whispered. "Like he was a lab specimen or something."

Dani nodded. "All they need is an excuse. If they're so eager to kill us, what are we doing here?"

That question was answered ten minutes later, when a tall Asian man strode into the hanger. A woman in a black jumpsuit followed him like a shadow. The man's arrogant gaze swept over the hostages as he walked among them. Most of the prisoners averted their eyes. To her shame, Dr. Reed did, too. But not Dr. Bascomb, The doctor's undisguised hostility only seemed to amuse their captor.

"My name is Jong Lee," the stranger said at last. "You will each tell me your names, your fields of expertise, so that I may determine your value. If I am satisfied by your answers, you will board the airplane outside. If I am not . . ."

Lee paused, gestured to the woman at his side. "My assistant Yizi will deal with any unpleasantness."

· · · · · · · · · · · · · · · · · · · · · · · · · · · · · · · · · ·

THE FOLLOWING TAKES PLACE
BETWEEN THE HOURS OF
5 A.M. AND 6 A.M.
PACIFIC DAYLIGHT TIME

· · · · · · · · · · · · · · · · · · · · · · · · · · · · · · · · · ·

*5:02:51 A.M. PDT*
*Runway 33R/15L*
*Groom Lake Air Force Base*

Tony's plan was to sneak over to Hangar Six, where
he'd stashed a Glock and a cache of ammunition inside an idle generator. But with daylight coming on
fast, and the fuel truck parked on the dimly-lit tarmac, pumping hundreds of gallons of JET A–1 into
the Boeing's tanks, the 737 was a target of opportunity too tempting to ignore.

　　Tony had scouted around Hangar 18 a number of
times. It was the largest structure on the base, capable
of holding a pair of Boeing 737s. Tony knew experi-

mental aircraft were being stored there, but because access was restricted he'd never been inside

He did know that welding tools and tanks were stored in a small cinder block maintenance shed next to the massive hangar. He'd been there a few days ago because that's where civilian welders had assembled the microwave tower that was later erected at the test site.

Under the fast-brightening sky, Tony moved without detection across the desert terrain, well away from the illuminated runways and building lights. He observed a contingent of prisoners being herded into Hangar Five. He'd hoped the raiders would ignore the dormitory and stick to the technology labs and testing centers. But it seemed the enemy wanted more than just machines. Either they were gathering hostages to use as human shields, or kidnapping highly trained technicians. Either way, Tony would do his best to stop them.

It took a long time, but Tony finally reached the shed. The door was locked so Tony used a rock to smash the padlock. It took several minutes and plenty of scraped knuckles, but he finally slipped through the door and closed it behind him. In the glow of the overhead light Tony gathered up everything he would need to make a modern variation on the old-fashioned Molotov cocktail.

Five minutes later, Tony left the shed with two hand-held welding tanks strapped to his back, and a striker thrust in the elastic band of his sweatpants. As he circled the massive hangar, the building's interior echoed with shouts and the sound of things breaking.

Cautiously, Tony approached the runway near the tail of the aircraft—and couldn't believe his luck. Most of the activity around the airliner had ceased. The men had finished loading the cargo bays, and had once again fanned out across the base in a search for more loot. The Boeing was guarded by only three men now. Better yet, the fuel truck was parked less than twenty yards away from the spot where Tony lurked. The man who worked the hose was standing under the wing, facing two guards who had gathered at the bottom of the portable stairs.

This was going to be a whole lot easier than Tony first thought. He watched the man at the hose abondon his post and move closer to his comrades. Crouching, Tony sprinted across the tarmac, covering twenty yards in seconds. He dropped to the ground behind the fuel truck, slipped a welder off his back and touched the starter to the nozzle.

The gas hissed loudly as a blue jet of fire spewed from the nozzle. Tony feared the enemy would hear the sound, but the whine of the fuel pump masked the noise. Tony ignited the second welder, and wth a tank in each hand, he positioned them on the hose rack so the blue flame bored into the side of the fuel tank.

Then Tony ran, circling the hangar in the hope that the building would be enough to protect him from the explosion to come. He counted to ten, then to twenty. Tony was about to circle back to see what went wrong when an orange ball of fire shot up into the purpling sky. A powerful wave of debris and hot gasses rocked the hangar, shattering windows and blowing out the electricity. That same scorching wind washed over Tony a split second later, knocking him flat on his back, singeing his hair and blistering the skin across his torso.

The first blast was followed by a secondary explosion, then a third. Keeping his eyes closed, his hands over his face, Tony waited a full five minutes before he peeked out over the edge of the pit. A grim smile creased his battered face when he saw the remains of the Boeing 737 scattered all over the runway.

Playing a hunch, Tony checked the display on the late Steve Sable's cell phone. His smile widened into a grin when he realized he must have destroyed the jamming system with the airplane, because now the cell phone had locked onto a powerful signal.

Tony knew there was only one man who could help him stop this invasion. By the wavering light of the burning debris, Tony dialed Jack Bauer's cell phone. . .

*5:39:26 A.M. PDT*
*Groom Lake Secure Terminal*
*McCarran Airport, Las Vegas*

Jack burst through the glass doors, leading with his Glock. As soon as he entered the terminal, he smelled death. Back to the wall, Jack moved cautiously along the corridor, shifting his Glock with his gaze.

"Clear," he called. Curtis came through next.

Glock in hand, he moved to the opposite end of the hall, checked all four points of the compass before he called "clear."

Finally Nina entered in a crouch, gun held low but ready.

It took them only a few minutes to determine the terminal was deserted, except for the dead.

"They launched their raid from here," Jack said. "They killed everyone and hijacked the airliner. Disguised as a regulation flight, they landed at Groom Lake and took over the base."

Nina averted her eyes from the carnage around them. "Tony said the attackers spoke Chinese. This might not be terrorism, Jack."

"Then we're at war," Jack replied, face grim.

"What's our next move?" Curtis asked.

Jack rubbed the back of his neck. "CTU has been mobilized, but it's almost sunrise and we don't have time to wait for reinforcements to arrive," Jack replied. "Anyway, I'm sure the raiders are prepared to deal with any large-scale assault. Tony estimated there were between twenty and thirty commandos, all highly trained—too many for him to stop alone. They have hostages, and they have radar and anti-aircraft missiles at the base. If they need to, they could threaten American lives, or turn our own weapons against us."

Nina met Jack's gaze. "So you're thinking what?"

"We'll split up here," Jack replied. "I'm going over to the main terminal, see if I can commandeer an airplane or helicopter. I'll fly in below the radar if I can."

Curtis frowned. "What about us?"

"The raiders are concentrated around the experimental hangars. I want you to join up with Morris and approach that section of Groom Lake Air Force Base by land."

Curtis shook his head. "There's only one road in or out of there. They bad guys are sure to be guarding it."

"Then it's simple," Jack replied. "Don't use the roads."

1 2 3 4 5 6 7 8 9
10 11 12 13 14 15 16 17
18 **19** 20 21 22 23 24

. . . . . . . . . . . . . . . . . . . . . . . . . . . . . . . . . . . . . . .

THE FOLLOWING TAKES PLACE
BETWEEN THE HOURS OF
6 A.M. AND 7 A.M.
PACIFIC DAYLIGHT TIME

. . . . . . . . . . . . . . . . . . . . . . . . . . . . . . . . . . . . . . .

*9:03:05 A.M. EDT*
*Central Intelligence Agency Headquarters*
*Langley, Virginia*

When Kenneth Wu, head of the CIA's Department
of Foreign Intelligence, arrived in his office, he found
a thick Fed Ex envelope on his desk. When he read
the return address—DIAMID, LLC—Director Wu set
his Starbucks coffee and breakfast pastry aside. The
package had come from a mole inside the Los Angeles Consulate of the People's Republic of China.

It took Director Wu ten minutes to peruse the doc-
uments, which outlined every detail of the attack on
Groom Lake, including the names and dossiers of the
leaders of the mission. When he was finished, the Di-

rector reached for his phone and called his boss, who promptly notified the President of the United States.

Captain Hsu saluted.

"Everything we loaded onto the plane was lost with the airliner, Jong Lee. The blast also cost four men. Commandos Sahn, Suh, Bah, and Shi-uhr," he said, rattling off their code numbers. Their names were unimportant.

"*Six* men," Carlos said miserably. "Do not forgot Enrico, and my friend Roland Arrias."

"An accident?" Jong Lee asked.

Hsu face remained impassive. "Possible, but unlikely."

"Then we have an enemy among us. One of the scientists, perhaps—"

"More likely a soldier," Hsu interrupted. "A member of the Air Force Special Operations Command. Or a particularly determined airman."

"In either case, we have a larger problem than our losses," Lee said with a frown. "I want your men to spread out across the base, find me this . . . *soldier*, and kill him. I also want Commando Chee to reactivate the base's defensive radar. He and Jyo will be in charge of base security. I expect we may have visitors shortly."

"But what about the hostages? We will be stretched so thin. Who will guard them?"

Jong glanced at the Americans lying about on the hangar floor. Most of them were sleeping. One young woman was sobbing quietly, a captured airman comforting her. "Three guards will be sufficient to keep them in check. Use the Cubans. They are less disciplined than our men, but this is one job they can handle."

Jong Lee glanced over his shoulder. "Yizi!" he cried.

The woman appeared at his side, AK–47 slung over her slim shoulder.

"Go to the flight tower and use the radio to send a coded message on the emergency frequency. Tell our reinforcements in Mexico that they will have to come get us," Lee commanded.

"That's absurd, the American military will shoot down any aircraft that invades its airspace," Pizarro Rojas cried. He was slumped on a stack of boxes near the doors. Stella Hawk, who had been sleeping with her head in his lap, awoke at the man's outburst.

Sneering, Carlos Boca spoke. "Even if your rescuers manage to reach this place, how can we fly out again without being detected? We've lost the stealth system in the explosion, and the Yankees will never let us get out of here alive."

Jong Lee smiled. "You forget our guests, Cuban."

Lee dipped his head in the direction of the hostages. "We will exploit our prisoners as human shields. When they try to stop us, we will tell the Americans we will free our prisoners once we cross the border, otherwise they will die. The United States government will agree to our demands. They must."

The hastily assembled teleconference with the President of the United States had just begun. Sitting around the table in CTU's briefing room were Ryan Chappelle, Alberta Green, Richard Walsh, and Christopher Henderson. In Washington, the President was joined by the Secretary of State and his own Chief of Staff.

The President was already in a foul mood when he appeared on CTU's digital monitor. This was his third conference of the morning and none of them had gone well. The first had been with his CIA director, the second with the Joint Chiefs of Staff.

He'd been scheduled to sign a new funding bill in the Rose Garden today, the crowning achievement of the President's second term. But between the terrorist attack in Las Vegas and the raid on Groom Lake, his public relations event had been shot to hell.

"You tell me you have assets in the vicinity of this raid," the President said without preamble.

"That's correct, Mr. President," Henderson replied before Chappelle had a chance to speak. "I have an agent working undercover at Groom Lake. He's the one who destroyed the aircraft the strike team planned to use in their escape. My man is still active, though there's only so much a single agent can do against a small army."

"What other actions has your agency initiated?" asked the Secretary of State.

"We've mobilized our strike team, Madam Secretary," Ryan Chappelle replied. "They'll reach Las Vegas within the hour."

"Too little, too late," scoffed the President.

"You're correct. It's not enough, Mr. President," Henderson said. "I also have three other agents in Las Vegas. Unfortunately, due to an ill-advised operational review—" Henderson glanced in Alberta Green's direction. "—those field assets have been deactivated pending a judicial review."

"That's ridiculous," roared the Chief of Staff. "Have them reinstated immediately."

Ryan Chappelle nodded to Alberta Green. "Could you take care of that?"

"Of course," the woman replied.

"He said immediately," Henderson said with undisguised contempt.

Eyes downcast, Alberta Green rose, gathered up her papers and left the conference room.

"The Chinese must be mad. This is an act of war," the President declared. "How can I end this crisis without bloodshed. My Joint Chiefs want to bomb Groom Lake, level the base. They claim that's a better option than the dissemination of top secret technology and I tend to agree."

"Give us a little time," Richard Walsh said. "With our assets in place, we can move against these commandos at once—"

"I have another suggestion," Christopher Henderson interrupted. "While we formulate a military solution, I think I know another way to influence the Chinese government. A little economic pressure may convince them to see the light."

Hope dawned in the President's eyes. "What do you suggest?"

Henderson rose and adjusted his tie. He leaned over the table to stare into the monitor.

"With your permission, Mr. President, I'm going to ask a close friend of mine to place an informal phone call to Zeng Ju, Premier of the State Council of the People's Republic of China . . ."

1 2 3 4 5 6 7 8 9
10 11 12 13 14 15 16 17
18 19 **20** 21 22 23 24

. . . . . . . . . . . . . . . . . . . . . . . . . . . . . . . . .

THE FOLLOWING TAKES PLACE
BETWEEN THE HOURS OF
7 A.M. AND 8 A.M.
PACIFIC DAYLIGHT TIME

. . . . . . . . . . . . . . . . . . . . . . . . . . . . . . . . .

*7:06:09 A.M. PDT*
*Orange Blossom Country Club*
*La Quinta, California*

Samuel L. Wexler, President and CEO of Omnicron
International, was ready to tee off when he got an
unexpected cell phone call from his old college roommate, Christopher Henderson. Wexler was immediately suspicious. In his capacity as head of a major
defense contractor, Wexler seldom received a social
call before ten AM, and never one from a departmen-
tal director at the Counter Terrorist Unit.

Henderson explained the situation at Groom Lake
to Wexler, who immediately knew what he had to

do to protect his company's interests. After the call ended, Wexler excused himself, tipped his caddy and drove his golf cart back to the club house. The CEO retreated to one of the plush lounges and used the country club's land line to place an international call.

It was early evening in Beijing, the work day ending, but Zeng Ju, Premier of the State Council, accepted the powerful American business tycoon's call. He was instantly sorry he did, because Samuel L. Wexler read the Chinese bureaucrat what the Yankees called "the riot act."

"Your man Jong Lee instigated an international incident that will have dire ramifications in the future relationship between our two nations," Wexler cautioned. "Beside the fact that you've committed an act of war, half the stuff your pirates are stealing is patented to my company. Now you don't think Omnicron International is going to sit idly by and let that happen, do you?"

"Why would the state of your patents matter to China, Mr. Wexler?" Zeng Ju asked, rather disingenuously, the CEO thought. It was time to slap the bureaucrat down.

"My company employs a hundred thousand workers in Hong Kong," Wexler replied. "Another quarter million factory workers on the mainland are employed by our subsidiary companies. Your nation relies on our contracts for work. That could all end today if you don't call off your raid."

"But—"

"I'm serious, Ju. I could idle half the factories in Shen Zhen with a memo."

"Mr. Wexler, please be reasonable. We have no control over the actions of the People's Liberation Army—"

"I don't want to hear excuses, Chairman. We will pull our contracts out of China if this invasion doesn't stop."

"But surely we can work out an agreeable solution to this crisis. You need us the same way we need—"

"Taiwan can do the work. Or maybe we'll just build a few factories in the USA. And it doesn't end there," Wexler warned. "I also have friends in Bentonville, Arkansas. If those folks decide to cancel their contracts, the Chinese economic boom will come to an abrupt and permanent end . . ."


*7:44:09 A.M. PDT*
*Over the high desert of Nevada*

It had taken Jack Bauer over an hour, but in the end he managed to cut through the red tape and commandeer an MH–6J "Little Bird" helicopter. This particular model was being used for desert reconnaissance by the Immigration and Naturalization Services, so it didn't have all the bells and whistles to which Jack had become accustomed.

The Little Birds he flew in his Delta Force days had a FLIR passive imaging system, and two 7.62mm mini-guns mounted on the sides, along with a pair of 7-shot, 2.75-inch rocket pods—features he could have put to good use on his present mission. Fortunately the MH–6J was nimble and quick, and capable of flying nap of the earth over varying terrain and weather conditions. Best of all, because the Bird was so compact, the craft presented a low profile on radar—though not low enough to completely avoid detection.

As soon as he lifted off, Jack Bauer contacted Tony Almeida on the man's stolen cell phone. Tony was hiding somewhere inside of Groom Lake Air Force base, trying to figure out a way to rescue the hostages. Jack and Tony established a time and place for a rendezvous, well aware that the chances for either of them to make that connection was probably negligible.

In the middle of the conversation, Tony's call abruptly ceased. Jack tried and failed to reach him again, and deduced the base was being jammed, either by the Chinese or by the United States military. Jack could not raise Nina, Curtis, or Morris, either.

Thirty minutes into his gut-wrenching, low-level flight, Jack slowed his aircraft and tested the GPS system. Like the radios and cell phones, the satellite signal was being jammed. Cursing, he glanced over at the area map displayed on his monitor. Jack determined he was less than fifteen miles from the base, and approaching out of the sun. Bauer hoped the blazing orange ball rising on the eastern horizon would be enough to mask his arrival.

*7:47:40 A.M. PDT*
*Somewhere in the Nevada desert*

The vehicle slammed through another ragged ditch.
Sand filled the open compartment and Morris pitched
forward. Seat belts straining, he was yanked backwards again as the sandrail climbed out of the hole.
The little man had been jolted so badly he nearly lost
the electronic device he'd been fumbling with.

"Dear God, woman. Would you please slow
down!"

Morris was yelling. Not because he was angry,
but because it was the only way his voice could be
heard over the ear-splitting roar of the rear mounted
engine.

Nina Myers shifted into low gear. In a cloud of
choking dust they climbed back to level ground.
"I can't slow down," she cried. "I'm already going too slow. The ground is rougher than this map
indicates."

"That what you get for listening to a pair of brain-
dead hippies," Morris shot back.

Sixty-five minutes ago, Nina, Curtis, and Morris
had "acquired a pair of sandrails—not "dune buggies," as the men who owned the machines were
quick to point out. Dune buggies were converted
vehicles, usually Volkswagen Beetles because of their
rear-engine design. Sandrails, or simply "rails," were
far superior. "The Cadillac of all terrain recreational
vehicles" were built from scratch using steel pipes for
frames. Rails were heavier and much more rugged

than buggies. They were wider and had a lower center of gravity. And sandrails also had more powerful engines.

The CTU agents obtained this pair from Your Desert Experience, a establishment on the outskirts of town that catered to tourists. Brad Wheeler and his brother Damon, the "longhairs in charge" as Morris put it, were happy to provide maps and suggest routes. They were happy because Nina had used her CTU credit card to pay them more money than the vehicles were worth "to rent them for an unspecified length of time." The smiling twins had even loaded the rails onto trailers and drove everyone to a site in the desert where they could get a head start.

Nina glanced over her shoulder, saw a cloud of dust trailing her six. That was Curtis, at the wheel of his own machine. He had no trouble keeping up with her, despite the blasted landscape.

"Can you raise anyone?" she asked her passenger.

Morris shook the radio in his hand. "Someone is jamming us pretty thoroughly," he shouted. "Either the Chinese, or our own military."

Nina came over a rise too fast to see the boulder, so there was no avoiding it. Not even the independent suspension system could deal with a strike like that. The front tire bounced off the rock, the sandrail leaped into the air, only to crash to the ground again. Morris' head banged against the roll bar before he was slammed back down in his inadequately-cushioned seat.

Morris adjusted the helmet, too large for his bald head, and moaned. "Mummy, are we there yet?"

Nina glanced at the terrain map taped to the dashboard.

"Not even close," she replied.

*7:56:29 A.M. PDT*
*Over Emigrant Valley*

Jack had just maneuvered over the top of the low mountain range. Now he put the Little Bird into a sharp dive. Descending into the valley, he spotted a plume of smoke in the distance. Jack knew he was over the base now, and fast approaching the edge of the runway, though it was still a mile or more away.

Peering through his mini-binoculars, Jack realized the smoke rose from the smoldering wreckage of the Boeing 737 sprawled across the scorched and pitted runway. Beyond the hazy curtain he could see the hangars.

Jack lowered the binoculars in time to see movement out of the corner of his eye. He immediately dropped the chopper lower, so he was skimming the desert at less than fifty feet. He glanced over his shoulder, spied the object streaking toward his aircraft on a plume of white smoke.

He waited until the last possible moment before he twisted the controls and spun the helicopter out of the path of the Stinger hand-held ground-to-air missile. Jack had timed his dodge just right—the sudden turn came too late and too fast for the missile's homing system to compensate. The Stinger struck the desert in a yellow flash.

Then Jack saw another plume of smoke ahead of him, two more to either side. He found himself pinned in the middle of a three pronged missile attack. No matter which way Jack turned, the Little Bird would be blown out of the sky.

The only way to go was down.

Jack cut power, pushed the chopper into a dive. At fifty feet, it took less than a second for the chopper to strike the sand. The impact bent the landing struts, and the helicopter teetered precariously on shattered legs. Jack spit blood, then released his safety belt.

Before the Little Bird tumbled onto its side, Jack dived out of the cockpit. Landing feet first, he sprinted for any cover he could find. Legs pumping, he did not look over his shoulder, even when he heard the chopper's whirling rotor blades bite into the ground, then shatter.

Their homing devices attracted by the still-spinning rotor, all three Stinger missiles struck the helicopter. The explosion caught Jack Bauer in its fiery grip. Helpless, the CTU agent was swept up like a grain of sand in a sandstorm.

· · · · · · · · · · · · · · · · · · · · · · · · · · · · · · · · · · · · · · ·

THE FOLLOWING TAKES PLACE
BETWEEN THE HOURS OF
8 A.M. AND 9 A.M.
PACIFIC DAYLIGHT TIME

· · · · · · · · · · · · · · · · · · · · · · · · · · · · · · · · · · · · · · ·

*8:00:09 A.M. PDT*
*CTU Headquarters, Los Angeles*

Ryan Chappelle received an urgent call, a tip from a
former colleague now working in the Department of
Defense. Face taut, Chappelle listened to the disturb-
ing news with angry disbelief. More than anything,
he was puzzled by the government willingness to flush
four highly trained and immensely valuable assets
down the toilet—*five*, if one were inclined to count
the troublesome Morris O'Brian.

After ending the conversation with his colleague, the
Regional Director of CTU, Los Angeles, attempted to
speak directly with the President, only to be told the

Commander in Chief was "in conference." He tried the Vice-President and ran into another wall.

Frantic now, Chappelle tried calling the Secretary of Defense, and to his surprise the man accepted his call.

"How can I help you, Director Chappelle?" Secretary Thompson asked in his Tennessee drawl.

"I wanted to inform you that we have four CTU Agents inside of Groom Lake right now," Chappelle replied.

A moment of silence followed the declaration. "There are a lot of people at Groom Lake, Mr. Chappelle. Good people."

Chappelle knew that when the Secretary of Defense casually demoted him from "director" to "mister," Ryan was in trouble. Still he persisted.

"I'm asking you to call off the B–52s, Mr. Secretary. Give my men a chance to deal with the situation before you resort to drastic action."

Another moment of silence. "I would like to help, but—"

"Secretary Thompson, these are very capable agents. One of them is the very best field agent in our Unit. I believe that even though they may be outnumbered six to one, my agents can and will resolve this situation."

"Excuse me for a moment, Director Chappelle."

*Promoted again*, Ryan thought hopefully.

He held on the phone for almost five minutes. When Secretary Thompson returned, he seemed irritated.

"All right, Director. Noon is our new go time. That means CTU has a little less than four hours to show us your stuff. If those pilots don't get the proper code phrase by noon sharp, I *will* give the order to bomber command to flatten that base. It will be Rolling Thunder all over again—"

"Code phrase, sir?"

"It's a randomly generated phrase created by our computer and disseminated over a secure channel. We'll send the phrase directly to you through a secure server."

"One more thing, Mr. Secretary," Chappelle said.

"Son, don't you know when to quit."

"No sir, I don't. Not when the lives of my agents are involved."

"What is it, Director?"

Ryan wasn't completely sure, but he thought he sensed a new hint of respect in the Secretary's tone. "I need to speak with my agents in the field," Chappelle replied. "I want to alert them about the time frame they are facing. To do that, the Air Force needs to stop their jamming for a few minutes."

"I'll talk to General Boyd. The jamming will be lifted for five minutes, commencing at exactly 0900 hours—that's nine o'clock, civilian time. Good enough?"

"Thank you, Mr. Secretary."

*8:30:49 A.M. PDT*
*Hangar Five,*
*Experimental Weapons Testing Range*
*Groom Lake Air Force Base*

After the loss of his escape plane, Jong Lee established a new command center in Hangar Five, where he could personally watch over the only functioning aircraft left on the entire base. The Blackfoot stealth helicopter figured prominently in Lee's original plan. That piece of advanced hardware was even more important now that the situation was in flux.

"It was not an attack," Lee declared. "One helicopter means a reconnaissance mission, not an all out assault." Jong's thin lips curled into a smile. "It gives me hope that the Americans have been shocked into paralysis."

"It is mysterious," Captain Hsu noted. "The Americans have positioned satellites over our heads. I have seen the contrails of high-altitude spy planes as well. They know much of what is going on here. Why send a reconnaissance helicopter?"

"Have you dispatched men to the crash site?"

"Yes, sir. Woo and two men are on their way now."

A runner arrived, dispatched from the flight tower across the tarmac. With the phones jammed along with everything else, Lee had to resort to nineteenth century-style communications between his units.

"Yizi reports that the jamming continues," the man said after saluting. "She has not communicated with the base in Mexico since the initial message was sent."

"Tell her to keep trying. If the curtain of jamming parts, I want her to be ready to send and receive messages at a moment's notice."

*8:50:49 A.M. PDT*
*Hangar Six, Experimental Weapons Testing Range*
*Groom Lake Air Force Base*

Tony Almeida spent a long, torturous hour crawling face down through a shallow ravine outside of Hangar Six. His filthy sweat pants clung to his legs and sand filled his sneakers. Though he was covered with grease and grit, the hot morning sun broiled the skin on his back and sent rivulets of sweat rolling down his flanks. He moved slowly to avoid discovery—Tony knew he was being hunted, he'd seen the men fan out across the base. They'd found other hostages, hiding in hangars or in bunkers, but so far he'd managed to elude them.

Finally, he was within sight of the side entrance. The door was locked, but Tony had rigged it so he could open it without a key, back when he was spying on Steve Sable. Risking detection, Tony rose and sprinted across the final stretch of sand. He made it to the door in seconds, yanked it open and ducked inside.

The dim interior of the hangar's forgotten storage room was at least fifteen degrees cooler than the air outside, and Tony was out of the direct sunlight—a double blessing. He was exhausted and thirsty, and the burn marks on his chest and legs throbbed, an ever present reminder of the torture he'd endured at the hands of the late Dr. Sable.

Tony slumped to the cool floor between two stacks of crates and paused to catch his breath. Just fifty yards away, at the front of the hangar, the hostages were still being held at gunpoint by an unknown number of guards. Tony dared not doze off, his mind remained sharp and alert while he rested his tired muscles. Mouth parched, he longed for a cold beer.

He heard an animal snort. Quietly, Tony rose to his feet, crept to a mountain of wooden crates and peered around them. A man was there, his back to Tony. He slumped in the battered office chair beside the work-bench, head lolled to the side. While Tony watched the man snored again.

Tony retreated to a massive spool of cable mounted on a rack. Irregular lengths of the black wire lay around his feet like dead snakes. He selected the most useful one and crept back to the sleeping man.

Tony moved around the work bench and behind the snoring man. It was one of the Cubans. Tony had heard the men speaking Spanish while he spied on them and recognized their accents, though how the Cubans and Chinese came together for this operation was beyond Tony's grasp at the moment.

Crouched behind the man, Tony saw a Makarov PM tucked his belt. He longed for that weapon more than he'd wanted the beer. Peeking between boxes and banks of machinery, Tony could see a guard standing over the hostages, who were still huddled on the floor.

He would have to strike quickly and quietly, or he would die in this dusty storage room. Hands rock steady, he looped the wire, then slipped it around the man's neck.

The Cuban's legs kicked out and, choking, he flopped in his chair, but the only sound he made was a faint gargle. The Cuban clutched at the wire around his throat, but it was sunk so deeply into his flesh, he could not get his fingers around it. Grunting, Tony yanked harder, crushing the man's trachea, the arteries in his neck. A final tug, and the Cuban's neck snapped. The struggling ceased. Tony released the cable and snatched the pistol from the man's belt.

He fumbled through the dead man's pockets, discovered two more clips of ammunition, a fake passport identifying him as a Salvadoran. When Tony was finished tossing the corpse, he carefully adjusted the man in the chair so he would appear asleep. Then Tony faded back into the shadows of the hangar, to plot his next move. . .

1 2 3 4 5 6 7 8 9
10 11 12 13 14 15 16 17
18 19 20 21 **22** 23 24

• • • • • • • • • • • • • • • • • • • • • • • • • • • •

THE FOLLOWING TAKES PLACE
BETWEEN THE HOURS OF
9 A.M. AND 10 A.M.
PACIFIC DAYLIGHT TIME

• • • • • • • • • • • • • • • • • • • • • • • • • • • •

*9:00:17 A.M. PDT*
*Somewhere inside the Nevada desert*

Nina and Morris circled back when they noticed Curtis was no longer following. They found him squatting on the sand next to his vehicle, which was tipped on its side. The sandrail had broken an axle and flipped over.

"It's finished," said Curtis, gesturing to a front wheel that was hanging askew, like a broken wing on a chicken.

"What do we—" Morris was interrupted by an electronic crackle and ran for the radio. "Come in CTU. We hear you," he replied.

There was a pause while the transmission was scrambled. Then they listened with mounting anxiety as Jamey Farrell explained they had only three hours to liberate the base or get out of the way of the bombers. "Be advised that contact with CTU will end in two minutes, when the signal jamming resumes," Jamey told them.

"If we're being jammed, how do we let you know we've liberated the base?" Morris asked.

"At eleven fifty-seven, the jamming will cease. The B–52s will release their payload three minutes later, unless you made a radio call, identify yourself, and deliver the code word."

Morris threw up his hands. "Code word! What's the bloody code word?"

"Coronet Blue," Jamey replied.

Morris shook his head. "Bleeding ridiculous spy games."

Nina took the radio from Morris. "Have you heard from Tony?"

"Ryan is talking to him now, over a cell phone that is not secure," Jamey replied.

"But they're giving him the code word, no doubt!" Morris bellowed. "Some secret *that* is."

"What about Jack?"

There was a pause. "We're trying to reach him, but so far we've got nothing," Jamey replied.

"What are we going to do now?" Morris said after the radio call ended.

"Is this a vote?" Curtis asked. "Then I say we go."

Morris crossed his arms. "And I say we don't."

"We're going," Nina declared.

Curtis cleared his throat. "We have a problem, then. There are only two seats in your rail, and no room to squeeze in a third person."

Nina pulled the safety helmet over her ebony hair. "Morris doesn't want to go. We'll leave him here."

"In the middle of the desert? I could perish out here," Morris protested.

"You'll be safe," Curtis said. "You're probably out of range of the bombs should they fall. And if all goes well, we'll send someone back to get you."

Morris watched them drive away. When they faded from view and the dust in their wake settled, he slumped down in the sand under the dubious shade of the ruined sandrail. The desert was getting hotter by the minute. Morris glanced up at the burning sun.

"Oh, what a bloody fine mess this turned out to be," he moaned.

*9:11:11 A.M. PDT*
*Hangar Six, Experimental Weapons Testing Range*
*Groom Lake Air Force Base*

After the sun rose, the morning began to heat up. Dr. Reed decided to ask permission for the hangar door to be closed, the air conditioning turned on. A Cuban guard pretended not to understand her, but she persisted. Finally he took her by the arm and led her to the hangar door, where the man in charge sat on a steel chair staring out at the desert.

"Why do you need air conditioning?" Carlos Boca demanded in a surly tone. He turned then, and openly appraised her from head to toe, until Dr. Reed felt naked in her sweat-stained pink teddy and flip-flops.

"You look comfortable enough, doctor. Request denied." Boca turned away, signaling her time was over.

The guard led her back to the hostages, but threw her down in a different spot. Because they were not allowed to move around, Megan could only make eye contact with Dani Welles, but could not speak to her.

"I tried asking for the air conditioning an hour ago," a young woman in dirty overalls said. The white label on her breast patch had the word CONSUELO penned in bold black letters.

"Are you from the terminal crew?" Megan whispered.

The woman nodded. "After the plane landed and the shooting started, I hid in Hangar 18. Some of the soldiers found me and brought me here."

"At least they didn't shoot you," Megan replied.

"Give them time. I've been listening," the woman said, her dark eyes staring at the floor. "These guys are Cubans, soldiers or former soldiers, I think. I know they consider us the walking dead. They're only waiting for orders to pull the trigger and finish the job."

For the first time since she was captured, Megan was glad she didn't understand what the men had been saying. It would only have made the ordeal worse.

She counted her captors. There were three men guarding them, all Spanish-speakers. She watched as the man called Carlos called to one of his men and issued instructions. The man turned his back on his commander and walked to the rear of the hangar, to disappear among the crates and machinery.

"What did he say? Where is that man going?" Megan asked.

"He said Manuel has slept long enough, and that it was time for the other man to wake him," Consuelo replied.

She breathed a sigh of relief. At least that Carlos guy didn't order them all to be lined up and shot . . . Not *yet*, anyway. Searching her memory, Megan recalled that there had been four guards, and that one of them had wandered off and never came back.

Tony heard the man coming and ducked between two stacks of wooden boxes. He was armed with the Makarov, and a two-foot long, straight cutting blade he'd unscrewed from the industrial strength wire slicer. It looked like a samurai sword, but lacked a pointed tip. Nevertheless, Tony found a use for it.

The guard passed so close Tony could have tapped him on the shoulder. Instead, he waited until the newcomer approached the dead man in the chair. Then Tony crept up behind the man and slipped the noose over his head.

When the guard was dead, Tony slipped the AK–47 off his shoulder, fished through his pockets and belt. This time he came up empty. One clip of ammunition for the assault rifle was not enough to do squat, not against upwards of thirty men.

On top of that, Tony knew this guard was sent to wake the first man he'd killed. Soon the Cubans in charge would be wondering where he went, too.

Tony would have to strike quickly. He wanted to finish off the last two guards before they could raise the alarm, then secure the hangar. With the help of the hostages, they could probably hold out for an hour or so, even if the commandos attempted a counterattack to retake the position.

In any case, Tony knew there was a time limit now. Ryan Chappelle had warned him about the bombing. Tony also knew Jack Bauer was coming—they'd established a rendezvous point and a time during their telephone conversation ninety minutes ago. All Tony had to do was hold out until the cavalry arrived, or until the bombs fell.

Either way, the siege of Area 51 would end in the next couple of hours. . .

Megan Reed's stomach rumbled and she shifted uncomfortably. She was hungry, thirsty and she needed to go to the bathroom. They'd had no water since six AM, around the same time they were last allowed to go to the restroom. More than a third of the prisoners were still asleep, and Megan admired those who managed to find peace despite the tension and discomfort.

*They must be shock, or suffering from some type of stress reaction*, she deduced, wishing she could sidle over to Dr. Toth and ask his professional opinion. Only then did she notice that the physician was sleeping, too.

Unfortunately her bladder was too full for her to sleep. She had to go, and soon. At first Megan decided to wait for the other guards to return before making the embarrassing request. Then she mentally kicked herself.

*What the hell is wrong with me? Do I have Stockholm Syndrome or something? I'm the victim here. Why make it easy on them?*

Megan raised her hand. "Hey there. You. Hello!"

Boca and the other guard glanced in her direction. "I don't know about these other people, but I need to use the ladies' room *pronto*."

Sneering, Carlos looked away.

"Hey, buddy," Megan cried. "I'm talking to *you*."

Face curled into a cruel sneer, Carlos Boca stood up, faced her. He slung his rifle over his shoulder and slowly approached the woman. Megan could tell he was angry. The closer he got, the more pissed the Cuban looked. The other guard watched from the sidelines, snickering. The prisoners around her grew uncomfortable, upset she was rocking the boat. But Megan didn't care.

*They're going to kill me anyway*, she thought. *At least I'll die with an empty bladder.*

Tony had been observing the hostages for a few minutes. The guards were so far apart, Tony couldn't see how he was going to neutralize them without firing a shot. But then, thanks to the reliably annoying Dr. Reed, he got his best opening yet.

While Boca loomed threateningly over the defiant Dr. Reed, Tony gripped the cutting blade with both hands, raised it over his head and burst from hiding. With a powerful downward thrust, Tony split the snickering guard's skull from crown to jaw. The dead man dropped without a sound, blood pooling around Tony's sneakers. Unfortunately, the guard dragged the blade down with him—it had wedged so deeply in the Cuban's torso, Tony could not yank it free.

Carlos Boca was still a few feet away. Turning, the Cuban tried to drag the AK–47 off his shoulder to fire. But Megan Reed grabbed the assault rifle and hung on with both hands like a tenacious pit bull. With the strap tugging at his arm, Boca had no choice but to release the weapon. Still, the Cuban commando was not unarmed. Boca drew a long stiletto out of his high boot and lunged at Tony.

The man was an experienced knife fighter, so fast Tony did not completely sidestep the blow. The razor thin blade raked his ribcage. Tony howled. Shutting out the pain, he locked Boca's knife arm under his own and stepped around the helpless man. A quick jerk, and Tony felt the bone snap in Boca's arm. Tony used his elbow to strike the man three times. The first blow smashed Boca's nose. The second shattered his jaw. The third strike killed him.

He stepped back and the dead man pitched to the floor. Tony reeled as blood streamed down his flanks. Megan was instantly on her feet to steady him.

"Antonio? Is that you?" she cried, recognizing him despite the layers of grit and grease.

Tony took in the woman's pink Meow, Meow Kitty teddy and matching panties.

"That's a new look for you, isn't it Doc?" he grunted.

"You've been wounded!"

By now, the hostages were starting to rise. "Get down, stay in your places. At least until I close the hangar door."

Tony limped to the control panel and hit the switch. It took a minute for the door to come down. When it did, he visibly relaxed but did not slow down.

Tony tossed Boca's assault rifle to a young airman with dark hair and Hispanic features.

"Go stand in that doorway—" Tony pointed to a narrow door adjacent to the blast-proof steel gate. "—pretend you're a guard. The longer the bad guys think they've got us, the longer they'll leave us alone."

Dr. Reed kept her arms wrapped around Tony while he moved across the hangar. She clung so tightly Tony wasn't sure who was supporting whom. Tony opened the idle generator and reached under the hood. The Glock was right where he left it. With his fist around the familiar weapon, Tony felt complete.

Dr. Alvin Toth touched his arm. "You're bleeding, young man."

"I don't have time to bleed," Tony replied.

"I saw that movie, too," Toth replied with a sly

smile. "I also have a First Aid kit right here. Let me fix you up . . ."

Tony nodded and leaned against the generator. He lifted his arm while Toth smeared a disinfectant on the ragged gash. Tony winced, sucking air.

"Be careful, Dr. Toth! You'll hurt him," Megan cried, arms wrapped around Tony's broad shoulders.

· · · · · · · · · · · · · · · · · · · · · · · · · · · · · · · · ·

THE FOLLOWING TAKES PLACE
BETWEEN THE HOURS OF
10 A.M. AND 11 A.M.
PACIFIC DAYLIGHT TIME

· · · · · · · · · · · · · · · · · · · · · · · · · · · · · · · · ·

*10:06:22 A.M. PDT*
*Hanger Five,*
*Experimental Weapons Testing Range*
*Groom Lake Air Force Base*

Yizi drifted through Hangar Five like a shadow. Ignoring the others, she approached Jong Lee. Her master had his back to the open door while he admired the sleek design of the experimental stealth helicopter. A few commandos were with him in the hangar. Many more had been deployed across the base, anticipating a military response from the Americans

"The jamming ceased approximately one hour ago," the woman reported in whispered Chinese. "I was able to re-send the emergency message to our base in Mexico. They acknowledged receiving it, but offered no timeline for our extraction."

Jong Lee frowned. He'd suspected the truth, but only now did he know for certain that he'd been abandoned by his own government. It was a stinging blow, but not unexpected after their setbacks. If Jong Lee were back in Beijing, he probably would have issued the same command.

"Very well," Lee said, his voice grim. "We still possess the only prototype of the Malignant Wave device, and the Blackfoot helicopter to carry it. It is time to retreat with what we have, rather than mourn what we have lost."

Lee called Captain Hsu to his side. "I believe an American counterattack is imminent. We will depart within the hour."

Pizarro Rojas watched the exchange, Stella Hawk by his side. The Colombian pulled away from the woman and strode over to the Chinese agent.

"You're leaving us, then," Rojas said bitterly.

Jong Lee did not reply. His face remained impassive.

"I don't need to understand Chinese to see what's going on," the Colombian continued.

"I must surrender to expedience," Lee replied. "Many valuable assets have been lost. There is only one way to achieve victory from this morass."

"You're not going run away without me," Rojas cried. He yanked the pistol out of his holster and waved it at Jong Lee.

"Baby, what's wrong?" Stella cried.

"This pig thinks he's going to fly away in that damned helicopter and leave us · behind," Rojas cried. He pointed the pistol at Lee's head. "But if he thinks—"

His words were cut short. Pizarro Rojas suddenly grunted, and the gun tumbled from his grip. Stella screamed when she saw Yizi's three-bladed sai sticking out of the Colombian's throat, the dark, thick blood bubbling out of the wounds.

She rushed to the man, cradled Pizarro's head in her arms as he fell. With manicured fingers she tried to stem the tide of blood that flowed from a punctured carotid artery. Pizarro managed to smile up at her before life faded from his eyes.

"You bitch!" Stella screamed.

Fingers curled, she clawed at Yizi's throat, raking the Asian woman's cheek, drawing blood. Yizi slapped Stella several times, until the woman sank to the ground.

"Put her with the other hostages," Jong Lee ordered.

Two commandos grabbed Stella Hawk under each arm. Wailing loudly, she tried to cling to the dead man even as they hauled her away.

When she saw the stranger emerge from the shadows, Dani Welles cried out. Everyone turned. Dr. Bascomb moved quickly to shield the woman while he aimed a captured AK–47 at the intruder.

"Don't move or I'll shoot," the scientist snarled.

Untangling himself from the clinging Dr. Reed, Tony jumped to his feet. "Wait, Doc. Don't shoot. This man is on our side."

Dr. Bascomb lowered the assault rifle. Tony stepped between them.

"Hello, Jack," he said. "You look like hell."

"I made it."

Jack Bauer's clothing was torn and scorched. Most of the hair on the right side of his scalp had been burned away when the helicopter exploded. He walked with a discernable limp, and Tony spotted a bloody bandage torn from his shirt wrapped around Jack's right calf.

It took a few minutes for Tony to bring his boss up to speed on recent developments. Bauer didn't exhibit surprise when he heard the Air Force was willing to blow the base up.

"It's a smart move. I'd do the same thing," Jack declared.

"Right now, the Chinese think we're still prisoners. But as soon as someone comes through that door they're going to find out the truth."

Jack nodded. "On the way over here, I noticed a lot of activity in the next hangar."

"That's Hangar Five," Tony said. "There's an experimental stealth helicopter in there, designed to elude radar. Once it takes off, the Air Force won't be able to find it."

"It's a two man craft," said Jack. "That would mean they're leaving most of their strike team behind."

"There's an experimental weapon installed in that helicopter, Jack. It called Malignant Wave and it's a real bitch. If the Chinese escape with the prototype, it would be worth any sacrifice."

Jack's eyes narrowed into slits. "Then we have to get inside that hangar. Stop that helicopter from taking off."

"That's going to be tough," sighed Tony.

Dr. Reed heard their words and stepped forward. "There's a back door to that hangar . . ."

"I tried it, doc," Tony said. "It's locked, and it's made of reinforced steel. If we try to break in, they're going to hear us."

"Beverly Chang gave me a copy of the key," she replied. "It's over there, in my locker . . ."

The airman guarding the door interrupted them. "Someone's coming," he hissed. "Two soldiers with a prisoner."

"Everyone get down," Tony cried, racing for the entrance. Jack was already there. They positioned themselves on either side of the open doorway, waiting to pounce the moment the soldiers entered.

When the commandos reached the narrow door,

they shoved Stella through first. Then the first commando stepped over the threshold. Tony seized the man, pummeled him to the ground with the butt of his Glock.

Stella recognized Jack.

"Jaycee!" she cried, stepping between Bauer and the commando he was supposed to take down. Jack thrust the woman aside, but it was too late. The soldier turned and raced across the tarmac, screaming a warning. Jack aimed his Glock with both hands and fired once. The commando's cries abruptly ceased.

Jack stepped away from the door. "They know we're free now," he shouted. "Everyone who isn't armed, take cover!"

Stella Hawk wrapped her arms around Jack Bauer's neck, tight as a boa constrictor. Mascara ran down her cheeks and her face was swollen and bruised. But her lush lips rained kisses on his lips, his cheek, his neck.

"I knew you'd rescue me," she sobbed.

Jack's eyes met Tony's. "Get her off of me," he snarled.

Outside, commandos burst from Hangar Five when they heard the warning cry. Tony picked up the dead soldier's AK–47 and fired on the men as they scurried across the runway. Three commandos dropped, the others turned around and bolted for cover.

Tony heard shouted commands, saw the soldiers begin to regroup outside of Hangar Five.

"Here they come," Tony warned. Legs braced, he stood in the doorway and fired another burst.

*10:52:56 A.M. PDT*
*The Tank Farm*
*Groom Lake Air Force Base*

Nina rolled the sandrail into a prefabricated storage shed hidden among a sea of aviation fuel tanks. She and Curtis climbed a steel ladder to the top of the tallest tank, to observe the situation at the hangars.

Before they finished their ascent, they heard the sound of gunfire in the distance. Scrambling to the top of the tank, Nina focused her mini-binoculars on the hangars.

"It's a firefight, not a massacre," Nina said, squinting through the lens. "It looks like some people are holed up in one hanger. They're putting up a good fight, but the raiders are rallying for another attack—"

"Another attack?"

"I count four dead men on the tarmac," Nina said, handing Curtis the binoculars. "The Chinese have tried to take that hangar at least once before."

Curtis frowned. "The commandos just drove a tow tractor out of the hangar with the weird aircraft inside. I think the Chinese are planning to use the tractor for cover in an attack on the other hangar."

Nina moved to the ladder. "We've got to get down."

Curtis followed her to the edge. "What's your plan?"

"I haven't got one," Nina replied.

"Look over there," Curtis said, pointing to a small tanker truck parked about a hundred yards away. "I think I have an idea . . ."

1 2 3 4 5 6 7 8 9
10 11 12 13 14 15 16 17
18 19 20 21 22 23 **24**

• • • • • • • • • • • • • • • • • • • • • • • • • • •

THE FOLLOWING TAKES PLACE
BETWEEN THE HOURS OF
11 A.M. AND 12 P.M.
PACIFIC DAYLIGHT TIME

• • • • • • • • • • • • • • • • • • • • • • • • • • •

*11:00:04 A.M. PDT*
*Hangar Six, Experimental Weapons Testing Range*
*Groom Lake Air Force Base*

Tony peered around the door, only to jump back when
bullets splattered against the doorjamb and peppered
the wall behind him.

"Get ready, they're coming again," he cautioned.

Tony risked another peek, saw the Chinese commandos advancing in disciplined ranks behind the
tow tractor. They were about fifty yards away and
closing fast. Even if he had a clear shot, Tony would
have trouble picking them off.

The hostages had knocked out the glass window on
the blast proof hangar door. Phil Bascomb had been

using the tiny opening as a gun position, providing Tony with cover fire. As the commandos closed on them, Tony glanced over his shoulder. "Tell Dr. Bascomb to lay down more suppressing fire," he cried.

The airman frowned. "Bascomb was killed in the last attack. Lucky shot came right through the hole. I think Dr. Toth has the gun now."

Tony was thrown by the loss. He'd liked the middle-aged, pony-tailed scientist from Berkeley. The irony was that man had protested the Vietnam War, only to die at the hands of a Communist enemy that had invaded his homeland. A ricochet snapped Tony back to reality.

"Tell Toth to start shooting," he yelled.

Shots rang out, inside the hanger and out. Tony dropped to the ground, peeked around the door. One commando had straggled behind the others and Tony picked him off, only to retreat again when a hail of gunfire blasted through the door. Tony rolled to a sitting position, leaned against the wall. He scanned the frightened faces of the others, who were depending on him to save their lives.

*We're running out of ammunition and shooters. We can't hold out much longer*, Tony mused. *I hope Jack made it into Hangar Five. If he can't stop that helicopter from lifting off, we're going to die for nothing. . . .*

The Blackfoot's dual engines produced a ear-splitting roar that reverberated inside the massive hanger. The noise more resembled the whine of a high-performance jet fighter than the sound of a traditional rotor-bladed helicopter. The Blackfoot also flew faster and higher than any helicopter ever developed—so high the cockpit was pressurized and the pilots were required to wear pressure suits.

While gunfire exploded outside, the commandos who served as the ground crew had completed the final flight check. Now they scrambled to get out of the way.

Jong Lee stood at the bottom of the cockpit ladder, clad in a form fitting, silver-gray pressure suit, helmet in hand. Leaning close, he issued final instructions to Yizi.

"The old men in Beijing care more about commerce than they do about China," Jong Lee said. "It is up to me to teach them a lesson, and force their hand."

"What will you do?" Yizi asked.

"Before I fly to the base in Mexico, I shall fire the Malignant Wave at downtown Las Vegas. The act will most certainly provoke a war. But with a weapon as terrible as Malignant Wave in China's possession, what can the Americans do but surrender?"

Lee frowned. "My strike will mean that when the

Americans come, they will seek revenge for what happened to their city, their people. You must fight them to the death. No one must be taken alive. I expect you to deal with anyone who tries to surrender."

"I understand, Jong Lee." Yizi's face was stony.

The man hesitated before boarding the aircraft. He wanted to say something more to this loyal and courageous young woman, but for the first time in his life, words failed him.

Meanwhile the figure of Captain Hsu emerged from the back of the hangar. He also wore a pressure suit, the featureless helmet and tinted visor covering his head, masking his features. Silently, the man stepped around Jong Lee and climbed the ladder.

Lee touched the woman's arm. She raised her eyes to meet his gaze. "Yizi, I want to—"

"Stop him!" a pained voice interrupted.

The real Captain Hsu stumbled into the center of the hangar, blood trickling from his nose and mouth. He pointed to the figure climbing into the cockpit, then pitched to the floor, a stiletto sticking out of his back.

*"Hùnzhàng!"* Lee cried, realizing he'd been tricked.

Lee raced up the ladder. On the way, the helmet slipped out of his grip. He abandoned it and dived for the hatch. Lee slipped through the automatic door before it closed.

Yizi raced for cover as the Blackfoot lifted off the ground. The stealth helicopter spun in a tight circle inside the hanger. When the helicopter's nose was facing the door, it leaped forward like a race horse leaving the starting gate. The craft paused to hover over the runway, then it suddenly shot straight up, into the bright blue desert sky.

Yizi ran into the sunlight, watched the aircraft rise until it disappeared in the billowing clouds.


*11:23:31 A.M. PDT*
*Runway 33R/15L*
*Groom Lake Air Force Base*


Nina sped along the concrete runway in a cloud of desert dust. She pushed the pedal to the metal, until the rail achieved top speed.

Ahead, commandos heard the sound of her engine. Some fired at the oncoming vehicle. Most scattered, running toward the open hangar.

When she was in range, Nina opened fire. Clutching the steering wheel with her left hand, she fired with her right. She and Curtis had removed the windshield before they left the tank farm in anticipation of this attack. She could aim better that way, and she didn't have to shoot through the glass.

Firing from a moving car wasn't easy, but it was something Nina Myers had learned at The Farm, and she felt a rush of professional satisfaction when two commandos dropped to the tarmac.

When she emptied her Glock, she tossed it into the empty seat beside her, grabbed Curtis' gun and opened up again. There were fewer targets this time. Almost everyone had run into the open hangar for protection.

Nina raced past the enemy and skidded to a halt in front of Hangar Six. The blast doors were pitted and pockmarked, but no bullet had penetrated the thick armor. Tony Almeida, clutching an AK–47, limped through the hangar's shattered doorway to greet her.

"You're just in time," Nina said, pointing to a second vehicle fast approaching.

*11:24:55 A.M. PDT*
*Runway 33R/15L*
*Groom Lake Air Force Base*

The battered tanker truck could not keep up with Nina's sandrail—not with a full tank of jet fuel, anyway. Curtis watched helplessly as Nina pulled ahead.

As their vehicles approached the runway, they both watched the high-tech helicopter blast out of the hangar and into sky. Though they were too late to stop someone from escaping, there were still hostages to rescue. By silent consent the CTU agents proceeded with their original plan.

Curtis smiled grimly when she saw Nina speed into the melee, saw dead men in her wake. Best of all, almost everyone ran to the hangar. Curtis aimed for the open door, lashed the steering wheel in place. Then he shifted a steel pipe waiting in the seat next to him.

The truck slowed a bit while Curtis positioned the pipe. Commandos in the hangar opened fire on the truck. When Curtis jammed the pipe between the seat and the accelerator, the truck surged forward.

*Time to go.*

Curtis popped the door and rolled out. He slammed against the concrete, felt his shoulder pop and cried out. He bounced, then rolled over once, twice, before landing on his back. Groaning, Curtis curled into a protective ball and closed his eyes. Shots pinged the concrete around him. He heard shouts, a crash—and then the explosion.

Flames filled the hangar's interior, incinerating everything and everyone inside. A few howling forms tumbled out of the building. Wrapped in burning fuel, they didn't scream for long.

The hostages burst out of the next hangar, guns ready. But there was no one left to fight. Yizi and the Chinese commandos were all dead.


*11:25:07 A.M. PDT*
*Over Emigrant Valley*


With Jong Lee clawing at his helmet, Jack steered the Blackfoot out of the hangar, then blasted it into the sky. The aircraft's flight characteristics reminded Jack of the Harrier's, but the vortex technology that powered the Blackfoot were far more powerful than the engines on the British fighter jet.

He'd intended to fly away before the other man boarded the helicopter, but Jong Lee figured out the plot and leaped into the helicopter to stop him. The Asian was a skilled and savage fighter, and Jack Bauer would already be dead if he hadn't been wearing the protective helmet.

Bauer knew he could not remain in control of the

aircraft and fight for his life at the same time, so he threw the helicopter into vertical ascent and engaged the auto pilot. While the craft shot straight up, Jack unbuckled his safety harness and grappled with his enemy.

The two men wrestled on the floor of the tight compartment. Jack was larger than his opponent, but he was also exhausted and injured, his reactions not at their peak. But the CTU agent had two advantages—he wore a helmet that protected his neck and head, and he was armed.

Jack rolled away from his opponent, yanked the Glock out of his flight suit. Jong spotted the weapon and dived for Jack's gun hand. The men slammed to the cabin floor again, with Jack's left arm pinned under him. Jong Lee gripped Jack's right wrist with both hands, squeezing until Bauer could feel his wrist bones scrape together.

Screaming alarms jangled inside the pressurized cabin. The Blackfoot had reached its flight ceiling. The craft could go no higher without stalling. Yet the auto pilot kept them on course—straight up.

The struggling men ignored the sound. Locked in a stalemate, Jong Lee could not let go of his opponent's arm. Meanwhile Jack could not aim the Glock. In desperation, Jack pulled the trigger anyway.

The shot shattered the cockpit windshield, causing the pilot compartment to rapidly decompress. Buffeting winds suddenly filled the cabin, ripping the gun from Jack's hand. Like everything else that wasn't screwed down, the Glock was sucked out the window.

Jong Lee's mouth opened wide. But if the man screamed, Jack could not hear the sound over the roar, the insistent alarm. Finally, Jong Lee released his arm. Free now, Jack grabbed the crash seat and hung on. The other man, his lips blue, eyes bulging, was sucked to the opening.

Amazingly, Jong Lee's corpse plugged the hole, and Jack managed to scramble into the pilot's seat, strap in. With Lee's dead eyes staring at him, Jack disengaged the auto pilot and struggled to regain control. But he was too late. The Blackfoot was locked in a fatal spin, the ground coming up fast.

Jack slammed his palm down on the ejector button. With a loud bang, the panel above his head blasted away and Jack saw blue sky. Then his spine compressed and the ejector seat rocketed out of the craft.

Twisting in the air, Jack watched the Blackfoot tumble through the clouds. Then Jack felt another jolt as his parachute deployed.

*11:57:24 A.M. PDT*
*Emigrant Valley*

Startled, Morris O'Brian jumped up when he heard the Blackfoot slam into the desert. The craft crashed a mile or more away from the wrecked sandrail. Morris watched the plume of orange fire roil and rise, topped by oily black smoke.

"That should get someone's attention," he muttered.

Morris stepped around the wrecked vehicle to gaze

up at the sky. He saw the parachute immediately, watched it descend until it came to earth on a bluff a mile away. Grabbing the still useless radio, Morris hiked to the low hill.

He arrived fifteen minutes later, surprised to find Jack Bauer in a torn pressure suit. The CTU agent was seated on a rock, head resting on his knees.

"Hello, Jack," said Morris.

Bauer looked up, squinting against the noontime sun. "Hello, Morris," he replied.

Jack's hair was askew—the hair that wasn't burned off, that is—and his face was battered like a boxer who'd lost a fight. Yet somehow Jack Bauer managed a smile.

Morris sat beside him. Both men stared at the blue mountain range in the distance. Finally, Morris broke the silence.

"That was a bloody long day, eh?"